HOT HOUSE

First Publication June 2022
Indies United Publishing House, LLC

ISBN: 978-1-64456-425-7 [Hardcover]
ISBN: 978-1-64456-421-9 [paperback]
ISBN: 978-1-64456-422-6 [Mobi]
ISBN: 978-1-64456-423-3 [ePub]
ISBN: 978-1-64456-424-0 [Audiobook]

Library of Congress Control Number: 2021951697

indiesunited.net

For Lee, the sun in my universe

Secrets, silent, stony sit in the dark palaces of both our hearts: secrets weary of their tyranny: tyrants willing to be dethroned."

– James Joyce

HOT HOUSE

A Thriller

Lisa Towles

INDIES UNITED PUBLISHING HOUSE, LLC

PROLOGUE

(Texting)

Hey
Hey
How'd it go?
Um
Did he buy it?
No
WTF…we had a deal
Wife came home early
Shit, what happened?
I slipped out
The window? LOL
Front door
Did she see you?
IDK. He's so smooth he could explain away another woman in bed with him
Would he have made the transaction?
I think so
Does he like it that much?
No, not it. You
Can you try again?
He won't deal with me
Why not?
He said sending a courier was insulting

So arrogant
From you, he'd buy anything
What did you think of him?
Nice smell, not bad looking for an old guy
You took a big risk for me
No big deal
Tomorrow then?
You know what he wants. I think you want it too
No way, gross
I know you Sophie
I just wanted to sell one of my pieces, my first sale, yknow?
He had a message for you
What?
Said you left your appointment book in his office
Really
What?
I don't have an appointment book
So what does that mean?
Means he's a player
Or he just wants to see you again
Maybe
He's a judge, what do you expect
I expect he'll get whatever he wants

CHAPTER ONE

6 months later

Nothing good ever happened on a day you spilled black coffee on a white silk shirt. I jerked upright at 7:55 a.m. having missed a seven o'clock meeting with a prospective buyer, still plagued with the thought of the dark gray van tailing me again last night. Sure, I could tell myself fairy tales about how prosaic gray was for an automobile color, or how Ocean Park was a suburban neighborhood with lots of kids that required transport. But that was no soccer mom in the van.

The first note arrived with uncanny speed, almost too soon when you consider how many steps are involved in investigating a murder. I mean, I'd barely scratched the surface when I came home and found an index card in my mailbox. Handwritten in tall thin letters with a fine, red Sharpie, "STOP". And back then, I'd barely started. I thought it was some kind of joke instigated by my senile neighbor who digs up objects from her front yard and delivers them to our front porches.

By the time I'd taken the judge's first two blackmail notes to the forensics team I contract work out to, a second card arrived—this time in a plain, white business envelope, no return address, same message. This told me two things: whomever was threatening Appellate Court

Judge Conrad McClaren was somehow threatened by my investigating the matter, and that finding the "who" and "why" now held more significance than I thought. But there was a third reason, one I'd barely even acknowledged to myself, about why I had to find these answers. The fate of my family and my heart depended on it.

CHAPTER TWO

A classy, dark green Land Rover, maybe ten years old, the kind you'd see in an REI magazine ad, pulled into the dirt lot, out of place in this part of LA's Fashion District. I squinted and rolled in the binoculars a quarter slide and lingered behind the dusty blinds of the tiny window knowing the neighborhood would (or should, I hoped) raise questions.

A man climbed down from the awkward height of the car and stretched his six-foot-three, maybe four, frame and took in the questionable surroundings. It's not much, buddy, I know. I have my reasons. I stirred three sugars into a clean mug of fresh coffee while I watched him approach the unsightly door of my work-trailer. I could see the wheels turning. I pre-empted our first encounter and jerked open the door with a thrust that activated the almost daily pain in my shoulder.

"Of course this is it, it's the only door in the building." I smiled at the wise, untrusting face and well-tailored suit jacket. A nice surprise.

A perfunctory glance at my chest, then the coffee, and his hand extended like a lever. "Derek Abernathy."

Unmistakable Beantown accent. Light hair, gap-toothed smile—I always liked that—bad skin, and earnest green eyes. My mother would say drug use from the bad skin, and she thought gap-teeth were indicators of a big heart. I'm usually wrong about first impressions. We'll see.

"Come in." I moved to the dingy, fake leather sofa, passed him the cup, and motioned him to one of the almost-matching chairs. He sipped, I saw a half-smile, but he caught it quick enough, then another sip.

"Nice place you got here." He looked around. A smart ass, good. A useful trait.

"Let's say the location is…advantageous," I said of my dingy work-office on East 8th between Downtown LA and the Fashion District. It was the hood, if there ever was one.

The eyes widened and glanced left and right. "For what exactly?"

Really? He didn't get it? I know, I dragged him out to this forsaken place through my cryptic Craigslist ad that read, "Business Partner needed for human behavior research."

I pointed east. "Next door is an importer/exporter specializing in Asian swords; down the hall they make fake IDs, passports, driver's licenses; and on the north side's a travel agent that books Hawaiian Zodiac trips."

"Oceanfront property in Arizona?"

I tried not to, but I let a crack of a smile slip through. I liked him. "Something like that."

"Couple meth dealers and you got yourself a party."

Derek Abernathy, I said his name to myself over and over.

"You haven't told me your name yet, Miss…Ms…Mrs…"

"Mari."

He nodded, like he'd categorized me into a certain something. "Mari-what?"

"E. Mari E. That's my name."

"Are you, like, a rapper?"

Now I was the coy one, folding my arms, sliding deeper into the couch, which pinched something in my shoulder.

"All right, fine. How'd you know I like Sweet'n Low?" he asked with an attitude now that wasn't there a minute ago. "And not only that but three. Where do you even buy that shit nowadays?"

"I'm a private investigator, Mr. Abernathy. It's my job to know stuff about the people I work with."

"Oh, is that what we're doing? Working?" He didn't hide that he was both amused and flattered.

"This is a conversation," I clarified.

"What do you need me for?" he asked, emphasis on the *me*. "You seem to know about me already."

I watched him squirm in the chair fumbling with a part of his sport coat he'd accidentally sat on. "Some," I admitted, "but not all salient facts can be found on the internet. Some are found when looking through... your garbage..."

"You didn't."

"Talking to your landlady." I cracked up now, couldn't help it. "Your paper boy."

"As in newspaper? What century are you from? And I own my home, for like two decades."

"I know, and in a much nicer neighborhood than this."

He wriggled out of the jacket now, folded it, and laid it neatly on his lap, then his elbow nearly tanked the coffee on the side table, catching it just in time. I stifled a laugh.

"Silver Lake's okay, a little too hipster for me. Too many funky coffeeshops with bad art on the walls."

"Are you an art aficionado?"

A sardonic snort and his eyes widened. "Let's say I know what's good and what's not."

Omigod, I thought, but held my reaction in check. "Look, we're both private investigators. What's wrong with a little collaboration?"

He sat back and crossed his arms, waiting. Now it was my turn to perform, and I knew after one second's meeting him that tight pants and a pushup bra wouldn't get me far in this case.

"Mr. Abernathy," I said pouring myself coffee, unsweetened, "you're good at something I'm not. There's a difference between locating someone who doesn't want to be found and pulling them out. I'm good at research, damn good in fact. I'm a blood hound. What you're good at, or so your reputation suggests, is the completion tactic. Drawing someone out, or 'collecting' as I call it, is one thing, but getting them to stay in one place long enough to identify them and make an arrest is another thing altogether, and with this clientele," I looked around the room, "you better move fast."

The man crossed his legs, pulled a pair of chic glasses from his front jacket pocket, and slid them on.

"That's a nice look for you," I said in earnest.

"I'm sensing the pitch is coming and I want to see your face clearly."

He was funny, and that alone was worth ignoring any less desirable traits. "I'm looking for a guy," I said, and the face changed from one that frequently smiles to a worn-down groove of mistrust. "What?" I asked.

He rose, showing me again that he was taller than me. Damn. I'm a six-foot-tall woman so that's significant. "Get yourself a bounty hunter then."

"I need a partner, all right?" I replied, one click too loud. I drew in a breath and remembered the goal. "I need backup," I revealed more gently, strategically unmoved from the couch and staring at the floor. "I've been watching you for weeks. I needed to be sure."

"Of what?" Annoyed now. "And watching what specifically?"

"Just tailing you driving around town, down to Encinitas to a bar next to that hookah lounge. No serious breach of privacy occurred, I assure you."

He slowly sat back down, shaking his head.

"All right, a blackmailer," I admitted, purposely giving him the impression that he'd gotten something out of me.

"You're the victim?" he asked.

"No, a federal judge."

"Really." Raised brow. "They hired you?"

"Sort of. It's a family friend."

"Well Miss E, by the looks of your trailer, I wouldn't picture you having family friends in high places but I'll take your word for it. So, the blackmailer witnessed a crime that this federal judge, your family friend, allegedly committed, and the judge wants you to find the blackmailer so we can...what exactly?"

I stood, grabbed my purse, my keys, turned off the coffee maker, and stood at the door.

"Wait. We're done?" he asked.

"I'll pay you five hundred dollars a day for every day that I need you," I said and pulled out my iPhone. "I'm texting you now so you'll have my mobile and I'll message you tomorrow. Venmo okay? Or if you're a dinosaur and prefer PayPal or cash, that can be arranged."

"You've been following me for weeks, you've got my mobile number, my Gmail...what's my mother's name?"

"Doreen. Deceased. Sorry." I made a lemon face.

"Don't I need to, like, sign an employment contract, read your business conduct guidelines for proper office behavior, read your EEOC statement?"

I waved my hand and nudged him out the door while I locked it.

"Who's your Human Resources Director?" he said, walking down the stairs.

"Oh, you'll be meeting him tomorrow."

He stopped and turned. "Really?"

"Nice to meet you, Mr. Abernathy, I'll be in touch again shortly," I replied and held out my hand. He was reading my face the way you read a legal document. "What?"

"My mother always warned me about tall women."

"Always listen to your mother."

CHAPTER THREE

Hating the heat like I do, not to mention the smog and traffic, I couldn't really say why I've lived in LA this long. My parents moved us to Moorhead, Minnesota on the border of North Dakota when I was seven, and we were only supposed to live there for a year. I vowed to never live in a cold place again. A small part of me missed the silent oppression of snow, the insulator of sounds and secrets. Down here in the constant sun and shimmery surf, there was nowhere to hide. And hiding had its advantages. But, by and large, Moorhead was the oily, dark secret I held back from the world, even from myself.

I knew my future partner would be waiting for us at or near the designated spot, The Cheesecake Factory in the Santa Monica Place Mall, cashing in on the element of surprise, watching our unsuspecting approach, sizing us up. Size, funny. As I veered into the mall parking lot, I imagined Derek Abernathy sitting on a stone wall somewhere in a leather jacket, maybe half obstructed by a tree or shrub. I found a parking spot far from the entrance, got out, slid back the side door and…

"Nice day."

I heard him behind me. Dammit. I tried not to flinch.

"I presume this is Trevor, your Human Resources Director?"

He'd one-upped me. How? Surveillance, talking to my neighbors?

Dammit. No problem. Now I owed him one. "Down, Trevor. Good boy."

Derek Abernathy stepped back as I expected, as everyone did when they saw my four-and-a-half-foot tall bodyguard.

"Great Dane?"

"German Mastiff, but yes." I touched Trevor's head lightly. He watched Derek with unblinking eyes but was more aware of my response to the man. "Hungry?"

Trevor's head flinched in my direction.

"Not you, sweetie." I smiled and pointed to the covered umbrellas ahead of us.

"How do those dogs do with cats?" Derek asked.

"Generally, they're good with other pets, but they have a tendency to chase cats. And the idea of Trevor chasing anything in my house could result in broken furniture, or worse. You're a cat guy, right?"

Pause and a smirk. "I've lived with more cats than dogs in my life, but both really. Cats sort of come and go for me."

Trevor sat upright on the cool ground next to our outdoor shaded table. A server arrived the minute we sat down. Guess it was a bit early for lunch. I ordered the California Guacamole Salad, which I knew I'd never finish. Derek ordered a turkey burger, and I kept handing tiny biscuits to Trevor from a bag in my purse.

"I would've thought he would eat half the restaurant."

"Actually, Great Danes have fragile digestion, so he can't drink or eat much at a time. But then again, you're not a dog guy." I tried not to smile.

"Here we go," he said, showing the gap between his front teeth. "Please, by all means."

"Though you seem like a dog guy, you have two cats, one inside, one outside. I'm rather proud of that little bit of detection I admit."

"Ever hear of invasion of privacy?"

"There was no intrusion upon your *expectation of being alone*," I said, knowing that my smug retort might make him admit to having attended two years of law school and then dropping out. "Besides, you weren't home at the time," I added.

"Names?" he shot back, not taking the bait.

"I'm too busy working to focus on trivialities."

"Ha! Your legal surveillance of an unknown suspect failed."

A server set down two plates, and for Trevor a smaller, kid-sized plate, into which I deposited a handful of his biscuits. He licked his chops as I set it on the ground under the table near my purse.

"Thank you," I said to the server, who asked if we wanted anything else. "I'm good, you?" I asked my companion, whose face was wondering what he was doing here. I opened a file folder and slid a 5 x 7 photograph across the table.

He nodded. "The judge," he said in a lowered tone.

"Conrad McClaren, Ninth Circuit Court of Appeals."

"Appellate judge, that's an interesting detail," Derek said with his mouth full. "Sort of brings a whole new twist. And Ninth Circuit, no less."

"Exactly, and high profile. He's been receiving regular demands for money via text message for the past three weeks, each time for a hundred thousand dollars, and always from a different mobile number."

"Threatening what?" he asked.

"We'll get to that in a minute."

"Have you traced them?"

I shook my head. "They were throw-away phones, untraceable. You're asking the wrong question."

"Did he pay?"

"No way," I shot back.

Derek tipped his head to the side and wiped a smear of ketchup off his mouth. "Let's see," he started, and I knew where he'd take this. "Your man McClaren's mid-sixties, right? From what I know of men who came of age in the Mad Men generation, their conception of women wasn't exactly based on equality." He raised his brows. "Getting warm?"

I blinked back, waiting.

"If my hunch is correct, McClaren, probably fifteen or twenty years ago, had some indiscrete encounter with a female that probably ended badly, is coming back to haunt him, and is something he wants to keep quiet considering his publicly-facing career."

I took a huge bite of avocado and reminded myself I was eating in public. His evolving theory was holding my attention.

"Now," he continued, "let's say the crime was plain old adultery. Then, in that case we probably wouldn't be sitting here. Let's assume he had a one-night stand, or a full-on affair, he tried to break it off, and the woman refused to just step away, given the economic potential of his exposure."

"Is that what you think happened?" I asked, determined to be coy.

Derek shook his head slowly, then leaned forward. "I think he killed her, and his blackmailer saw what he did."

"You may be right, *Detective.*" I smiled at the one detail Derek most wanted to hide.

He hung his head. "Okay, okay. I see you've done your due diligence…"

"Don't get excited." I put up my palms. "I just need to know who I'm getting into bed with, so to speak."

"It's a long story." He stood and tossed down his cloth napkin.

"It always is." I watched him walk around the corner.

Though it didn't matter much to me how or why Derek Abernathy left the LAPD so soon after becoming a detective, I liked how he cared what I thought. And it's not that all I think about is leverage, necessarily. Just that having the upper hand in an invisible negotiation can't hurt, and I'd obviously struck a nerve.

I walked Trevor around the mall parking lot before driving him home because he needed some light exercise after every meal and because I needed time to think. Derek would be useful. He wasn't just smart. He was wily, and resourceful, and experienced. Triple punch. But we weren't at that stage yet. I knew of someone else I needed more right now.

CHAPTER FOUR

I knew if I entered the gallery through the back door, I'd be more likely to smell nail polish than through the front, which had better ventilation. Sure enough, fresh organic coffee and acetone.

"Morning, Carrie," I bellowed up the hallway to my gallery assistant and settled into my office knowing she'd been listening to music and painting her nails for the past hour instead of going through the gallery's emails, responding to customer inquiries, and sorting through the artwork list for the following month.

"Morning." Carrie poked her head around the corner. "I was just finishing the inventory…a day early," she said with a wink.

"Great, it was due yesterday." Such a bullshitter. Always the back-door braggart, finding ways to self-aggrandize her nonexistent accomplishments.

I settled in and booted up my laptop, sliding my feet out of the new pair of kitten heels, quickly burrowing them into the Mukluks I kept under my desk. Ah, much better. How I hated dressing like a grownup.

"Some guy came in showing pronounced interest in the David Korty."

"Pronounced interest. Was he drooling or something?"

"He spent twenty minutes looking at it. And no, I didn't get his contact information, but he said his name is Abe."

I loved David Korty's work and had sort of earmarked that piece for myself. "Great. Thank you, Carrie. Can you find Duga for me? I need him today."

Carrie had been with me two months and I knew she'd be frantically scanning my gallery contacts right now. I waited another five seconds, then, "Oooh, the Tibetan fellow who takes care of Trevor?"

I loved how Duga's voicemail message said simply, "Do it," which I'd always thought aptly summarized his personal style and view of the world. In his tradition of brevity, I'd get a text in the next few minutes with his present location and a question about which of his many services I needed this week. My phone buzzed. Duga.

In Simi Valley till Sunday but can come down if you need me. Trevor okay?

I need you tomorrow if possible…and not for Trevor.

Can be there by 3. Do you need your windows cleaned?

'Windows cleaned' was our code for surveillance. I started typing back a response, secretly pleased with our secret language, when I heard the metal scrape of the front door and a man's voice. Carrie would no doubt be touching up her lipstick and hiking down her too-short skirt, all the while forgetting that her job was to talk about the actual paintings hanging on the walls.

I heard her talking. "I'm sorry she's not. Did you have an appointment?"

At least she got that part right. I heard the clomp of her heavy shoes on the wood floors. Was it possible I hadn't alienated my seven a.m. buyer after all, and they came by the gallery to buy the Lisa Pressman painting that still reminded me of a Diebenkorn? I pictured my new silk blouse in a heap on my bathroom floor. Ruined.

Carrie's voice echoed down the hallway. "Miss Ellwyn, there's someone asking for you."

"Who is it?"

"He said—"

"It's all right I'm coming." I shoved my feet into my big girl shoes, then froze halfway down the hall at an unlikely face.

"Marissa Ellwyn Gallery. *You're* Marissa Ellwyn?" Derek said with a raised brow and parted lips, the space between his teeth showing. Already, I knew that look. Shit.

"Mr. Abernathy, what a surprise. I didn't know you liked fine art,"

I said, emphasis on the fine.

Carrie watched us awkwardly, then retreated to the reception area.

"What are you doing here?" I smiled and grabbed his outstretched hand, digging my nails into his flesh.

"I'm an investigator, Ms. Ellwyn," he mocked. "It's my job to know things about the people I work with."

Lord, just kill me. I folded my arms and leaned on one hip, thinking how my dress matched the Mark Rothko lithograph behind me and would have made a good promo shot. Another day maybe.

"So I have two jobs, what's the big deal? A girl's gotta make a living, right?"

"Jobs? More like lives," he hissed back, pointing outside toward the parking lot. "Mari E, as you call yourself, drives a 15-year-old dented Honda and wears a weathered hoodie artificially inseminated with the smell of cigarette smoke and vanilla cologne. Mar-ISSA, on the other hand, drives a freaking Porsche and buys her eight-hundred-dollar Ferragamo shoes in Beverly Hills, which she wears to her Culver City art gallery!" Still whispering, barely. "Now, you're gonna tell me what's really going on here or I'm out right now. I have no time for games like this."

"Oh get off your high horse," I shot back. "I didn't tell you anything untrue the other night. Okay, I didn't tell you the whole story, and we'd just met for God's sake. Calm down, Detective."

In came Carrie's shoes again during the standoff. She was carrying a tray of two demitasse cups. "Espresso?" she asked with a perfect hostess smile.

Never ask the universe questions like, "How much weirder can this day get?" As I grabbed my Louis Vuitton off the side chair in my office, I heard Carrie-the-manicurist talking up a Janet Lippincott and sounding surprisingly intelligent. Derek, true to form, was swigging espresso like it was a shot of Jim Beam. Give me strength.

CHAPTER FIVE

We agreed to meet after work, where I would apparently be giving him a more thorough explanation than earlier in the gallery. He met me in the gallery parking lot. I said I'd drive to a spot where we could talk. Now, towering over me, he glared down into my car.

"Afraid you won't fit?"

"Um…your steering wheel's on the wrong side of your dash." He struggled to maneuver his body into the cramped bucket seat. The door was pushed open all the way and the seat as far back as it would allow. He managed it with his knees crammed against the glove box.

"You need some help?" I snickered.

"I'm taller than you," he whined.

"I bought this car when I was visiting London a few years ago. I fell in love with it."

We drove in silence on the twenty-minute ride to Venice Beach, which I knew would be crowded enough for us to be virtually invisible. Completely by accident, I'd managed to time it so we'd be facing the horizon when I pulled up and miraculously found an empty spot facing the beach. The sky was blood orange and darkening quickly. Ah, LA sunsets, killing me again.

After a momentary silent vigil, uninterrupted by a caravan of skateboarders, my companion unclasped his seat belt and turned slightly left.

"You've got a lot to hide, Miss E."

"Mari."

"Is that what you're called in your other life, too?"

"Okay." I removed my sunglasses and sighed. "Okay. Yes, my legal name is Marissa Ellwyn. So what?"

"The same Ellwyn family who settled in southern California in the 1930s, and your father's uncle was freaking William Randolph Hearst?"

So this meant he'd not only researched me but he had other means at his disposal.

"That's my family, yes. I'm on the fringes of family acceptance…"

"…and all the money. Okay, I'm starting to get it now. Your family doesn't know you're a private investigator and they think you're a successful gallery owner. Why would they care? Criminal justice doesn't quite have the cache of fine art I suppose."

I nodded. "That's part of it. PI work is a reminder to them. I used to work in…" I paused and checked his face to see if he was going to finish my sentence. He didn't know. "Intelligence."

"As in CIA?" His mouth puckered.

"I investigated a case that got me shot and almost killed. Some small-time marijuana grower was also a courier for a much bigger operation running roofies and ketamine from Texas to an offshore oil rig and back. You can imagine the complexity of the operation and investigation. Big Oil, Navy, Coastguard," I explained. It was partly true anyway.

"…and the Coast Guard's under Homeland Security. Right?"

"Right," I confirmed, "bringing another entity into the picture, which meant more red tape and barriers to potentially tear it all down."

"You got to the top of the food chain, so to speak?"

"Yep, and now I've got a bullet embedded halfway into a bone in my shoulder. They'd have to break two bones to get it out, followed by a bone graft, steroid injections, and a five-month recovery. No thanks."

He kept his eyes pinned to my right shoulder. "I bet that still hurts."

"You sort of get used to it."

When Derek's head wasn't turned by the topless roller-skater gliding past us, I knew he was even more of a broken stereotype than I'd thought.

"My father went after the guy who shot me: a European organized crime boss, Jacques Martel. He and my father haven't been seen since." I turned and caught the last orange glimmer in the gray sky. It hurt just saying it out loud. "Hence, my off-hours job in a bad neighborhood. It gives me time and privacy to dig up everything I can find on where he might be without being interrupted."

"When did this happen?" he asked.

It was a fair and straightforward question. I felt my face change, my shoulders roll forward, and my body tighten all over. I guess I just didn't want to talk about how long the hole in my heart had been there, and how it started. "A year next Monday."

He turned all the way to face me. "You've got a past. So do I. It's okay. How do I fit into this tangled web?"

I sighed and unclasped my seat belt. "Judge McClaren's blackmailer, if we find him, could be used as a bargaining chip."

Derek slid his sunglasses to the top of his head and widened his eyes against the striped vista. "You think McClaren knows where your father is? Why?"

"He might have been the last person to see him before he disappeared."

"Is that a theory or do you have good intel?"

I shrugged. "Theory, so far. But I'm hoping."

"How do you know," he paused, "sorry to ask this. But how do you know he's…not dead?"

"I don't," I said, in what I knew would be one of many lies I told my future partner. It was a lie because I did know he was still alive. I felt it, in my heart, in my body.

"I'd like to see the whole case file."

"There's a file box on the back desk in my office. There's not a lot in there yet but I left it out for you. Bobby Bishop in the office next door will let you in, he works in the mornings."

"You've got it all figured out then," he mumbled as I took the onramp to Highway 10 back toward Culver City, an orange smudge over the water behind us. "I still don't know what you need me for though."

"I told you…"

"I remember what you told me. You said you needed backup."

"I do. I mean, I will. Soon."

CHAPTER SIX

What I hadn't told my new partner is that the file box with the judge's case file was a decoy, made up of 1990's era customer files from my friend Bobby Bishop, the crooked travel agent next door to my office.

I also knew I would be followed, so I'd smartened up in the past two days and would be, if all went as planned, following my pursuer—the infamous gray van. Change the balance of power and you can change everything.

For the second time, I was watching Derek Abernathy through binoculars, this time crammed inside Bobby Bishop's vintage Ford Bronco in the lot outside our dingy office trailers. The man moved carefully up the walkway, like he expected to get jumped on the way in. Bobby, who unlocked the office for him, turned on the overhead, and left Derek to himself. Staring at the coffee maker, crossing his arms, moving towards my desk—go ahead there's nothing in it, I thought, half amused at his curiosity about me. Finally, he walked to the back desk, leaned over it to finger the files and then hoisted up the whole box and headed for the door. He turned back, exchanging some words with Bobby while I crouched completely under the seat knowing he probably suspected I'd be here somewhere nearby. Bobby texted me as soon as he left.

He's done. Should I lock up?
Sure, I typed back.
Seems like a nice guy.
Don't start, it's early
LOL...*he asked about your relationship status*
You told him I'm celibate?
Nymphomaniac
Very sweet of you, okay if I stay here another few minutes?
Im not leaving for an hour, take your time, call if you need backup
Still trying to take care of me?
Always xo

I watched Derek put the file box in his trunk, eyes peeled left and right as he snaked his smart-looking Land Rover down the dirt road. I stayed, crouching my six feet of flesh and bone uncomfortably on the floor beneath Bobby Bishop's glove box...listening. From this vantage point I couldn't risk sitting up to look through the windows, but I knew whoever had been sending me index card "STOP" messages was no doubt watching me and my new partner, not to mention the gallery. I waited twenty minutes and still there was no sign of the gray van. Time to call in an expert.

CHAPTER SEVEN

Friday morning, six a.m. and I was wide-eyed staring out the sliding glass doors to the balcony I helped build with Duga last summer. I hadn't yet made coffee, my coveted ritual, and didn't really need it today. Something else had shaken my mind and heart; maybe the retelling of the Martel saga, or the compassionate expression on Derek's weathered face. Or maybe the idea of feeling targeted. The floor quaked and Trevor jumped to attention on the kitchen floor. I knew what earthquakes felt like, but this would be Duga, who always arrived before the sun came up. I swear Trevor could smell Duga's special doggie cookies three blocks away.

"Ruff!" I heard him pacing the kitchen floor—he must feel the vibration of Duga's footsteps.

"Calm down, you'll get your cookie." I reached for my bathrobe, which had slid onto the floor. As I crouched to pick it up, Trevor howled one of his deep, throaty, menacing barks, three at a time. What the hell? I scrambled to pull my sleeves into the robe and find my slippers under the bed. Then I stopped. Was that breaking glass coming from the kitchen? Holy fuck.

"Trevor!" I shouted, pulling my Beretta .9mm pistol out of its holster. I skidded around the corner and glimpsed a man in a black ski mask on my kitchen floor and Trevor standing with one foot on the man's throat staring back at me. *Breathe, Mari.*

"Goooood boy," I said in my calmest voice, scanning the broken glass from the breached door, the gun just out of reach of my assailant and Duga on the steps now behind them.

"See anyone else out there?" I shouted.

"No one," he replied. "Are you okay?"

"We're fine."

"Good boy. Trevor, come," Duga said and snapped his fingers.

Trevor checked with me first. I nodded and he backed up two steps away from my visitor, removing his massive paw from the man's larynx. I kicked the man's gun across the kitchen tile and yanked the ski mask off a clean-shaven, unfamiliar face. Barely twenty years old.

"Slide back a few feet," I told the man. "If you try to get up, Trevor will probably kill you."

The man eyeballed Trevor, then slid as directed and sat up with his hands covering his throat.

"Who are you?" I asked.

The man stared at Duga and Trevor, then me.

"He won't talk. Call LAPD," I said to Duga.

"They're on their way."

When two officers arrived ten minutes later, I handed over the assailant's gun, showed them my Private Investigator's license and gun permit and, within minutes, they'd hauled the man away. I made coffee for Duga and me. He brushed Trevor and talked to him in the special way he'd cultivated to keep him calm, understanding how high-strung Great Danes can be. Duga and I never talked business over the phone because he believed every person's phone was potentially bugged, and the same for texting.

I liked how Duga stepped quietly through my house, quietly through life, careful not to disturb what he encountered, like a Buddhist monk. He moved from Trevor's massive doggie bed and picked up a mug of Starbucks Italian roast. "This is why you needed me today?"

I laughed, enjoying the irony, knowing it probably kept me from crying. "I've been followed by a gray van for the past week, and I've been getting notes in my mailbox." I pulled the most recent one from my purse and held it out. "I'm sure the man breaking in here was another escalation of those threats. I'm investigating a federal judge in a blackmailing case and I think I'm getting in someone's way."

Duga's thoughtful eyes blinked back. "Give me twenty-four hours. I'll find out what I can."

"Thank you, my friend. Can you take Trevor with you today? I don't want to leave him alone." I surveyed the shards on the floor. "I'll arrange for the glass to be replaced, which will involve more strangers coming to the house and that will be even more upsetting to him."

"Sure." He snapped his fingers and Trevor slid out of the bed. "Where's your new partner?" Duga asked, grinning.

"Oh, so you're following me too now?"

"Many people know Derek Abernathy, not just me and you."

I paused to consider his riddle. "And that means…"

"I like the idea of you having a partner. Especially today," he said gesturing to the door.

"Fair enough. I'll be careful." I rubbed and kissed Trevor's head and realized I liked the idea of it too.

CHAPTER EIGHT

Three hours later, my side door had new frosted glass and a peek hole installed. Down five hundred dollars with no food and six cups of coffee, all after a sleepless night. With a brief text exchange to coordinate, I was about to meet my prospective partner, Derek Abernathy at Worldwide Tacos near the LAPD Baldwin Hills Crenshaw substation. I caught sight of him midway through the usual long line. He stepped out to greet me.

"You'll lose your place." I slid my sunglasses up.

"It's okay, I have my priorities straight."

Classy.

We walked to one of the picnic benches positioned between the taco stand and the substation parking lot. "You come here often?" I asked, as this was his suggestion.

He nodded toward the two-story white and gray building. "I was over there consulting with someone on a case I've been working on."

"Oh? What case?" I don't know why I was so curious, but now that my home had been breached, I felt suspicious of everybody. Or was paranoid a better word?

He was talking about journalists with his other case, but my attention was diverted by the long taco queue, a row of cars waiting to get in the overcrowded lot, and two jets flying overhead. I was observing my surroundings like any sensible person would, secretly scanning the streets for the gray van, knowing its connection to this morning's surprise visitor. Whoever was driving that van very likely intended to kill me this morning. Deep breath, in, out.

"Mari…Mari?"

I realized he'd been saying my name. "Sorry."

"Are you okay?

I shook my head. "Sorry, not really. My house was breached this morning and I'm a little off."

"Breached? How?"

"A man in a ski mask with a gun type of breach."

"Holy shit, are you okay? Are you hurt? How about Trevor?"

"Trevor." I stopped to laugh and kept on laughing picturing Trevor in a Superman cape coming to my rescue. My eyes filled up in front of Derek, a man I barely knew. God dammit.

He grabbed my hand across the table. "That's alarming. It would be for anyone. Let's get a patrol car to sit out in front of your house tonight. Really. I know people here," he said, looking at the substation. I snickered to myself.

Searching for tissue in my handbag, I heard him on the phone.

"Ivan, it's Derek Abernathy, yeah, good good, I'm at the taco stand. Can you come out? I want to introduce you to someone…yeah, okay thanks."

Just when I thought my day couldn't get any worse. I was glaring with my palms in the air.

"What? I'm asking to put a squad car on your street tonight."

Ivan. Jesus, I needed him right now like a root canal. Assessing how far away my car was, it was probably too late for me to escape him. I saw his too familiar outline in the side doorway of the police station. He raised his hand to block the sun's glare and waved to Derek, then sauntered up to us John Wayne style. The friendliest of smiles with dubious intent. He and Derek shook hands like they were old friends. Oh, my God no. Disastrous. I tried not to laugh.

"Mari, I'd like you to meet Ivan Dent, Chief of Detectives, and recently promoted too," he boasted, Ivan standing there like a freaking cat that ate the canary. Boy did he ever.

"Ivan," I said and raised a brow, my hand swallowed up by his ginormous mits. "Thought you were in San Fernando."

"Yep, then Inglewood, and now here," he replied, Derek getting the picture.

"You two...know each other obviously," he said in a defeated tone. "Mari's home was breached today and I wanted to get a squad car out to monitor her street tonight, but..." He let his voice trail off in the awkwardness of the moment. "Or did you know about this already?"

"No," Ivan shot back and sat at the table. "Are you okay? What happened? How's Trevor?"

"He probably saved my life."

"Please please, allow me to put a car outside your house tonight."

"Hell yeah I will. I'll take all the help I can get right now." I looked to Derek, who was now sitting beside Ivan across from me.

"What are you two doing here today?" Ivan asked, looking at me. "You working a case together?"

"The two missing journalists." Derek nodded. "A family member of one of them contacted me and I'm looking into it for her, just as a private matter for the family. But the case is still open, right?" he asked Ivan.

"A little cold but still open," Ivan replied. "We haven't made any arrests yet so you're free to dig up what you can, and if we end up stepping on each other's toes, we can fight about it then."

"That's fair," Derek said. "And I've only just started on it this week so nothing much to report yet."

"Who are they?" I asked. "Or were they?"

Derek turned toward me on the picnic bench. "Two journalists working together to track down the killer of a French college student who died six months ago. Two weeks ago, one of the journalists disappeared, and the other one was found dead in San Diego."

I paid close attention this time, remembering what I'd read about the college student's case. There'd been nothing about it in the news for months. "Sonia-something, right?"

"Sophie," Derek confirmed. "Sophie Michaud, a French art student studying at UCSD, her first year here. What a shame."

"And what are *you* digging up that's causing bad guys to go crashing through your door?" Ivan this time, leaning forward in his paternal voice.

I told him about the federal judge, the blackmail notes he'd been getting, and what little information I had to go on.

"So you don't yet know what he's being blackmailed for?"

"Only theories so far," I admitted.

"Who is it?" Ivan whispered.

I leaned forward in the tacit language of investigative work, protecting victims and their identities until circumstances dictated a different approach. "Judge Conrad McClaren, a federal appellate judge in San Francisco. Ninth Circuit."

Ivan looked at the sky, blinking. "McClaren?" He looked at Derek. "Isn't that the judge involved in the journalists' case with Sophie Michaud?"

"Wait…what?" I glared at both of them. "You knew this?" I said directly to my supposed partner.

"Yeah, I knew there was some judge vaguely connected to the student the journalists were writing about. I didn't know who it was until now."

I felt heat rising in my chest. "Vaguely connected? What does vaguely connected mean?"

"Look, Mari—" Ivan started.

"I need to see that case file. I need to see it now. McClaren's a family friend."

"You know I can't share details of an open case," Ivan said, his eyes begging me not to make a scene.

"Cut the crap, Ivan. My partner here's working on the same case, apparently. And that means—"

"Your partner?" Ivan interrupted, looking now at Derek. Poor Derek.

I rose and put my glasses back on, now towering over both of them. I liked how that felt. "You listen to me. I've been followed for the past week, I've been getting harassing notes stuck in my mailbox, and an armed assailant broke through my kitchen door at fucking six o'clock this morning. You *will* let me see that case file because it's likely this case is why my life is now in danger. Got it?"

CHAPTER NINE

Well, that may be the only argument I've ever won against Ivan Dent after our fiery eighteen month whatever-it-was, which ended around the same time as my father's disappearance. All told, though, Ivan took me in, comforted me, and essentially nursed me back to vim and vigor after I was shot, when the case I'd spent two years building came to a head. I put myself in the line of fire to take down one of Europe's most notorious drug czars, Jacques Martel, and it nearly worked. I got close enough to look him in the eyes, after which a bullet from his pistol lodged in my shoulder and thrust me overboard to bleed in shark-infested waters. My team got me out in time, but the scent of blood and salt water was permanently imprinted on my nostrils. Even now, the smell of low tide sickens me. The body remembers with a precision the mind can't fathom.

Ivan's terms: Derek and I could view the entire casefile—in this case what they call the Murder Book for Sophie Michaud, from within the precinct—and it had to be in one sitting. Guess I'd be spending all day in a stuffy, too-small conference room with bad lighting.

I got there at eight the next morning and Derek arrived five minutes later with a cardboard tray of coffee from Starbucks and a crumpled bag in between them. God bless him.

The table was way too small for the amount of material in those boxes. Derek sat across from me sizing me up. "Is it safe to assume that at one time you were referred to as Mrs. Dent?"

"Seriously? That's how you're proposing we start the day?"

"Sorry."

"Whatever. Let's get to work, Detective."

"I'm no longer a detective," he corrected.

"And I was never Mrs. Dent," I hissed, pulling one of the coffees out of the holder too hard. Surplus coffee spilled on the table and rolled down to my pants. Bad coffee karma lately. I wiped it up with one of the napkins stuffed in the bag, and a few more tucked in a pocket of my handbag. I peeled the top off the café latte and took three swallows. Perfect amount of sugar. How did he know? "That's good," I admitted, sipping the warmth. "Thank you."

Derek sipped from his cup and opened his eyes wide.

"What??" I was already annoyed and we'd only been here five minutes. "Okay, fine. Ivan and I met when I was first starting the case that got me shot. We lived together for almost two years."

"He says it's Trevor's fault that you broke up."

"Love it. He would say that, wouldn't he? Maybe that's true. Trevor's a kindred spirit. All right, so now you know. My turn. How do you and Ivan know each other?"

"Ivan Dent hired me and fired me a year later. He's the reason I'm no longer a homicide detective."

"Then why—"

"Yeah, group therapy's over for today," he snapped.

"Fine." I held up my hands and reached for the file box Ivan had left for us on the long white conference table. When I did, a clump of garden soil plopped onto the table in little thuds.

"Is that dirt?"

"My neighbor." I sighed and remembered Mrs. Whittimore. "She's close to a hundred and I don't know how she lives alone." I brushed the dirt onto the linoleum floor. "She digs up flowers from people's gardens and delivers them, roots and all, to their front porch."

"Like a dog digging for bones," he said, looking off like it reminded him of something.

"Something like that. Why don't you tell me about the journalists."

Derek rose to take off his suit jacket, revealing a pressed, white, button-down shirt tucked into dark jeans. He was clean-shaven, well built, and obviously spent time working out. Runner? Volleyball? No.

Seemed like more of a gym guy. He pulled two muffins out of the white bag, placed one on each napkin, and pushed it to my side of the table while he broke his apart.

"Two women—" he held up two fingers—"working together on the same case like Woodward and Bernstein. And similar in some ways, too. Bob Woodward was more experienced, Bernstein was 'hungry' as he put it, so he made up for his lack of experience with passion. Elise Turner, the more experienced reporter, took Nina Richmond, a novice just out of college, under her wing and brought her into this case to expose her to a high-profile murder case."

I'd pulled my 11-inch MacBook out of my bag and started typing notes. "Murder case of the student?"

"Right. Her real name is Sasha Michaud but she went by Sophie, a French art student."

"Exchange program?" I asked.

"No, she was enrolled full time at UC San Diego, and not here on a student visa because she's got dual citizenship. French father, American mother."

"Interesting," I commented. "Why's the case up here?" I asked, as opposed to San Diego. "Did she die here?"

"Debatable, from what I've read of the file so far." Derek sighed and crossed his arms over his chest. "Let me answer the first question first. I'm working on the case because Elise Turner's mother hired me. Turner's been missing for almost a month."

"Okay, so she got too close to something?"

"I suspect so, and her protégé', Nina Richmond, was found dead in the same manner as Sophie Michaud."

"Which was…what?" I pulled my fingers from the keyboard to listen.

"That's the second question and an interesting one. Where did they die? Both women were found early in the morning on Mission Beach in San Diego, with similar marks on their necks. Apparently strangled."

"What part of the beach?" I asked.

He smiled. "Good question. Mariner's Point, over by Sunset Point Park." Derek's eyes were squinted.

"There's more. What?" I asked.

He rubbed his chin and the rest of his face. "The postmortem revealed that both bodies had been moved to the beach from somewhere else."

"Both of them? And were they both moved from the same place?"

"Both yes, but I don't know yet where they were moved from. So, without knowing where they were killed, or Nina Richmond anyway, I don't know where to look for Turner. So far, I've started talking to her family, coworkers, and neighbors to place where she was last seen and who she saw or talked to her the day she died."

My phone buzzed; it was a text from Duga. I dialed his number. "Hey, Duga. What's up?"

"I have those groceries you asked me to pick up for Trevor. Can I meet you and give them to you?" he said in our encoded language, which meant I'm too paranoid to give you information over the phone and I need to tell you in person. I gave him my location.

"Okay, where'd we leave off?" Derek asked.

"Elise Turner," I said. "And I'm gonna meet Duga at the taco stand in a few minutes."

"No problem. Elise Turner and Nina Richmond, reporters with the San Diego Union Tribune, got as far as Sophie Michaud's brother in their investigation of her death. Apparently, he also had some connection to Judge McClaren."

"Wait a minute," I said. "Did the judge have a direct connection to Sophie? Or was it through her brother?"

"It was through her father, actually. He's a French diplomat," Derek replied and smiled.

I took in his detail. "Geez."

"I know."

"Let me get this straight," I said. "The girl, what, nineteen—"

"Eighteen."

"Okay, eighteen years old, was a dual citizen of France and the US, and here studying art at UCSD, and she's the daughter of a French diplomat. She had some kind of connection to a US federal judge, now she's dead and the two journalists writing the story are either dead or missing, and the judge is being blackmailed. Sounds like this crime could have been politically motivated."

"Could be." Derek nodded, finishing the bottom half of his muffin.

"I assume the French government will have initiated an investigation of their own by now. No?"

His lips formed a *nailed it* expression. "The legal jurisdiction of the French government in the case of Sophie's death is questionable, but

I'm assuming the family has already initiated their own investigation into the matter."

"Were they questioned?" I asked.

"Yes. Questioned and cleared."

"Either way, it complicates matters for us," I surmised, typing some additional notes. My phone buzzed again. "Duga's here. I'll be back in a few."

"Are you gonna actually eat any tacos there today? And who's Duga?"

"Tacos? It's nine-thirty in the morning."

CHAPTER TEN

I wondered what Duga would be bringing me as I moved past the squad cars in the lot and up the incline to the adjacent lot. Not only information, but he sometimes brought odd toys, trifles, and trinkets. Crystals, jade charms, Chinese herbs, and once, the day before I got shot, a fortune cookie whose message prophetically read "Danger lurks around every corner."

I hadn't quite gotten around to explaining Duga to my new partner, or to myself, if I was being completely honest, like his habit of appearing out of thin air. There had never been anything romantic or sexual between us, but certainly intimacy, like more than family even. He was a business associate that sometimes substituted as my dog whisperer, bodyguard, and shaman. Like always, I got to the taco place and he was nowhere to be seen. Then I half turned, and he was a foot away from me.

"Jesus, Duga." My hand slapped my chest. "Don't do that to me."

"Morning," he said and drew me into a safe embrace. Add hug-master to his list of job titles. When he got me in his arms, he pressed his mouth to my ear and whispered close. "Don't go to your house today." He pulled away and motioned me to the same picnic bench I'd sat on yesterday with Derek and Ivan.

"Lord. What now?"

Duga sat beside me on the bench, both of us looking out into the waking sky over the water. "Your house has been breached again."

"Oh…my God…are you kidding me?" I felt sudden nausea. "The kitchen window again?"

"No, bedroom window." He paused and scrutinized my expression. "What are they looking for?"

"Is Trevor okay?" I asked, my heart pounding.

"I don't think he heard anything, and he wasn't drugged."

"What do you mean he didn't hear anything? How could he not?"

"I checked him out and he's okay. He's at my house now."

"Duga, what the fuck are they looking for? What about the van?"

"They tailed you here this morning, but no sign of them now. The plate came up as Wackenhut. Security firm with eight locations around town."

"They're a front organization for the CIA," I whispered.

He paused, and I knew that meant that Duga's brain was kicking into bodyguard mode. "I see. And the cards you've been getting in your mailbox have no prints on them. They must be wearing rubber gloves because my team found residue of talc but nothing more. I checked and there's nothing in your mailbox right now. Do you want me to contact the glass company and have them replace your bedroom window?"

I nodded, absently. Another escalation. How many more would there be?

After Duga left, I walked slowly back to the precinct where Derek was waiting. I tried hard not to look over my shoulder every two seconds, but there was no traffic noise right now. When did that ever happen in LA? Get a grip, Mari, keep walking. Duga said he'd make up his guest room for me. I think Trevor liked it there better than my house in Ocean Park. Glenwood had wider streets and smoother concrete for his paw pads.

As I decided how much of this I'd tell Derek, I went through the list of what I'd done so far in my investigation of the judge and his texting blackmailer. Like I'd been trained, I thought about time. When did the messages start, and why now? I'd been thinking the messages were related to a case, and maybe one of Judge McClaren's bench rulings on an appeal, and maybe someone opposed one of them. My brain was working, and maybe my assumptions so far were wrong. My hand fumbled with something in the right pocket of my blazer, something cold and shiny…and heavy. I pulled it out just as Derek opened the door to our conference room.

"Hey, what's that?" he asked, looking down.

"Well…" I rolled it in my fingers and wow, Duga strikes again. "It appears to be a tiny brass elephant," I said and laughed.

"Good luck charm?"

Duga's Tibetan, and in Tibet elephants are said to bring you fortitude and strength. "Something like that."

"What happened with the van?"

"Well, the Company's keeping tabs on me, looks like." I made my way around the table back to my laptop, my half-eaten muffin and cold coffee.

"You mean—"

I nodded, the Company referring to CIA. "I worked in the intelligence community, but…must be something more to this case than we can see from here. Duga also told me someone broke into my house again, this time my bedroom and they were obviously looking for something."

"What? When, today?"

"This morning, I guess."

Derek shook his head. "What are you on to here?"

"What are *we* on to? Maybe the same thing."

CHAPTER ELEVEN

I paced the floors of the police precinct conference room while Derek Abernathy ran through a summary of Ivan's casefile, or the Murder Book for Sophie Michaud.

"We're only just learning about her and she's already not your run-of-the-mill teen tragedy."

"Why?" I asked.

"Straight A student in her Visual Arts program, and in her elective classes as well: International Business and Political Science. On top of that, she placement-tested out of three lower-level math classes and was getting an A in Multivariable Calculus when she died."

Sophie Michaud was a first-year art student, a gifted artist who already had an exhibit on campus, no police record, smart, successful, looking like a prodigy. My mind had been trained to find the weak link, especially when it appeared there weren't any. So, as Derek moved from her academic to her personal life, I was already forming an opinion of Sophie as an extraordinary young woman who may have made some enemies along her short path of success. And, in an investigation, those early judgments were as critical as they were hazardous. Useful to clinch what your gut was telling you, while a formed judgment inevitably closed off your mind to other avenues of inquiry. I grabbed my laptop.

"What are you doing?"

I motioned him to me and smiled. His eyes widened. "Come here, I won't bite."

"You sure?"

He pulled a chair next to me and watched my screen. I opened Chrome and pulled up Instagram on one tab, Facebook on another, then LinkedIn, and Pinterest.

"You're thinking like an eighteen-year-old."

"Yep. Not sure she even has anything up on LinkedIn—that's really for when you already have a career." Seven Sophie Michauds came up initially.

"Try with an f," he said.

"Okay," and I typed Sofie Michaud, got a few more hits, and sat back in my chair. "Facebook," I said and switched tabs and typed Sophie Michaud with both spellings. Forty-five entries to search through. "Shit."

"Wait." Derek opened the murder book. "The original postmortem—" he flipped pages, "had two names."

I waited.

"Here. Her real name was Sasha Michaud, but she went by Sophie. Both are listed here."

"As Sasha Sophie?" I asked.

"Yes, with the 'ph'."

"Interesting." I twisted the right lower corner of my hair under my right ear lobe, a habit I'd picked up from my mother, and one that always seemed to help me think. "Who ID'd the body?"

"Hannah Moraga, no idea who she is, and a school counselor. And there's mention of a Jonathan Michaud, though not sure if he identified the body or not."

"Family…gives us something at least."

"Brother—" he read through the report—"has an apartment in San Diego. Sophie was living with him and a roommate."

Derek stepped back three paces and glanced at the window with a heavy sigh. I loved his exaggerated movements, like thirty minutes of digging through a file was real work. I indulged him because he was doing all the work for me. But something told me I had mine coming.

"And presumably Ms. Moraga was the roommate," he added, still reading. I took two more bites of the now-hardened muffin top. As usual, it was sweet enough to induce a diabetic coma, which was fine. I needed all the help I could get today.

I went back to my laptop and typed Sasha Michaud and then Sasha Sophie Michaud into LinkedIn and found a page that put a tiny flash in my chest. The woman in this picture looked early twenties but could have easily been eighteen, not-smiling, looking away from the camera. I studied the details: the strawberry blonde hair lighter on the tips, chic haircut, dark eyes with an unmistakable *don't fuck with me* attitude to them. I knew it was her, but I'd learned to substantiate hunches. Scanning the profile, it identified UCSD, photography, art, a list of the classes she'd taken so far, a link to a Childish Gambino video. Derek pointed at my screen.

"Your finger's blocking what you want me to see," I said.

He moved it an inch to the right, and it showed that the location of the profile we were looking at indicated Paris, France. "She's French." He was towering over me now, nodding and smiling.

"What?" I asked.

"I was reading about it while you were out with Dunga or Duncan."

"Duga! Come on, it's four letters. Are you jealous of him already? We barely know each other yet," I chided. "He's like my mentor."

"Really? What skills is he helping you improve?"

It was a fair question, worthy of introspection. Maybe later. "At the moment, staying alive."

"Sorry, I know you've had a traumatic morning." He placed one hand on my shoulder. It felt warm, and very large. He sat beside me again. "Sophie is, Sophie *was* the daughter of a French diplomat. Nicholas Michaud is the French Minister of Culture, and the family's from Paris. Sophie's mother is American so that explains Sophie's dual citizenship."

My brain scrambled to pull the strings together. "And the brother lives here?"

"Yeah, Jonathan Michaud, a businessman who the roommate reported is never home."

"What a mess."

CHAPTER TWELVE

Two knocks. Ivan Dent opened the door to the conference room and stood tall in the doorway. He'd put on weight since my last visit and he was hoping I hadn't noticed. He watched me through narrowed eyes, chewing one side of his lip.

"Long hours now, huh?" I asked.

"Don't say it." His hand went up.

"Still going to the gym?" It was an evil question, intended to humiliate him about his twenty-two-year-old 'personal trainer', Melissa.

"Yes I'm still working with Melissa. She's done a wonderful job getting my knee back in shape."

I'll bet she has. "Kicking us out?"

"You're doing that thing with your face," he said, Derek watching the dynamic between us.

I closed my laptop. "I don't have a *thing*."

"Honey, don't get me started," Ivan said in an affected tone, letting his half-Cuban heritage emerge.

Derek and I put the files and Murder Book back in the large box and cleaned up the table while Ivan kept his eyes glued to me.

"Don't call me honey, *fatty*," I whispered as we wriggled past him into the hallway toward the side door exit.

"Dude, she just called me fat!" he bellowed to my partner but loud enough for the entire precinct to hear because that was his way. Ivan Dent was larger than life. It was what I loved about him. Once.

"Do you have copies of the articles the journalists wrote on this case?" I asked Derek, ignoring Ivan and heading out to the parking lot.

"There's only one so far," he said, "but I heard they have drafts of two other unpublished articles."

The word unpublished stopped me in my tracks. "Why unpublished? And how do you know this?"

"A former client of mine works there, and I don't know why they weren't published. I can look into it if you want," Derek offered.

I'd find the published article online. But I desperately needed to get to the gallery today. That meant going home to change into my other life and checking on Trevor.

"I've got some things I need to take care of today. Let's meet again tomorrow morning if you're free."

Derek leaned against the car with his arms crossed. "Sure, I'm free tomorrow, and we should use that time to figure out the connection between your blackmail case and Sophie Michaud."

He was right.

"However, I don't think you're going anywhere alone right now. Do you have somewhere else you can stay tonight?"

"Duga's got Trevor, and he said I could stay in his guest room. Believe me, it's not ideal."

"What, does he have, a dirty house or something?"

"Dirty, that's funny. You could literally eat off his floors, so much so that I'm shocked he allows Trevor there. I just, you know, like my independence." I sighed. Get through today one step at a time, I thought. I agreed to let Derek escort me home while I changed clothes and that I wouldn't go out tonight without a chaperone.

My phone buzzed. Ivan. I tried to suppress my eyeroll. "Yeah," I answered, holding out the phone, "and you're on speaker in case you were planning to start an argument." I winked at Derek.

"Just letting you know there's no ID yet on your assailant who broke into your kitchen. No record and nothing came up from his prints."

"What about FaceFirst?" Derek asked about the facial recognition tool.

"Nothing on that yet. I'll check again after lunch and let you know. Derek, do I have your mobile number?"

"Unless you deleted me from your contacts, you should."
"Ouch!" Ivan joked.

CHAPTER THIRTEEN

After tossing and turning in Duga's guest room bed that night, I woke early and slipped past Trevor, who was snoring peacefully in Duga's special doggie bed. I changed into my Marissa Ellwyn attire, which I'd stuffed into an overnight bag: black pencil skirt, blue and black Banana Republic floral blouse, and low heels. I was ready for anything, or at least for coffee.

Truth be told, I wanted to get to my gallery. It had a corner back office with the most beautiful lighting, a lemon tree outside one of the windows, not to mention my good laptop with the 17" screen. It's where I'd been researching my father's disappearance and, more recently, the judge's blackmail case. I'd driven to San Francisco to talk with Judge McClaren, his wife, his law clerks, his paralegal, and his admin assistant. I came back with a whole legal pad worth of notes, chronicling the dates of all the blackmailer's communications, everyone's personal opinion of office visitors who fit the "edgy" profile, and not a single commonality in the list. Via email and phone, I'd established a picture of the judge's movements and activities the week the first note arrived as well as a summary of all the appellate decisions the judge had written in the past year. So far I wasn't seeing any correlation between these facts and what we'd just learned about Sophie Michaud.

Cognoscenti's, Culver City's best coffee spot, served lattes with oat milk, almost everyone did now, and the frothy brew started to wake up my brain by the third sip. I loved the concrete floors of this place offset by bright orange chairs. I was always the odd demographic, twenty years older than the mostly college-aged students. It had a glassed-in breezeway in the back, which was perfect for quiet introspection. I settled at a small table and absently checked the newsfeed on my iPhone while glancing at the world waking up. Halfway through the headline story on politico.com, a text alert slid down my screen prompting me to call my security company. What now? I scanned my phone contacts for Prestige. I was alone in the breezeway so I placed the call from my table.

"This is Marissa Ellwyn. I got a text just now. Is everything okay?"

After the usual ninety forms of verbal authentication, they confirmed that they'd texted me because a man had been knocking and then banging on the entry door to the gallery three hours before we opened. The man wouldn't give his name, but Security had no trouble detaining him as he refused to leave until I showed up. I guzzled the rest of my latte, a ruthless thing to do to fine coffee, and texted Derek to meet me at the gallery ASAP.

ASAP, huh? he jibed. *Nice having backup?*

Actually, yes. Are you free or not?

I'll be right behind you.

He was right. Why hadn't I worked with a partner before now? I'd had about enough surprises for one week, and I felt my chest tightening to prepare me for whoever needed to see a gallery owner with a life-or-death emergency. I was three blocks away from the gallery and I swear I recognized Derek's hair in the car behind me. "Hey Siri, call Partner," I said. My phone dutifully dialed the number I'd added yesterday.

"Hey," he answered.

"Just curious, when you said *right behind you*, did you literally mean that you've been following me today? This is a straight yes or no answer."

Pause. Sigh. "Duga asked me to. He's on surveillance of the gray van and wants to spend the whole day tailing it. He said to tell you your bedroom window's fixed and that he'll return Trevor after you've installed the alarm system you promised to install last year."

"He'll return Trevor tonight and I'm looking into an alarm system," I clarified. "He's a good protector." Maybe too good.

I told him about the Prestige call as we pulled into the parking lot. A thin, wiry-haired, sweaty guy paced outside the front door clenching his fists. He froze when he observed us pulling in. Derek was closest to him and got out and introduced himself. I watched them shake hands and the stranger nodded. Judging by the sobering expression on the other man's face, Derek was saying something. Then he motioned for me.

"This is Marissa Ellwyn, the gallery owner," Derek said. I liked this formal version of him.

"Hello," I said, and extended my hand.

Handshake analysis: sweaty palm, weak grip, eyes blinking too fast. This guy needed a tranquilizer gun.

"I'm-I'm-I'm Thomas Barnes," he blurted. "Can we talk inside?"

Thank goodness Carrie didn't work on weekends, so there was nothing to explain away when the three of us entered the space. I dragged my desk chair into the main gallery and the two men sat on a bench by the east wall opposite me.

"So, now that we've all met properly, what exactly is so urgent?" I asked.

The stranger looked over his right shoulder and leaned sideways to glance down the alley, looked out the front windows, and then a scan around the gallery's interior.

"Mr. Barnes?" I repeated, not hiding my irritation. Derek quietly observed.

"Judge Conrad McClaren's office was burglarized last night."

Derek and I stared at each other. This judge was literally everywhere I turned this week. "You mean his office in San Francisco?" I asked.

"Yes."

"You drove down here when?"

Before the man answered, Derek moved toward the front door, looking out at the street and standing guard. Not a bad idea, all things considered.

"No actually, I live here," Thomas explained. "I no longer work for the judge."

"So how'd you know about the break in?" Derek asked without missing a beat, still by the front door. "Unless you did it yourself."

"One of his other clerks called me. Seems that the judge asked for your help specifically," Thomas replied, looking directly at me.

"Wouldn't he just call me?" I asked. "He's a family friend and he certainly has my number. Besides, I was just up there two weekends ago."

"He asked his clerk, ah, his current clerk, well one of his numerous current clerks, to ask me to come and talk to you, and he gave me your address. Here, I mean. The gallery address. I mean, because I live down here, which is closer to—"

Give me strength. I disappeared into my office to grab a notebook and pen, hopefully to help me organize the chaos coming out of this guy's head. Derek brought our visitor a glass of ice water to stave off an anxiety attack.

"When did you stop working for the judge, Thomas?" I asked when I returned.

"Two months ago."

"Why was that?"

"I, um, moved. What I mean is, I was living in—"

"Yep, I get it," I said. "You were living in San Francisco working for one of the most high-profile federal judges in the country and you just quit and moved to SoCal to hang out at the beach all day? Weather's nicer, I'll admit."

"I, well, bartend actually, pretty good money, too."

This guy will be a perfect surveillance job for Duga, I thought. "Okay, that makes sense," I lied, eyeing my partner, who was looking on his phone, face frozen solid. "Who was the other clerk who contacted you?"

"Walter Judge."

"That's his name?" I asked.

Thomas affirmed and sipped the water Derek brought him.

"You'll need to leave us your phone number before you go. What exactly did Judge McClaren ask you to relay to me?"

"For you to come up to San Francisco and, you know, help him figure it all out."

"Figure all what out?"

"Well..." Thomas drummed is fingers on his knee and tapped his feet. He hadn't seemed like a junkie at first, but I was quickly changing my mind. "I know you're working on his blackmail case, and he wants you to help him figure out who's targeting him like this."

I glanced at Derek, who raised a brow and nodded, encouraging me to go on.

"Like what? You think whoever's blackmailing the judge is the same person who ransacked his office?"

"I'm sure of it." Thomas nodded his head a little too quickly.

"Really? Because that doesn't make sense. The blackmailer probably thinks they already have something incriminating on the judge, and the break-in implies that someone thinks the judge is in possession of something needed by someone else. Is that how you'd look at it?"

Derek turned in response to a sound at the curb, and I saw a gray car pull up and park. I'd plopped my purse, with my gun, on my desk when I ran in to retrieve the desk chair. Now it was about twenty steps around a corner. Shit.

"It's the security company. I'll go out." Derek closed the door behind him, keeping an eye in the room while he talked to an officer on the sidewalk.

I pretended to write something on the legal pad on my lap, glancing up at Thomas every few seconds. "Where'd you go to law school, Thomas?"

"I dropped out. I was going to Stanford and got through two, almost three years."

"So you dropped out right before you were about to finish?"

"Yep, I thought it was the best idea under the circumstances."

"Which circumstances were those?" I got up and adjusted a painting on the wall to give him a moment to frame what would inevitably be another lie.

"Well, the ones I was telling you about. I didn't like the direction things were going in the office, so I changed course."

I nodded, wondering if nine in the morning was too early for a martini. "Bartending sounds fun and a nice change of pace. Where do you work?" I seriously worried that the man might have a heart attack in front of me.

"A wine bar, and then a bar on the Santa Monica Pier."

"Aren't you up kinda early then? Did you work last night?"

Slight laugh. "Yeah, till two-thirty. I don't sleep mu— What I mean is I don't really *need* that much sleep. I never have."

"I'm jealous. Must give you a lot of time to get things done."

The man's face hardened with a contracting of the mouth and eyes. "Look Ms. Ellwyn, I might have given you the wrong impress—"

I opened my palms and smiled. "Not at all, you're fine," I said.

"You're bringing me information about a man I've known nearly all my life and a situation where he needs my help." I took two steps toward the door. The truth was that before two weeks ago, I hadn't seen Conrad McClaren in twenty years. "Tell Walter Judge that we talked, and I'll reach out to Judge McClaren later today. Sound good?"

He managed a faint "yes", then thanked me by offering his even sweatier palm and made it worse by wiping it on his pants, *post*-handshake. OMG hilarious. I had him write his name, address, phone, email, and the two bars he worked at on the legal pad I was holding, because I remembered Ivan Dent had a handwriting analyst on his team. Now I just had to think of a reason why Ivan owed me a favor.

CHAPTER FOURTEEN

Finally I had time to make real, freshly-ground, French press coffee in the gallery's micro-kitchen. I heard Derek's footsteps canvassing the space, and I wondered what he thought of modern art. I carried out two mugs.

"Can I go back to bed and start this day again?" I asked.

Derek plopped down on the narrow bench; it wobbled under his weight.

"Don't spill that on my floor, please," I said. "What happened with the security guard?"

"They said he was agitated and on the verge of tears, and demanded they call you. He said you were expecting him, but not till later today."

I shook my head. "What an operator."

"What did you get out of him while I was outside?"

"Dropped out of Stanford Law School in his third year, says he quit his federal judicial law clerk job voluntarily, which probably paid over $100k, by the way," I added, "moved down here and bartends at two venues in Santa Monica. He says another of the judge's law clerks, a Walter Judge, and yes that's his name, called him and said the judge wanted him to tell me about the office break in. Why? I guess because of the convenience factor that he lives down here now and so do I."

"You were up there a few weeks ago, right?"

"Two weekends ago I drove up to see the judge and discuss the blackmail case and the notes he's gotten so far. I spent time at his home, talked with his wife again, saw some of the new art he's acquired recently, a—"

"Is he an art collector?" Derek asked.

"Not officially, but he loves fine art and has money to spend."

I watched my partner working these facts over in his brain. His gaze landed on a painting on the far wall. He rose and stood in front of it.

"No touching," I said, only half joking. "You wouldn't believe how many people actually reach out and touch paintings in art galleries." I moved toward the painting and stood beside him to stand guard. I know he's gonna try to touch it.

"I like this."

"Really?"

"Yes." He elbowed me. "Does that surprise you?"

"Sort of. Mira Dancy, called Blue Exile. I like it, too. We can fight over it later. I want to see how Duga's doing with his surveillance, and I need to see Ivan." I went to grab my purse from my office.

"Speaking of surveillance," he said, "I think Thomas Barnes might be a good pet project for Duga if he can fit it into his schedule."

"Agreed. I got Thomas' address and I know where he works."

Derek smiled. "I can do better. I know what he loves."

"What?"

"Chess, and there's a chess park on the waterfront in Santa Monica."

"Chess, interesting. How'd you find that out?"

"Social media profiles."

"So, that's what you were doing outside."

He grinned.

"The chess park is right near the bars he works at, too." I inhaled and exhaled deeply as the thought formed in my head. "I'm not sure about him, though."

"Well, we just met the guy."

"That's not what I mean. I'm trying to figure out if the judge is at the center of everything, or if Sophie's at that center. I think right now I'd like to know if there was a connection between Sophie and Thomas Barnes. That's what I'm gonna work on after I see Ivan." I grabbed my purse and closed my office door behind me. "I'm gonna lock up. Let's go out the back."

"I didn't get a chance to tell you what I found out at the newspaper," he said, as I pressed the alarm code and locked the back door.

I stopped, half turned, and the sun blinded me. I fumbled for the sunglasses in my bag and kept walking towards the parking lot. "About Elise Turner, the journalist?"

"Put it this way…I think you're asking the right question about who's at the center. I mean, we've got a homicide—no, two homicides—a blackmail, several B&Es, and harassment, if you count the notes in your mailbox."

"Don't forget the van that's been tailing me. And we might discover that Sophie was connected to all of these threads."

"I was thinking the judge," Derek said.

"Why?"

"I found one of the draft articles Turner had shown to her editor, which hadn't been published yet."

"And?"

"She'd uncovered a connection between the judge and Sophie that had ethics violation written all over it, or worse."

"Jesus. I hope—"

"Sophie, the week before she died, apparently sold him something, or he bought something from her that might have been a piece of art. This is the theory the article was proposing anyway."

"One of Sophie's art pieces?"

"Well," Derek paused and stopped walking. "There was also speculation in the article, unsubstantiated, that Sophie might have been selling sex."

"Come on, that's ridiculous. To the judge?" I leaned on my car. "I've known his family since I was ten." I looked up at the sky. Blue, empty, like it was waiting for something. "And you think this is why it wasn't published?"

"The editor's not publishing the article, or not until there's a way to substantiate that theory with some evidence or witnesses to corroborate the claim. It might be nothing," he added, but his face said something different.

"I'll call the SFPD and see who's been assigned to work the burglary case of the judge's office break-in," I said, "and maybe tomorrow we can pay Thomas a visit and see what he'll tell us about Sophie and the real reason he's no longer a law clerk."

"Right."

We got in our own cars, but he stopped before pulling out and rolled down his window. "One more thing: if the judge bought a piece of art from Sophie, where is it?"

CHAPTER FIFTEEN

My gallery, Emmy Fine Art, was in Culver City midway between the Crenshaw LAPD station and my house in Ocean Park, which was 1.1 miles from the Santa Monica pier, where we suspected we'd find Thomas Barnes tomorrow at the Chess Park. This mattered because I'd been followed now for weeks, still getting notes in my mailbox, and was driving around alone today. I loved living alone and I'd never been afraid before. But today I reminded myself to watch my surroundings and be sensible.

I was dying to know the history behind Derek and Ivan, why Ivan dismissed him, what kind of case went south, and what circumstances led to the end result. But I honestly couldn't fit one more person's traumatic story into my head right now. I needed to concentrate and focus. I found myself checking my makeup in the car window reflection before heading back into the precinct. Ivan. Why should I care after all this time? The human heart had its secrets.

From the parking lot, I texted Ivan to say I was outside and needed to talk. I knew the 'need to talk' phrase would intrigue him enough to let me interrupt whatever case he was running down. And the fact that I'd been targeted lately would give him an irresistible urge to go into rescue mode. He texted back to meet him at the East door of the precinct.

So naturally, I tore in through the front door and announced myself to the main dispatchers on the ground floor. This would red alert everyone about Ivan's ex in the building, which would cause an epic stir. I'm so bad.

I watched Ivan jog down the stairs, awkwardly talking to someone behind him, eyeing me, and trying not to trip. I was glad in that moment that I'd chosen the lighter, less imposing lip color.

"Miss Ellwyn, hello!" He grabbed my hand too hard and gave it one brisk shake. Surprising it didn't fall to the ground. "Come with me, please, right this way."

I grabbed back my injured hand and followed him down a different hallway into a different conference room twice as large as the previous one. He stood aside while I walked in, then pressed the door so it clicked.

"Why did you do that?" he asked, obviously not amused. "I said side door for a reason."

"I think you might have broken my hand." I wriggled my fingers for effect. I did care that I'd obviously upset him, but only insofar as it might impact the favor I was about to ask. "All right, I'm sorry," I added. He knew I wasn't.

"Okay." He sat and put his forearms on the table and motioned for me to sit. "Okay. What can I do for you? Did you two get what you needed this morning?"

"Yes and no. We actually need another few hours to read through the material. But I didn't want to put you out. Mainly I was wondering if you still have a graphologist on the payroll. Didn't you contract that out to some older lady? I can't remember her name."

"Yeah, Louise Chen. She's still here. Not here physically at the moment but I can sub out work to her. She's neither cheap nor quick."

"I'm happy to pay her fee. I have a sample I can leave for her. I just need someone to make me a copy of it before I leave."

Ivan nodded. The typical bags under his eyes were even puffier today, and his eyes looked red. I handed him the page from my legal pad. He disappeared for a few seconds and came back to the table.

"You're not sleeping again?" I asked.

"No. I mean yes. You know what I mean."

"No, I don't. What's going on?"

Ivan Dent lowered his head and buried his fingers in his hair. It was a beautiful head of hair that I used to adore, and he had way more of it than most men his age. He looked up, suddenly. "Same as you, right? It's all the same case, but it's like this octopus that keeps growing new legs."

"Arms," I corrected.

"Actually, they have both arms and legs."

"What new legs have cropped up today?"

"Wait here," he said, slipped out of the room again and returned with a folded newspaper and a photocopy of my legal pad page. He opened the newspaper and tossed it on the table. The headline read, "Mission Beach Strangler".

"Sophie Michaud's oddball, unsolved case, has suddenly taken on whole new meaning. Today's the first day there's no TV station van parked in the lot waiting to ambush us when we step out for lunch."

"The journalist?" I asked, remembering what Derek had told me about Nina Richmond.

"Both she and Sophie Michaud were killed in the same way, in the same place, and bodies discovered the same time of day."

"Were they both autopsied?" I asked, remembering the impressive forensic pathologists at the Forensic Science and Technical Division of the LAPD. "And autopsied by the same pathologist?"

"Sophie, yes," he said. "Strangulation. But I don't know about Nina Richmond. Why?"

"For the sake of continuity, would be interesting to have the same pair of eyes viewing both victims, since they apparently died in the same manner of strangulation and maybe by the same person."

"Look, don't jump to conclusions yet," he said. "But, yeah, maybe. I'll check on it. Other than Derek, what's your connection to this case?"

"None, well, not at first anyway. I was hired to look into a blackmailing case of a federal judge in San Francisco, someone my family's known for a long time. It turns out he may be connected to the Sophie case because one of the two journalists was writing an article and about to name that same judge."

Ivan stared in the same way that Derek had when I mentioned a federal judge. Like the very thought of it put the investigation into a different category. "Who is it?"

"McClaren."

"Doesn't sound familiar. Is that who the handwriting analysis is of?"

"Actually, no. His former law clerk, guy named Thomas Barnes." I'd circled the section on the page where Thomas had written his address, phone, email, and where he works, to distinguish it from my own handwriting, which I did *not* want analyzed, especially by someone Ivan had access to. "Are you guys investigating this in coordination with the San Diego PD?"

"Unfortunately, yes. It became my case when Nina Richmond was killed, and we discovered she was a journalist writing a story about the death of Sophie Michaud."

"But I thought both bodies were discovered on Mission Beach," I recalled.

"They were," he said, "but Nina was from LA, and she worked for a newspaper in San Diego and another one here. So the two cases are related and both PDs are involved in the investigation. Once the lawyers get on board it's gonna be interesting."

"I was surprised to learn that no suspects have been brought in on Sophie's case."

"Oh, we've brought in plenty of suspects in the past six months. Just no one strong enough to build a case around yet," he replied, and I could tell by the slight downturn of his mouth that I'd hit a nerve.

"That's the part we hadn't quite gotten to. I could use another day," I added, hoping.

"Sure, just give me a little notice and I'll set you up again."

"Is there anything in your case file about a piece of art?" I asked.

"Art? Like a painting?" he asked. "Not that I recall, no. Why?"

"Probably nothing," I said, only realizing in this moment what Judge McClaren's and my burglar had likely been looking for.

CHAPTER SIXTEEN

I don't know why I didn't tell Ivan about the second break-in at my house, or the van following me around town, or the little notes cowardly placed my mailbox. And I was glad he hadn't asked about Trevor, because I'd never be able to lie about that, and I knew Trevor wasn't well right now. How could he be? He loved Duga but he was staying in a strange house and those breeds desperately need structure, more than most dogs. I promised myself Trevor and I would be sleeping in our own beds again tonight.

I stopped at Cognoscenti's for a coffee and croissant and brought them back to the gallery and camped out in the office. Sunday afternoons there were perfect for thinking because the gallery was technically closed. My paranoia seemed to increase every day, so I turned all the lighting on to display our artwork to foot traffic and because I felt a little bit safer. I typed an email to Derek about meeting at the Crenshaw Station again tomorrow to review the rest of the casefile, most notably the list of suspects they'd brought in during the six-month period since Sophie's death. The problem, though, was that they essentially had no suspects. How could that be, and what had they been doing for six months? I know they'd brought in at least a dozen potential suspects, but no one with sufficient cause to fully prosecute. The question was, why?

I knew I should be driving north right now to San Francisco, to coddle Judge McClaren and gather details on his break-in, talk to his staff, and make it seem like I was actually investigating what happened, including the blackmailing case, which the judge confirmed was still going on. I just didn't feel like making a six-hour drive right now, alone no less, and somehow his case felt suddenly smaller in comparison to the unsolved and brutal murder of an eighteen-year-old girl. She'd been strangled, after all—much more personal than shooting, so her killer obviously, or probably, knew her. I knew assumptions could be dangerous, but it was a place to start. *Sophie Michaud*, I typed on my laptop, *what happened to you?*

I deleted the words and instead typed *Richard Ellwyn* into a Google search and filtered the results to just the past month, knowing the likelihood of finding anything new was pretty much zero. I changed my search criteria to include Jacques Martel, the drug lord I'd hunted down and found before my father disappeared. Nothing new in the search results.

I'd pretty much assumed, at this point, that Jacques Martel had either killed or kidnapped my father. After he shot me during our standoff, my father went after him. It was possible he'd killed him instead of kidnapping him, and a tiny spot in the center of my chest tightened at the thought. But the complex logistics of killing another human being and concealing the act often outweighed any of the advantages. Money could be a motivator, a de-motivator, and maybe the biggest inspiration for bumping someone off. But for Jacques Martel, he'd have the difficult job of hiding the body and concealing the crime to prevent law enforcement tracking. Martel had lived, after all, off the grid for over a decade, such that no one had found him. No one but me, that is. There'd been nothing by way of clues about my father's disappearance so far and, more importantly, no reports of his death. Tomorrow marked the one-year anniversary. Something told me Richard Ellwyn was, somehow, somewhere, still alive. Dad, where the hell are you?

I hadn't touched my croissant. It wasn't surprising that thinking about my father squelched my appetite. I packed up, locked the gallery, set the alarm, and texted Duga that I was picking up Trevor, desperately craving my favorite yoga pants and my own house.

Duga called me back. "We're walking on the pier."

"How's he doing?"

"Great, he gets good exercise when Uncle Duga takes him."

"Aww come on, that was a cheap shot."

Laughing. "Sorry. How are you feeling?"

Of course, I thought. Thomas and the Santa Monica Pier. "Hey, are you near the Chess Park down there?" I asked, ignoring his question.

"We just passed it. Why?"

"One of our witnesses, that guy Thomas Barnes I told you about, used to be a chess master. Kind of a small, nervous, wiry fellow with light brown curly hair. And constantly sweating."

"I can go back and look if you want, but I think there were the same three old men who hang out there every day: two playing and one watching."

"Okay never mind, we're going there tomorrow anyway. Can I meet you at your place and pick up Trevor? I'm dying to go home."

"Mommy misses you," I heard Duga say, followed by one of Trevor's whiny moans.

While Trevor ate his favorite Blue Buffalo dog food out of a brand new stainless dish back home in Ocean Park, I found the perfect surveillance spot in my living room. Looking out the south windows, I had a clear view of both Ashland and Highland Streets, but I was artfully concealed by the green canopy and tangled branches of the mulberry in my front yard. I took Duga's advice and parked in the garage and left the lights off in the house to make it look empty. This was a tactic and a risk, but I was ready. I reminded myself that I have a Great Dane, a gun, and I'm an excellent shot. So far, no gray van, but I wasn't even sure the gray van was used during the two break-ins.

I was convinced I wouldn't be able to walk barefoot through my house until I'd vacuumed several times and had it professionally cleaned again, fearing tiny shards of invisible broken glass everywhere. I'd checked my mailbox on the way in—no notes, thank God. In fact, there hadn't been any notes since I last made inquiries about the judge. I grabbed my almost used up legal pad from our last meeting and scanned through my notes. Phone calls to his family members, his law clerks, his paralegal, his admin and, wait, I'd forgotten about this. A security guard in the Ninth District Appellate Courthouse had been about to give me five minutes of his time but was called away by someone on his team. I wrote the security guard's name as DeRon, no last name. I'd track down that lead tomorrow.

CHAPTER SEVENTEEN

Sometimes I liked working backwards. One phone call and I determined that DeRon was actually DeRon Richards. I called the mobile number he gave me when I was in San Francisco investigating the judge's blackmail case. And now I could add the burglary to my line of inquiry. DeRon remembered me, luckily. He was on a break and asked if I was at the courthouse.

"I'm down in SoCal actually but I should be coming north there again next weekend. I wanted to follow up with you about the matter I spoke briefly about when we met."

"Yes, Judge McClaren," he replied formally, like he was at a military tribunal. "I don't know the judge personally, Ma'am."

"Yep, I know, you mentioned that, and that's fine. I'm wondering how I could find out if your security feed on incoming visitors showed any sort of wildcard characters in the week prior to the initiation of the blackmail notes."

"We'd need a court order to release those, and even then it takes up to a week before video is available."

"Judge McClaren said a court order had already been signed to release them, and I should wait for a call within a week. It's been almost two weeks."

Pause. "I'll check on that, Ma'am."

"Thank you, and while you're at it, I learned there was a breach in the judge's chambers last night."

No response.

"Were you aware of this?"

Another pause. "I wasn't aware of that, no," he replied with emphasis on the 'I'. Can I ask how you learned about it?"

"One of his law clerks, Thomas Barnes, contacted me."

"Reggie?"

Reggie? "A Thomas Barnes, whom I remember hearing about from some of the other law clerks, mentioned the break-in to me yesterday. Did you say Reggie?"

"That's what everyone calls him. I didn't realize his real name was Thomas, but it's Reggie Barnes so I'm sure it's the same guy. He hasn't worked here in three or four months."

"Do you know where he's working now?" I asked, curious to see if he even knew Thomas was living down here.

"Not really, no. I heard his mother lives in LA, and that he'd been fired for questioning a decision the judge made on an old case."

I hated the racket my frantic typing was making, but there would be no way to scribble fast enough to keep up with these useful details. I also couldn't help wondering why DeRon Richards was being so forthcoming about these details. "Do you know which decision Reggie was opposing?"

"No, I don't keep track of the legal proceedings here. Just the people whose lives are affected by them."

•—•••—•

I couldn't wait to share the juicy tidbit with Derek.

"Good morning," Derek answered on the first ring. "Someone's at your door."

I listened and heard nothing. "I don't think so. Dude, check this out, our friend Thomas…is known as *Reggie* within the federal court system."

"That's good intel. Where'd you find that out?"

"Well—"

"And someone *is* at your door."

"For God's sake, are you surveilling me now too?" I shuffled to the front door, and there he stood with a tray of coffees, in familiar orange and white paper cups. "Ha," I sort of half gasped and grinned. Nice surprise, today of all days. "Well, come on in then."

"I can't, I have an errand to run. I'm just dropping off a few things. Where's your boyfriend?"

"Asleep at the foot of my bed," I said. I could hear Trevor breathing from here. I went and checked on him and came back to find the tray of lattes and a bag on the console table behind my sofa.

"You're too much." I shook my head. I had a rule about men who bring me coffee. "Are these from Cognoscenti's? You know that's my favorite coffee place, right?"

"I pay attention." He smiled.

"Where are you off to?" I grabbed one of the cups.

"Interviewing a witness on another case."

"Missing persons?"

"Yep, Venice. Shouldn't be more than an hour or so. And I really gotta run." He moved back to the open doorway and looked out. "Ah, I love Ocean Park, all the tall trees and Craftsmans," he said with a wistful gaze down my street. I did too. "One more thing to drop off," he said, turning and reaching deep into the pocket of what looked like expensive suit pants. He pulled out a watch and displayed it carefully in his opened palm. Worn, scratched, gold color, with roman numerals. I think my dad had one just like it years ago.

I looked up at him, waiting. A low rider car drove past my house playing loud hip-hop.

Derek took another step inside leaving the door wide open behind him. "This was my dad's. He gave it to me a long time ago. I keep it because I remember how shiny and regal it always looked on his wrist when I was a little kid. It looked like a grown man's watch and I always liked it because of that, or maybe because I wanted to be like him when I grew up. Anyway, I remember today's a sad anniversary for you, so I thought, I don't know, I'd sort of lend you my dad in some way until you track down yours."

Don't cry, don't cry, I said to myself, willing my eyes to hold back the flood of emotion flowing up from my chest. I opened my mouth to speak and closed it again. Omg, where did this guy come from? I'd mentioned, only in passing and several days ago, that today was the one-year anniversary of my dad's disappearance.

"Is your dad still alive?" I managed in a crackly voice.

"Oh yeah, he still lives in Southie, South Boston, where I grew up. He's like the Burgess Meredith character on 'Grumpy Old Men'."

I stared down at it for a moment, then delicately grasped the watch from his hand and fastened it around my right wrist, considered the wrong wrist for a watch according to some. The metal felt unmistakably warm on my skin.

"I knew I recognized that accent," I whispered, happier for a lighter moment. Derek turned to give me privacy for the emotions he'd obviously pulled up.

"He's kind of a piece of work. But boy would he love you."

Mic drop.

CHAPTER EIGHTEEN

It took me a good thirty minutes to regain composure after the outpouring from Derek's surprise, and, symbolically perhaps, my shoulder was killing me today. My dad had been officially missing a full year as of today, and I hadn't seen him for a month or two before that, for no other reason than busying myself with responsibilities that were clearly lower in priority than staying close to family. I'd spent about three months working on my guilt after he disappeared, knowing that wherever he'd gone was a direct result of the bullet Jacques Martel shot at me out of his Glock pistol on the Carpinteria Offshore Oil Rig five miles off the coast of Santa Barbara. So I most certainly would wear Derek's father's old, beat-up watch and who knows, maybe it would inspire a miracle.

Two hours later, Derek got to the Baldwin Hills/Crenshaw station before me, where we'd agreed to meet Ivan for another review of Sophie Michaud's Murder Book. He waited in the same conference room while I narrated a long list of requests, okay demands. I wanted the Autopsy Fact Sheet, Historical Summary, Evidence of Injury, and Toxicology.

"Anything else?" he asked.

"A list of suspects, and I'd like to know the order and sequence of when they were brought in for questioning. Should be in the

Chronological Record in Section 1."

"Good," he replied. "What else?"

I sighed, thinking. I was heading east on 87 about to merge onto Highway 10, about five minutes away. "I was wanting to know who identified the body, actually both bodies—Sophie Michaud and Nina Richmond the journalist. But more importantly, I'd like to know who discovered them and called them in."

"Are you thinking it's the same person?" he asked.

"We could get lucky and find that, but it's not likely. Anyway, that's what's on my list for this morning. See how you do with it."

"Ivan says to say hi."

I almost heard his Cheshire cat grin through the phone. Lord, the two of them together talking about me made me want to drive up to San Francisco, not just today but right now.

I disconnected, and noticed I liked the feel of that watch on my wrist. Somehow it felt like a good support today, the warm, metal disc and a thin strap of leather holding together the pieces of my broken heart. *Come on Dad, you need to help me find you. I need a sign. I know you can hear me, somehow. You want to be found, right? Prove it.* And on cue, almost, as I turned off Highway 10 onto South La Brea, I spotted the gray van.

Okay, sure it's possible it was just "a" gray van, but now that I was behind it for once, I recognized the same tinted windows, white walled tires and, sure enough a Wackenhut license plate border on the rear plate. Shit.

"Hey, Siri," I bellowed, "text Partner." I'd already added Derek to my contacts under the name 'Partner' as a lame measure of security, knowing still that anything on or connected to my phone was potentially vulnerable.

"What would you like to say?" Siri replied.

"I'm following the gray van right now."

Siri repeated the message correctly and then sent it.

I knew Derek was probably telling Ivan about the van, my two break-ins, and the notes in my mailbox. I was being perfectly safe and observing every possible precaution. Even still, I knew I shouldn't be here alone right now, pursuing my pursuers. I turned left on a side street following the van with four cars between us. My phone rang, luckily Duga. I told him what I was doing.

"Where are you right now?" he asked.

"I don't know actually. The van's making frequent turns."

"Do they see you? Or a better question is, are you armed?"

"Yes, I'm armed, and I'm on one of those Don streets in Baldwin Hills, like five minutes from Crenshaw PD. I think I'm on Don Diablo. Are you nearby?" I asked him.

"I'm coming from the other direction, 9th and Stocker. Should I stick around and see if he comes out of Baldwin Hills in my direction?"

"That would be great. I'm hanging up. I gotta concentrate and make sure I stay four cars behind. That's my rationalization of safety."

Two cars had turned onto Don Diablo, and the van was now exactly seven cars ahead of me, so I was in the perfect spot for discreet surveillance. The next call was Derek, probably sitting with Ivan and determined to keep calling until I picked up. Sigh.

"Hey there," I answered, "I'm trying to concentrate here so I can't really talk. How's your research going?"

"Well," chuckle, "I just heard the story of how Ivan and you met. His version anyway."

"Slow day at the PD, huh?" I joked, knowing Derek had me on speaker.

"I told him you showed up for a flying lesson an hour late and I was about to leave and you begged me to take you up," Ivan chimed in.

"Some of us are doing real work today. I'm off. I should be there shortly."

"What are you up to this morning?" Derek asked. "Where are you?"

I heard Ivan ask Derek if he'd met Duga yet. I ignored his question and disconnected the call, just as the van turned left on Don Miguel. I was still about six cars away. I might not see him before he turned again. Shit.

"Hey Siri, text Duga and say *he's coming your way.*"

For a while there, Siri was misinterpreting all my verbal texts. She read this one back correctly and hopefully, by now, Duga was pulled over on Stocker with binocs ready to spot the van driver. Three more cars, two cars, geez, come on. I'm gonna lose him, I know it. I pressed Duga's number on my car console.

"I'm just turning now and I don't see the van, dammit."

"No sign of them from my end either," Duga said.

"Are you freaking kidding me?" My heart thudding in my chest, paranoid that they'd spotted me and were tailing *me* now. Keep cool, I told myself. I kept moving forward, looking left and right in people's driveways, parking lots, trying to keep my eyes on the road. Had they made me? Had they ducked into someone's garage, or driven over the median and were now going the opposite direction? I needed to slow down and think. I kept my eyes peeled for Duga's gray Honda as I turned onto Stocker. Nothing yet. I drove slowly in the right lane, a tall embankment on my right and some apartment buildings on the left. Duga, where are you? I dialed his number. Three rings, four rings. What the hell? Was I safe right now? I did not feel safe. In fact, I felt like I was being watched. I pulled over behind a white SUV, concentrated on regulating my breathing, put my car into park, and left the motor running so I could look around.

I sent a quick text to Derek. *May need your help, I'm on Stocker/Don Miguel.*

He wrote back with an *OMW*.

I tried to use my rearview and side mirrors to check my surroundings instead of betraying my paranoia by whipping my head around every five seconds. I saw a car pulling up to the curb behind me, someone in a baseball cap getting out and walking toward me. My right hand found the opening of my purse, reached in and unsnapped the holster. I pulled out the gun, safety on, and held it in my lap without taking my eyes off the rearview. Omg. I laughed to myself. It was Duga. He opened my passenger door and sat on the front seat.

"You…about…gave me a heart attack."

"Put your gun away, please," he said.

I did.

"I just had a conversation, well, a strange conversation with the driver of your van, and I got his picture," he said and winked.

"What…how? And what's with your disguise? Where did this happen?"

"Three blocks down the road."

"Did they make me?"

"I think so," he nodded, "they pulled over probably to get a look at your position. I put on this Jurassic Park baseball cap and brought my map and asked them for directions to Disneyland in Cantonese. I started to speak a little English but kept stopping to find the right world hoping to give you time to catch up."

"Nice work, you're a pro." I'd lost track of how many languages Duga spoke. "And the picture?"

"I snapped it and then dropped my phone under their van so not sure they knew I took it. Take a look."

Derek pulled up beside us with his window down. "Everyone okay in there?"

"Yeah, all good. Duga talked to the van driver and got his picture," I said.

Derek nodded and leaned forward with a smile and a wave. "Hey, nice to meet you. Why don't you both come down to the station and we can take a look at that picture and check the facial recognition database."

Duga nodded. "Sure."

"We might not need it," I said, shaking my head.

CHAPTER NINETEEN

Duga texted me the photo and took off to go to one of his many other jobs: caretaker for an elderly Tibetan monk, a tea consultant at Descanso Botanical Gardens up in La Canada Flintridge, Youth Advisor for the LA Youth Network, and a meditation instructor at the two Shambhala Buddhist Meditation Centers. From what I'd gathered over our ten-year friendship, Duga never earned any money from his numerous side hustles, he rarely spent money, and didn't seem to need it as a currency for meeting his needs, though he always cashed my checks when I paid his expenses. I asked him once if his house was paid for and he answered that he had a sort of arrangement about the house. I thought maybe the meditation center owned it, but his property tax bills came to him in his name: "Duga", no last name.

I followed Derek back to Crenshaw where Ivan was waiting for us in the same conference room with the Murder Book for Sophie Michaud and some supplemental casefile reports. He and Derek were eyeballing each other as I walked in the room and collapsed into one of the uncomfortable chairs.

"Is it five o'clock somewhere?" I lowered my head on the table. When I picked it up they were still in some tacit communication. "What?"

"Did you tell her?" Ivan asked Derek, who shook his head. Ivan passed a white business envelope across the table that had two folded sheets in it, neatly typed, and labeled, Supplemental Autopsy Report.

"What is this? From the casefile?" I asked.

"It was just delivered to me by runner from the M.E.'s office," Ivan whispered.

"Why are you whispering?"

"Seems there were two autopsies done on Sophie Michaud," Derek explained.

Ivan waved his hands. "Not really. Two autopsy reports were prepared at the time of Sophie's death six months ago. The second one made it into the official file, with the manner of death as homicide and the cause of death as strangulation. No one, well most of us, didn't know about the initial autopsy report that was prepared until today. This," Ivan pointed to the folded pages, "is a Supplemental Autopsy Report from the Medical Examiner indicating that what the initial autopsy report had, and the second one omitted was," he cleared his throat, "there was evidence Sophie may have been sexually assaulted. Postmortem."

"This case…my God." I looked up at Derek who was shaking his head. "You weren't kidding about the octopus," I said to Ivan.

"There's more," Derek interjected, looked at Ivan, and sat down across from me. "There was evidence Sophie had sex the night she died, within, what," he looked at Ivan, "twelve hours before death?"

"Right," Ivan confirmed.

"The lab report indicated two semen samples and concluded sex was consensual."

I leaned my elbows on the table and rubbed my eyes. "So the external exam of the body didn't show evidence of a struggle from nail clippings and hair and fibers?"

Derek looked at Ivan, who had presumably combed through all the forensic evidence already.

"I'd have to study them more closely," Ivan admitted.

"The most interesting part, I think," Derek said, "was that the M.E. couldn't confirm whether the two semen samples came from the same person or two different people. Their findings were inconclusive."

I blinked a few times to register this new finding. "Sorry, I don't understand. Both samples presumably came from the same place on Sophie's body, right? So what would make anyone think they came from different people?"

"Time," Ivan said absently. "If one sample appears to be older than the other, or if they didn't necessarily come from the exact same location on Sophie's body, if you know what I mean, that could be why it was ruled inconclusive pending further testing."

"You're saying it's possible Sophie had sex the night she died, and she may have been raped post-mortem?" They didn't answer and I took a moment to take this in. Two different men, one before death, one after death. "Who in the M.E.'s office conducted the autopsy?" I asked both of them. "And why were the findings inconclusive?"

Now Ivan sat beside Derek across from me. The room smelled stale and the air felt static. They just stared straight ahead at the wall without answering. "What," I asked, "is there more? How much weirder can this case get?"

"Weirder," Derek nodded.

"The LA County Medical Examiner-Coroner's office employs around 250 forensic pathologists. There's some confusion about who conducted the autopsy and who wrote the report—both reports. Apparently, the pathologist who initially conducted Sophie's autopsy and wrote the first report, which included the report of post-mortem rape evidence found during the external exam, no longer works there. Then the M.E. had another pathologist review the initial report, conduct a supplemental external and internal exam, and write up a second report. And in that second report, this one," he touched the pages on the table, "there's no mention of post-mortem sexual assault. This report is preceded by a letter from the M.E. acknowledging this discrepancy and the confusion it has caused, with plans to inform Sophie's family of the new findings."

"Jesus." I exhaled and sat back. "Are they here?" I asked, then remembered that she was French and was getting her bachelor's abroad.

"Sophie lived with her brother in San Diego, and her parents are in Paris," Ivan answered.

"Don't forget the roommate," Derek added. "Hannah Moraga."

"Okay, let's back up a few paces." I arranged the facts in a sort of sequence in my head. "You said the two presumed attackers, ante- and postmortem, were possibly two different men by the semen analysis. Do we have an identity match on either of them?"

"Not yet. According to the roommate, Sophie had a waiting list of guys who wanted to date her, but she wasn't interested and rarely dated.

She gave us two names; we brought them in a few months ago, blood samples, interviews, fingerprints—both dead ends."

"No criminal records for either of them?" I asked.

Ivan shook his head. "No. I have a meeting in ten minutes. Feel free to stay and continue reviewing the case file while I'm there and I'll come back in an hour, after which I'll be dealing with the shit storm this new report is gonna cause with the press. Fun times."

CHAPTER TWENTY

That left Derek and I time to finally examine the picture from Duga's sting operation. I gave him the details while I pulled up the picture from the text message. I glanced but it looked too blurry to make out a face.

"Did he flag down the van or how'd he get it to stop long enough to talk to them?"

I smiled to myself. Explaining Duga to anyone was impossible. "Red light I think."

"He just walked up to it and asked for directions in Chinese? That makes no sense."

"Get used to it." I texted the picture to Derek and we sat studying it from each of our phones. "It's blurry but I can see the guy's face well enough. Doesn't look familiar."

"Does to me," my partner said. He reached for the Murder Book. "Section 14, Witness List and Statements," he narrated, flipping through it. "Here we go," he rotated the book so I could see. "Looks like this guy, doesn't he?"

I held up my phone and displayed the photo of the van driver to compare with the witness page. Both men had angular-shaped faces, medium brown combed-back hair, and tall foreheads. "I guess. Sort of. Who is this?" I pointed to the image.

He looked down at the witness report. "Jonathan Michaud. Sophie's brother."

I sighed and shook my head. "That makes no sense. I thought he was a traveling businessman or something. How would he have time to be driving around town following me? And why?"

"Maybe it's not only him."

"I think it's time we drove down there," I thought aloud.

"His house?"

"Campus. I read that Sophie was officially living with her brother, but unofficially she'd been staying with a roommate on campus."

"Hannah Moraga," Derek nodded. "She's also a freshman."

"I'd like to go and check out the brother's home and also the dorm room where both girls were staying."

I watched my partner's face change, and I knew what he was thinking. Ivan.

"The case is still open, right? So I should only need permission from Ivan, who's the lead investigator, and he'll probably warn me not to talk to any witnesses."

"You can't go down there alone, not after everything that's happened." Derek said it like a parent grounding a teenager.

"I'll be fine, it's not even two hours away." It was the shallowest of arguments; he knew I didn't mean it.

Derek put up his index finger. "And...he can ask us not to formally interview any witnesses, but we'll inevitably need to talk to a number of people just to find our way to the right building."

"Good loophole."

I lost that round, and an hour later Derek and I were driving past San Clemente on I-5.

Before we left, I'd gotten a text from my gallery assistant, Carrie. She had miraculously sold two of our largest pieces from our most high-profile artist that morning and she needed to take next Friday off. Was selling two paintings too taxing for her? Whatever. I agreed, knowing this case would be taking more and more of my time with less of me available for my gallery management and community responsibilities, and I needed Carrie as the face of the gallery in my absence. And God knows she'd appreciate the career advancement opportunities of my constant absences. She's probably been introducing herself as me.

Derek had been searching in silence through what looked like pictures on his phone, and I let my mind churn through all the details. Mid-February now, it was light-jacket weather. I'd named all the seasons out here according to types of clothing. And I always seemed to have the wrong attire for the climate. The ocean was covered in dense fog the whole way south so far, with little specks of sun peeking through every half hour or so.

"What are you looking at?" I asked, finally, "or is that classified?"

He turned and his eyes landed on the exposed watch on my right wrist. He raised a brow and nodded gently. "I told you, you drive and I'll research."

"What are you researching?"

"The rest of the casefile. I was reading about who called in Sophie and Nina Richmond, the younger journalist, and was—"

"Wait a minute, you didn't take pictures of the casefile while we were—"

"Come on, give me some credit. I'm reading the newspaper article that the journalists published. They obviously had access to the case file because everything's in here that we saw this morning."

"Why would journalists have had access to a police file on a homicide victim?"

"Yes, excellent question. Why would they? Anyway both victims were called in by an anonymous caller."

"That's too bad, it could have been an important lead. Do we know the gender?"

"I'll find out."

"Also, if there was a trace of where the calls came in from," I added, my brain in overdrive now.

"I'm on it."

"Another thing I was thinking about was Nina Richmond's autopsy. I don't remember seeing that in Sophie's case file. They're separate but related case files and that should be in there."

"It should," Derek agreed, "but there isn't one."

"Oh God, another lost autopsy report?" I groaned.

"Her family's playing the religious card."

"No way. Really? I think there's only four or five states left that are allowed to do that. So they wouldn't agree to any kind of autopsy because it wasn't allowed by their religion?"

He nodded. "Looks like a number of back and forths with the family, according to the log, and they declined every request."

"She was how old?" I asked.

"Twenty-four or something."

"Seems so odd. Wouldn't they want to know?"

"Not bad enough, I guess. Are you hungry?" he asked. "We should stop at Mission Beach on the way back north. There's a great taco place near there."

I knew the place. "La Playa's?"

"Yeah. Now I'm hungry."

"Do you eat anything but tacos, Detective?"

"Do you eat anything but huevos rancheros?"

"Lattes. Do they count?"

CHAPTER TWENTY-ONE

Though the argument had been between Ivan and Derek, I could hear through the phone that Ivan didn't like Derek and I being down here in San Diego.

He seemed to understand the need to see where Sophie lived, as it was a feature of the investigation he hadn't done himself. And while the investigation details in the casefile covered technical minutia like the distance from Sophie's dorm to the Visual Arts building where most of her classes were, it left out some of the more important features of college life for an incoming freshman. What was the campus vibe like, was she popular, was she a loner? Did she feel comfortable being on campus, and what did she do with her time outside of classes? Fitness, working in the art studio, studying in the library, was she a runner? Ivan would be lucky to have our combined perspectives on his unsolvable case.

I let Derek go up the stairs ahead of me at the Revelle College Apartments and Residence Hall building on the southwest part of campus. We were both well dressed, and tall, giving us a commanding presence. I hoped the other students might think we were somebody's parents or, better yet, professors. All the better.

"You sure this is the right building?" he asked me on the stairs.

A young woman with long, straight brown hair with a streak of pink in it stopped on her way down. "Can I help you guys find someone?" she said.

Derek and I halted like two deer in headlights. We'd prepared for everything but this.

"We're looking for Room 308B," Derek said finally, with an apology in his voice. The girl's large eyes stared down unmoving, then a quick eye-shift to the left to gauge onlookers. Her face was a perfect oval with a sad downturn to her mouth.

"That's my room," she said quietly. "Are you guys cops?"

"We're not cops, no," I answered, mimicking the tone of her voice.

"You'd think I'd be used to this by now," the girl said.

"We're working in collaboration with the LA Police Department on an open investigation."

"Sophie?" the doe-eyed girl said, her eyes suddenly glassy.

"Are you her roommate?" I asked, knowing the answer.

Three guys tore around the corner of the staircase from an upper floor and flooded past us. The perfect diversion, and Derek took advantage of it. "Should we, maybe, talk someplace a little quieter?"

"Sure, follow me," the girl said, leading us to a security door to the second-floor residence halls of Revelle College at UCSD. She opened the unlocked door of a typical two-person dorm room and stepped slowly to the window, leaving the door open behind her, sliding her arms around her body. I followed first, then Derek, and we were careful to not close the door or move too deeply into the room. Derek touched my elbow and pointed to an odd, dark stain on the carpet. He snapped a picture of it, then bent a few inches lower to take another one. Thank God he'd turned off his volume.

"Do you need to talk, Hannah?" I asked in my most comforting tone and speaking slowly. She half-turned. "Are you Hannah Moraga?"

She nodded.

"I'm Mari, and this is Derek. We're Private Investigators working with the police to help uncover what happened to Sophie. Just in case something was missed the first time."

"You don't have to talk to us, Hannah," Derek added, "and we're not here to interfere or invade your privacy. We're mainly looking around campus today just to familiarize ourselves with it."

She sat on one bed and motioned for us to sit on the other. Derek and I exchanged a quick look and took advantage of the opportunity.

"How are you doing?" I asked as a sort of blanket opener, shaking my head, implying that no one under the circumstances would be doing okay.

She paused before answering, obviously measuring her words. "I'm not failing all my classes anymore, but the first few months after Sophie, um, di-ed," her voice cracked, "was rough. I almost dropped out." She looked at the floor. "She was my best friend."

Hannah Moraga was either a great actress or genuinely broken by this loss. I noticed how oddly quiet it was on campus, on a random weekday, late afternoon. "You're not usually in class now?" I asked, giving Derek more time to find a way into the conversation.

"It's President's Day so there aren't classes. I just got back from the library."

"Where's that?" Derek jumped in.

"Straight up Gilman." She pointed. "It's not far.

"Which way is the Visual Arts building where Sophie was studying?"

"Arts and Humanities is up Gilman and on the way to the library."

He nodded. "Okay, I'm trying to get a sense of Sophie's path to classes, the library, and what her typical routes might have been. It seems like an easy campus to navigate."

"It's not that bad. I transferred from UCSF and that campus is much larger," Hannah replied.

I made sure my face was absolute stone. Thank goodness Derek seemed to be doing the same. San Francisco, Jesus. Okay, we needed a quick subject change, though Derek's navigation tactic was smart.

"Other than walking, how do you guys get around here? Does Uber come on campus?" he probed.

"Yeah Uber, Lyft, and they have scooters you can sign out. Sophie rode her bike sometimes, but mostly kept it at her brother's place."

Bike? There'd been absolutely no mention of a bike in the case file; I would have remembered it. I typed bike in a Notes file I'd opened on my phone in the parking lot.

"You don't have that address, do you?" I asked.

"It's here. Hold on," she moved to the desk in the middle of the room. "518 Arbor Drive. It's a townhome."

"Thanks." I added the address to my Notes file. "You've been there?"

Another pause. "We stayed there together for the first few weeks of school, but it was getting expensive to Uber here every day. This is my room, and my roommate dropped out the first week so I had room for someone else."

"But you otherwise like it there?" Derek asked.

I made note of Hannah's body language. She was perched on the edge of the bed, sitting on her hands with her shoulders hunched forward. Feeling powerless would be normal in this situation and this social dynamic, but I reminded myself not to trust her yet.

"It's a nice house," she said absently, "but a boring neighborhood with nothing around it. The pool was nice. It was okay until her brother came back. He travels a lot and, for some reason, didn't like the fact that Sophie had brought a friend to stay with her. It's not like she brought a guy there or something."

"She didn't have a boyfriend?" I jumped in, glad for the opportunity to ask about the men in her life.

The girl shook her head. "No one regular, but let's just say there was a waiting list." Her tone was wistful, and a little bit bitter.

"Are the guys pretty nice around here?"

"The engineering students, not so much. Sophie and I are—were in the art department, and artists are cool. And the gardens too, some nice people there."

"Gardens?" I asked.

"Campus has a lot of community gardens around. Sophie was into gardening and had a couple of plots at Roger's Community Garden."

"Where's that?" Derek asked, with his notebook out and visible now.

"Five-minute walk that way." Hannah pointed in the direction opposite to the library, so closer to the street on the outskirts of campus.

"An herb garden, or vegetables too?"

"Both, I think. It's the biggest community garden here. They grow orchids there too, I think, indoors though."

CHAPTER TWENTY-TWO

There was so much to unpack from that conversation it was a struggle to keep my mouth shut until we got to the parking lot.

"Can you—"

"Let's get in the car first," I said. "Who knows if we're being watched right now."

"Yep, you're right." Derek climbed into the passenger seat of my car and wore all of the day's stress on his face. "So, what have we got?" He sighed and we both sort of cracked up at the same moment. "I know."

"I'm not sure where to start. Hannah Moraga used to attend UC San Francisco and transferred to UCSD, which means she had opportunity and access to Judge McClaren, and she may have known him. I can't yet speculate as to why, but that's just too much of a coincidence."

"Agreed." Derek wriggled out of his suit jacket. "Summer in February, welcome to San Diego."

I pressed the button for the air conditioning but kept the car in park.

"And the bike! Why was there no mention of this in the ninety-seven pages of material we've been sifting through for the past two days?" I sighed.

"I guess no one knew about it, but why not, if they talked to Hannah?"

"They probably never asked her specifically about that. We need to get that bike," I said with fresh determination. "The thing about the brother is another one. She made it seem like he had a bit of a temper. Or was I reading too much into that?"

"She said he was unhappy with Sophie bringing a friend home, and yeah she made it seem like he was significantly put out, enough to make them leave and move into campus housing. Are you thinking maybe he didn't want anyone snooping around the house? I'd love to know more about that—"

"Me too but I'm not holding my breath. So…what's with the stain on the carpet?" I pointed to his phone, which he was staring down at and squinting. He held up the first image, then swiped to show a second one closer up.

"There were two stains actually, though the first one wasn't that visible to tall people like us." He zoomed in to a small, reddish spot. "Could be ketchup, but I think ketchup might be a little more orange because of the tomato ingredients."

I leaned in close. "That looks dark reddish brown to me." I held up my palms again. "And where exactly was this in the casefile?"

"Could be new, maybe it wasn't here then. I don't know but I'm actually more interested in the second stain, the larger one." He held up his phone again with a picture of a larger stain.

"Zoom out a little."

But now Derek was looking over my shoulder at something outside the car. He motioned for me to turn around. Out of pure instinct, I slid my hand into my purse and then turned fully to see Hannah standing two feet away with her arms wrapped around her frame. I rolled down the window.

"Hey Hannah, what's up?"

"I, um, sorta forgot something."

"Okay…" I said and gave her time to form her words. I could really see her now, out in the sunlight. Dark hair, very light skin; thin, wearing an oversized black shirt. She glanced up into the sky, bent down to peer at Derek, who waved and motioned her to come closer.

"We're looking at a campus map," he said, "and trying to find where Sophie's art studio would have been." He held up his phone to show her. Crafty. "I assume she had a studio, right? She was an illustrator?"

"No, a painter, oils, but she was into digital art," Hannah said.

"Oh okay, so that's all done in the studio?"

The girl nodded. "Visual Arts is down this street." She pointed ahead and to the right. "Take your first left. There's a pay lot there."

"Great, thank you," Derek said.

The girl was looking behind her for the second time. Who would care that she was talking to two strangers?

"So what did you forget, Hannah?" I asked, threading back to her original thought. I motioned her toward us but she didn't move.

"I'm not sure who else to tell about this. Everyone's like starting to recover from the shock of her death so I didn't want to bring it all up again. But we're getting, I'm getting bills stuffed under the door every day now. I have a stack of them I've been holding and I don't know what to do with them."

"What kind of bills?" Derek asked.

"Sophie's tuition, books, other university fees. I don't know if she was paying those before, or her brother. I've called him over and over but haven't gotten a response."

"Can you give me his mobile? Or here's my card," I held it out, "text it to me. We'll give it a try and see how we do. You certainly shouldn't be getting Sophie's bills. Those should go to her brother, or her parents in France. I'm sure this can get sorted out, don't worry."

The young face contracted, scrunched down from the top.

"What?"

"Sophie's parents are dead."

CHAPTER TWENTY-THREE

There was no time left for Mission Beach, tacos, or a visit to the brother's house, with both of us feeling greater urgency to report these new findings to Ivan. Sophie's bike, if it was even at the brother's house, may or may not contain forensic evidence that could lead us to the truth of her killer and their motivation. And at this point, everything I'd learned so far about this case hung in the balance of authenticity. I didn't know what to believe.

I was driving like a lead foot north on I-5. Normally I would have been talking nonstop. Today I used the monotony of the road to process what we'd just learned. There was a bike that no one knew about. A stack of unpaid bills for Sophie's tuition from the bursar, and the brother not answering his phone.

"The parents…I don't even know what to do with that," Derek commented, breaking the silence.

"I know."

"I read in the casefile about her father's position as Minister of Culture. I've been looking online and I see nothing about her parents being dead. What the hell? Are they, like, *not* her parents? Or is it worse than that? Have we been duped here, or was Hannah duped into thinking her roommate was an orphan?"

"Text Ivan and tell him to meet us at my house tonight. We should be there in an hour."

"I'm starving."

"I know, me too. Use my phone; you can order us something from GrubHub and have it delivered when we arrive."

"Dinner for three?" he asked.

I bristled at the thought of Ivan in my house. "I guess so."

While Derek was on the phone with one of his clients for part of our ride back, I arranged my thoughts enough to relay something even remotely coherent to Ivan. What I hadn't asked Hannah was whether anyone had talked with her before. When we were in her room, she mentioned seeing the police at her dorm before, but now I was second-guessing everything about this case. For instance, who was the original police investigator brought in after Sophie was first discovered? Who else was brought in to assist? Who were the interviewers of the first set of witnesses, and was Hanna on that list?

I'd started feeling nauseous shortly after we left San Diego, the same way you feel when you've eaten something that was ill-prepared, partially cooked, or just doesn't agree with you. The stomach just simply knows when something doesn't belong in there. My body warned me, sometimes, about impending danger through sudden stomach aches or migraines. Of course I had a stomach ache. I was having a hard time digesting these new facts and, meanwhile, based on our visit from Reggie, I owed Judge McClaren a call. What I still didn't understand was why he'd asked Reggie Barnes to get in touch with me instead of just calling me himself.

Derek was texting with Ivan now.

"He said he'll meet us at your house. He asked if Trevor is gonna be nice to him."

"I don't know, actually. Having both of you there might be upsetting to him." Derek looked up. "For real. And you're both very tall men so there's that too."

"Trevor likes me," he boasted.

I laughed. "He's deciding, is more like it."

While Derek went back to his text conversation with my ex-lover and the lead Homicide Detective with the LAPD, I caught sight of something in my rearview mirror that suddenly turned nausea to an all-out roiling. Derek saw me looking.

"What?"

I kept my eyes balanced between the road in front of us and my rearview, estimating how far back it was.

"The van?"

"About ten cars behind and weaving in and out of traffic pretty fast. We need to get the hell out of here."

"I'm checking 511.org now. One second, stay in this lane," he said, and turned his head back to the right, "now get over one lane to the right."

I obeyed, kept driving straight, and tried hard not to look in the rearview. "What the fuck do they want from me??"

"You're in their way," he said in a voice way too calm for the situation. That told me something about him and reminded me of my training. I was trained to never react to a situation. Breathe, I told myself. Breathe.

"Get ready to cut over two lanes and get off at the next exit, wait for me, three, two—"

"Now?" I said, checking the lane beside me.

"After the white SUV."

I was breathing deeply and ready.

"Now," he said.

I did it, one more lane surprisingly devoid of cars at this moment, and then the ramp. I was there, heading down a hill and I realized that's why Derek chose that exit. Now when the van drove past, it wouldn't see my car because I'd be fifty feet lower. Genius.

"Turn left here, under the freeway, and make an immediate right and get on 261."

"Stay on 261 or get on 241?"

"261," Derek said, looking down at his phone map, "and now turn left on East Santiago Canyon Road. Yep, you got it. Slow down and turn right in here."

"Irvine Regional Park?"

"Yep." He pointed up ahead. "What do you hear?"

I listened but couldn't make it out. "Just a lot of noise."

"Right, follow that noise."

The road wound left, then right in a big circle to the back of the park. There was a parking lot jam-packed with cars, and two empty spaces in a middle row. He pointed.

"That one," he said.

"What's going on here?" I asked.

"Field trips, community programs, soccer games, it's always packed this time of day."

"You've been here before?"

"Yeah. Perfect camouflage."

I turned off the motor. "Better call Ivan and have him meet us."

"Good idea, and you need to leave with him."

I turned and stared, suddenly numb. Were these people trying to force me off the road? What seemed like an annoyance at first, probably because I'd understated it to myself, now felt like a lightning rod of fear in my chest and hands.

"In a different car, you're right," I said. "Can you drive this, with the steering wheel on the wrong side?" The mental image was comical, but I had no humor in me right now. I felt sick, cornered, and targeted. Because I was.

Derek put his hand on my forearm and held onto it for a moment. "That was some nice driving back there."

"Right."

"We're here and we're both in one piece," he said. "I think I saw the driver."

I raised my eyes to his. "Did it match the picture Duga took? Jonathan Michaud?"

"Yes."

"Does he know where we were today? Thank God we decided against going to his house, though he obviously wouldn't have been there."

"Yeah, maybe we should have." Derek looked down at an incoming text. "Ivan's on his way. Asks what the hell we're doing down here, says he'll call when he's close."

CHAPTER TWENTY-FOUR

I used the automatic control to recline my seat. "Yours reclines, too," I said, closing my eyes.

"I'm too pumped up to relax. You rest, I'll stand guard."

"But then you'll be the target when you drive home in my car," I realized. "How is that a solution?"

He was still reading his phone. "For one thing, I'm not the target and neither is your car. You are. But from here I'm gonna take 91 to Compton and then get on 710 north and then back roads to Ocean Park, completely avoiding Highways 5, 10, and 1, which are the most obvious and visible routes north from San Diego."

"Well, Detective, if we make it to my house tonight, I'm a bit of a martini connoisseur."

"Really?" he asked, still looking at his phone. Meanwhile my eyes were wide open and on patrol in every direction. "Vodka martinis?"

"Definitely not. Using gin allows the complexity of the juniper berries to blend with the other flavors to make it more aromatic and memorable."

"Memorable, okay. What's your recipe, or is that classified?"

"Easy recipe that requires precise proportions. Boodles Gin, dry vermouth, orange bitters, and lemon rind on the glass. No olive."

"Stirred or shaken?" he asked. The banter was a breath of fresh air.

"Stirred but stirred well and long enough to get a good flavor blend. This method requires a lot of tasting to get it right," I added, now feeling a bit more in the mood to actually drink a martini. I looked at the watch on my wrist, smiled to myself, and hoped Ivan would get here soon, which was an odd thought.

"What kind of vermouth do you use?" he asked.

"What are you reading so intently?" I asked, my jangled nerves now starting to affect my speech.

"Ivan just texted, and I don't recognize the name of the exit he was near. Wait, I see it now, coming from that direction. Okay…" he said and typed the response.

"I use Dolin Blanc Vermouth because it's more citrusy than herby and makes a nice palette pairing with the curved lemon rind I float on the glass."

"Do you have actual martini glasses in your house?" He turned to face me now, like it was serious question.

"Sure, I'm not a heavy drinker but I'm very selective and take my drinks seriously. Martinis and lemon drops are my poison, in case you were curious."

"I am." He smiled when another text came in. "He's just pulling in now." He was typing. And just then, I got that same feeling I had on the freeway when I first detected the van behind me.

"I don't know why, but I have a feeling…"

"They're not here. Ivan will pull up right next to us and you'll get in his car and ride back to your house with him. I've already told him about my alternative route. Let him drive and I'll be calling you on the way."

"I'm sure I'll be fine," I lied. The van was here; they were watching me. I could feel it.

My neck and shoulders were sweating. I distracted myself by looking high out the front window. The tops of trees swaying in the wind, a hint of rain in the air, the mood of the sky changing every five minutes.

"Here he is," Derek said.

I turned and saw Ivan's black SUV and, through the side window, a look on his face I hadn't seen in a long time and didn't exactly miss. With the motor still on, Ivan stepped out, closed the driver's side door, walked around the car, scanned our surroundings and opened the rear side door.

"Let's go," Derek said, "give me your keys."

"No, give *me* your keys," Ivan commanded. "I'm driving this car; you two take mine." His set jaw told me there was no arguing with *that* Ivan. No adrenaline left in my body, I sighed and got out of my car.

"Why, what's your plan?" Derek asked.

Ivan stood up straight and sighed. "This is my suspect and it's my ass on the line every day this nightmare case stays open." The two men shared a momentary standoff, then Derek nodded and motioned me into Ivan's car, and handed Ivan my keys.

"We think it's Jonathan Michaud, Sophie's brother, driving the van." Derek moved past Ivan to get in the passenger side.

"We know," Ivan confirmed. "We ran the plate and the vehicle's registered to Wackenhut. He works for them."

Derek and I stopped and stared, wide-eyed, knowing only now what this meant. The puzzle's image was taking shape.

"You seem to be missing a steering wheel."

CHAPTER TWENTY-FIVE

Derek called Ivan as soon as we all took off and continued the conversation on his car's Bluetooth. We followed my car closely down a series of winding, unfamiliar, empty roads, steering clear of the freeway.

"Does he have a record?" Derek asked.

I knew that if Jonathan Michaud worked for Wackenhut, he really worked for the Company and that meant two things were likely: some kind of Special Forces training, so therefore he'd have a visible military record, or else he'd have no record at all, whereby he publicly didn't exist.

"French Army Special Forces Command," Ivan replied. "That's all we could find. Has lived in this country for five years and travels extensively, usually to Europe. How'd you do on campus today?"

Derek ran through our report. He asked Ivan who investigated the original case.

"Why do you ask?" Ivan didn't like the question, and him being defensive about this question told me he had something to hide. "You think some things were missed? That's always possible."

"We went upstairs to see where Sophie lived and just happened to come upon her roommate, Hannah, who was happy to talk to us in her dorm room." Derek was careful to cover all the bases there. Ivan kept listening. "She mentioned that Sophie had a bike, and I didn't remember reading anything about a bike in the casefile so far. Do you know if anyone talked to Hannah, or else anything about a bike?"

"Hannah was interviewed as one of the first witnesses and she was distraught, so one of the counselors at school suggested we continue the conversation after she'd had a little more time to process what happened," Ivan said.

"Did she identify the body? And if not, who did?" I asked.

"They both did, as I recall, Hannah and the counselor, because Sophie's parents live in France and the brother, who lives locally, was out of the country at the time."

"What about the bike?" Derek asked.

"Wait a minute," I interjected, "the topic of her parents came up today."

"Why?" Ivan asked.

"Because Hannah said Sophie's parents were dead." I let the words hang in the air for a few moments. "Have you had any interactions with them since the case was first opened?"

"I know the brother didn't respond to our calls. The roommate gave us his number. We contacted the parents when her body was first discovered and had some phone interactions, but they were cleared."

"And the brother's address, did your team go out there?" I asked. "If they did, they likely would have seen Sophie's bike."

"I don't remember anything about a bike coming up in our initial investigation," Ivan said. "I'll send a car out to the brother's house to look for it tomorrow. Might tell us something, and we can at least dust it for prints."

"Something else about Hannah Moraga," Derek said. "She transferred to UCSD from UC San Francisco."

"Is that supposed to mean something to me?" Ivan asked.

"The journalists writing about Sophie's case identified a connection between Sophie and Judge Conrad McClaren, the federal appellate judge of the Ninth Circuit. I was curious reading the file how an eighteen-year-old girl might have known a federal judge. It's not like they traveled in the same circles."

"So you think maybe the roommate knew the judge and introduced them?" Ivan asked. "And just for the record, I don't necessarily believe everything I read in those articles. There were some wild and baseless allegations, as I recall."

"Baseless?" Derek jumped in. "I mean, you do realize that one of those journalists is still missing and the other one is dead, and died in the same way and in the same place as Sophie? I think whatever they were alleging may have had some foundation."

"Calm down. I agree with you. I'm just saying that someone wanted to silence the journalists and stop their line of inquiry for fear of exposure. But the judge may not have necessarily been the detail the assailant was trying to protect. Right? It's just one possibility."

Derek looked at me and lip-synched a *What the fuck*??

"You're right," Derek answered Ivan, "it's just speculation at this point." He eyed me when he said it.

We disconnected the call and agreed to follow each other all the way to my house and talk more when we got there. There was no mention of martinis on the phone before we hung up. As soon as we did, I knew what we were both thinking: it sounded like Ivan was covering for the judge. But why?

I sank down into the deep, lumbar-supported bucket seats of Ivan's insanely large SUV. His ego was as big as California, so of course his car had to be, too. I was thinking about my trip to San Francisco, how I wanted to talk to that security guard again, DeRon Richards, talk to the judge and hear his description of what happened in his office. I also needed to talk with his clerks again, maybe ask about Sophie and get a sense of how familiar they were with her. And I would fly up there and take Uber around the city—a transport that offered a lot more discretion than a car that could be followed. We hadn't yet told Ivan about the issue with Sophie's unpaid bills from the school, which should have been either sent to her parents or her brother. And the incident of the stain on the carpet was something Derek could follow up with the crime lab for samples while I was in San Francisco.

Coming out of the woods now, we made a few sharp turns. Derek steered too deeply into one turn and I jostled against the passenger door.

"Sorry, not used to this car," he said.

Ivan was a little farther ahead of us, but we were the only ones on the road, with no one in either direction. By now we should be close to crossing over I-10. I couldn't even see Ivan now.

"Where is he?" I asked just as my face rammed into the dash. "What the—" I smelled metal and was sure my nose was bleeding. Derek struggled to orient the car correctly in our lane while I wiped blood dripping from my nose. He was half on the uneven shoulder with Ivan nowhere in sight. I slowly turned my body to the left to look out the back window.

The crashing sound of metals colliding caught me in a moment where I was in a sort of mental stasis—quietly observing our car bumping up and down—on a perfectly smooth road.

"Did we run over something?" I managed.

"Someone hit us from behind. Call Ivan."

I fumbled for my phone, but it was no longer in the console between the front seats. I bent and palmed the floor and found it between my feet. I stayed down there, half-afraid to sit up and see what was ahead of us. I pressed redial on Ivan's number.

"They're next to us now," Derek said.

"Shit, they're gonna force us off the road!"

"I don't think so," he decided. "They could've done that already."

"There's a ditch right here. Try to get up a few hundred feet to where the embankment evens out."

Derek gunned the motor to accelerate. The gray van, falling behind us half a car-length, quickly closed the gap. My eyes were glued to the rear-view mirror. They'd almost caught up, and by now I could see the driver, who was presumably the brother of our victim, Sophie Michaud. He looked young with dark hair and angular features. Another man, shorter, fatter, sat beside him, talking with headphones on. They'd caught up and were veering left to get beside us on an otherwise narrow road. There were more cars on the road, several in front of us, and some coming in the other direction on a two-lane. As soon as there was a gap, the van pulled left and jerked hastily in front of us, miraculously without touching Ivan's SUV. Ivan! I'd forgotten about him and now I could hear him yelling into the phone in my hand.

"Sorry. I'm here."

"Are you all right? What's going on back there?"

"I'm bleeding but I'll live. The van's beside us now. I think he's trying to force us off the road. Where the hell are you?"

"Ahead of you, but not far. I pulled ahead to get a better vantage point," he said. "Stay on the line, don't hang up. Please confirm you heard what I just said."

"Oh shit."

"What?"

"The van's in front of us now," I said.

"He's slowing down," Derek said, slowing the motor to keep a safe distance.

The van in front of us came to a sudden stop. In one lightning moment, our car stopped short, hit the back of the van, the van doors slide open, and two men in dark suits got out. When a revolver was thrust at his temple Derek instinctively put his palms on the steering wheel.

"Don't move," someone said.

"I am not moving," Derek answered.

"Get out," the man said from the driver's side, eyeing the other man standing outside my door, which he'd just opened.

Naturally, at this precise moment, there were no cars coming from either direction. I'd managed to slip my phone into my jacket pocket before the van stopped in front of us and had time to zip the pocket. I knew Ivan could hear the exchange. Hopefully he'd keep his mouth shut so I could keep the phone connected, and maybe he could track wherever I was about to go.

I heard a loud crack, which sounded like the other man's gun barrel colliding with the side of Ivan's car. Derek, still in the driver's seat, was leaning out to the left with one hand grabbing his assailant's hair and banging his forehead on the top of the driver's side door frame. Once. Twice. The man caved in at the middle. Derek managed to gut-punch him through the open window, then worked his body around the man to climb out of the car. The other man shoved all his weight against him and pulled back, preparing to use his boot as leverage.

"Hey," my assailant bellowed from the other side of the car. "Let's go. Leave him. Now."

God help me.

CHAPTER TWENTY-SIX

One man led me to the back of the gray van, which had been tailing me now for weeks. He handled me gently, his fingers on my arm. Minor nuance but notable.

"You can't see where we're going, so you have two choices," he said in a surprisingly civil tone of voice. "This," he held up a hood, "or I can drug you. You'll be groggy for a day or so after."

"Hood," I replied, for so many reasons. It had happened before. I'd be awake so I could listen for cars, sirens, people, trucks, foghorns. I would be able to smell the air, fumes, low tide, smoke, and my senses would be awake to tell me whether my life expectancy was rapidly decreasing. I was sitting in an actual seat; the man strapped on my seat belt and gently placed the hood over my head.

My hands were positioned behind my back. He didn't bind them or cuff me. Interesting.

I felt surprisingly calm considering I'd just been abducted at gunpoint and my partner's life was in danger. But I knew he wasn't what they wanted. Somehow, I sensed that Duga, my secret guardian angel, was watching. Besides, I still had Derek's father's watch on my wrist.

"You guys are being very courteous. I wish you'd just tell me what you want," I said, raising my voice to be heard through the hood covering my face.

"Just following orders, Ma'am, on both counts." It was the same voice as the suited man who spoke to me before, a man who didn't seem to care that I'd seen his face and could later identify him. And I wasn't sure if the two men who had climbed out the back of the van were the driver and passenger that we'd seen up front, or two additional men in back.

This was no typical abduction. This was a delivery. These men had been assigned to do me no harm. I was being picked up and transported to a secure location, hence the hood, to have an in-person conversation with someone who didn't want to be seen by the public or by anyone non-essential. Jacques Martel? Or my father? My heart thudded in my chest just thinking about it, but I knew better. Logic told me that this van would need to stop for gas at some point, which could tell me how far we were going.

It was too quiet. That meant we were still on back roads. They were avoiding detection from Derek and Ivan, and I suspected they were driving together at this point comparing stories. The next thing would be to get gas and probably switch cars with another Wackenhut vehicle.

The two men weren't talking to each other, not a word. No exchange of information, chit chat, nothing. These men were seasoned intelligence officers, emotionally made of stone, ready to sacrifice themselves at any moment, committed with every fiber to the success of the mission, and committed to excellence in the completion of every step on the path to that end. The van slowed slightly, then veered into a lot.

"We'll be changing cars in a moment," the same man informed me. "When I open the back door, I'll guide you from one door to another. It can be a very simple operation, or not. It's up to you."

"Understood," I said.

We stayed there parked in whatever lot we were in for less than five minutes, then I heard another vehicle rolling into the lot and live parking beside us.

"Now," the man said. He opened the door, crawled in to unclasp my seat belt, and instructed me to get out.

I did and climbed into the cushy backseat of a sedan. The man strapped me in and closed the door. A moment later, both front doors opened, I heard the words "Right. Yes," uttered by one of them, followed by the combination of two noises: a foghorn and what sounded like a large bird of prey. I'd been wondering if we would be headed west or north. The foghorn could be from Marina Del Rey and the bird could be from the Ballona Wetlands Wildlife Reserve, which was a few miles south of Ocean Park and on the way to Santa Monica. The driver took us down a bumpy road, which probably meant a beach access road or else an unpaved road.

We were leaving Del Rey Lagoon.

After about ten minutes, the car slowed to allow for dense traffic, then I felt us veer off the highway. I expected my well-mannered abductor to explain the next steps in the process to me. Instead, one of their cell phones buzzed, the driver picked it up, said yes five times, followed by a "Yes, Sir." Were they making plans about what to do with me, or plans for what to do after they tortured information out of me? But what information did I have, really?

I remembered the phone in my pocket was still connected to Ivan. But to grab it, I'd need to make a somewhat awkward and obvious movement with my left arm, and right now I was being invisible.

"Stay here," my abductor commanded.

Both men got out of the car and closed the doors again. I heard the vibration of them mumbling outside, probably preparing to move me to another car, probably because the last one had been detected. I leaned forward two inches and slid my left hand into the pocket of my jacket. I rotated my phone with my fingers to find the volume button and pressed what I thought was the button to increase it. Next, taking advantage of the fact that I was alone in the car and couldn't be heard, I thought of a way to tell Ivan where I was. I used the fingernail of my index finger to tap the word "Lagoon" in Morse code. Pilots are required to be able to communicate in Morse code. Did he still remember it, did he hear it, and would he know which lagoon?

CHAPTER TWENTY-SEVEN

My intelligence training had prepared me to give proper attention to logistics. For example, it was still technically daytime. They'd brought me to a parking lot at the Del Rey Lagoon, or so my inner navigation guided me. They're gonna pull a six-foot-tall human female out of a car with a hood over her head and stuff her into a much smaller car, and do this undetected? In 1990, maybe. But now, in the age of smart phones and small form-factor tech that can be instantly shared across a thousand different social media platforms, it becomes a lot riskier. My gut told me that these men wouldn't hurt me, but my *red alert* was still activated, and I was ready to run if needed. Now I wished I hadn't disabled location tracking on my iPhone.

The rubber tires crackled on the gravel, then stopped. The whoosh of high tide against sand buffed out a flock of gulls flying east to west. Amazing what the ears can detect when the eyes stop working. The hood my captor pulled over my head felt like a pillowcase—smooth and cool—wasn't entirely uncomfortable, other than the uncertainty of my release and personal safety. Someone opened the driver's side door.

"Here we go," my captor said, and tapped my knee with his hand. "One more time now. From one backseat to another." I grabbed the man's forearm instead of his hand so I could get a sense of his body and clothing. A suit jacket with a scratchy, thin, summer wool-feel to it, and a long-sleeved shirt underneath. It bunched up when I grabbed it, and I rotated left and crept out to the gravel. Just as my feet touched the earth, a hand gently pushed my head down and an arm wrapped around my side body to guide me out of this second car and into a third. I prayed their hand wasn't low enough to feel my cell phone. I settled into the backseat of a smaller car, so small that the top of my skull touched the inside roof. The man's arm wrapped around me to clip my seatbelt, again leaving my hands free. I kept them clasped behind my back in the guise of compliance, sneaking one finger down into my jacket pocket to raise the volume. Please, God, don't let Ivan sneeze or cough. The motor started, the rear side door closed, and we started moving. I slid down an inch to keep the top of my head from chafing.

I wasn't sure how many captors were in this car. Obviously a driver, but I assumed there was also a front passenger, or how else would they know whether I was taking off the hood to see where we were going?

"How long will our drive take?" I asked.

Short pause. I'm sure the two captors looked at each other, deciding how much to tell me, and the risks of my knowing how close our destination was to a populated area.

"Hour at the most," the driver said.

I used my other senses to pull what usable intel I could. We were traveling about 70 mph, and most likely in the middle lane because I heard cars on each side of us. No lane changes so far. And if my orientation was correct, we were going north from the lagoon. We were going too fast and the road was too straight to be Highway 1, which was always choked up this time of day. So we had to be on 405 heading toward Culver City, which crossed Highway 10 further north in Santa Monica. So an hour northeast of here would take us somewhere northeast of Beverly Hills, like Beverly Glen, which comprised windy roads, huge, old estates, and mansions. I smiled under the pillowcase hood. I knew where we were going.

I said nothing and continued playing the part I'd been assigned in this ridiculous theater. I was the meddling private investigator poking and prodding in the wrong places, threatening the integrity of operations and the security of assets. I'd been abducted against my will and would be taken to a safe house for a private interrogation. I knew how these things went. I was just normally on the other side of them.

My God, what about Derek? Had he been injured? I had to calm my nerves, or I'd never be able to breathe with this hood over my head. My curiosity of whether my call to Ivan was still connected consumed me, but I resisted the urge to do anything but sit quietly. Making trouble would only elongate my captivity, increase the chances of harm, and compromise my mental and physical strength. Would Ivan recognize Morse code from my tapping on the phone screen and would he know what I meant by 'lagoon'? Neither he nor Derek would automatically know where I was being taken, and the car was too quiet for me to get away with another round of fingernail tapping. I had to think of another way to contact them.

We now had about thirty minutes left, I estimated, because I'd felt the turn we made to exit Highway 405 to a winding road leading to the UCLA Westwood campus, which connected to North Beverly Hills Boulevard in Holmby Hills, and led north to the gorgeous hills of Beverly Glen. Some of the homes in Holmby Hills were the size of an entire city block, with wings instead of bedrooms, Olympic sized infinity pools, and vast gardens. Hannah had mentioned that odd, ill-fitting fact about Sophie gardening. Something about it just didn't feel right, nor did it match the profile of her so far. She apparently had been using two plots in Roger's Community Gardens on the UCSD campus. What was growing there?

CHAPTER TWENTY-EIGHT

We were climbing. I remembered the northeast slopes of Beverly Hills, but in all the time I'd lived in LA I think I'd only been here once or twice. The hills, grand and spacious, framed the landscape of curved, narrow streets, tall, pillared mansions, majestic gates, and silent opulence. My captors made a series of turns, doubling back on themselves twice. They must be lost. I'd only been to this house once before and the main North Beverly Glen Boulevard led straight up the hill to the estate at the top on the left, somewhere between Beverly Glen and Bel Air.

The car stopped; someone spoke into a gate speaker. Something buzzed and I heard a metal gate creak open. The car backed up a few feet, then proceeded straight ahead and down a long, winding path. At the end was a circular driveway and we parked on the far side of it, I assumed to make a fast getaway if needed. In this orientation, I was in the backseat on the right side, and my captors exited the car, closed both doors, locked it, and walked away from the car, presumably towards the entrance of the estate. I heard them talking to each other and I could feel the vibration of their footsteps.

Without moving more than what was critically necessary, I pulled one hand forward, reached into my pocket to grab the phone, and held it under my hood.

"Ivan," I whispered. "Are you still there?"

"We're here." It was Derek, also whispering. "Are you hurt?"

"Not so far. I think we're in Beverly Glen, something's going down soon. Gotta go, will keep the phone on." I dropped it back into my pocket and put both hands behind me again.

I touched the watch on my wrist and held onto it. *Thank God.* I heard footsteps coming back toward the car. In a purely game-time decision, I felt the seat in front of me and it had a pocket. I considered slipping the phone into it, thinking I would typically be searched when I got inside. But nothing about this encounter tracked with a typical abduction. So, in that case, maybe not. I kept the phone in its present location in my pocket and prayed.

I'd been investigating something that's beyond this current case, bigger than Sophie Michaud, and bigger even than the blackmailing of a federal judge. I knew the cost of solving this case may be too high. My escort returned, opened the back door, and stood aside. I crept out of the car; he hooked an arm through my elbow and walked me to the house. There were no sounds, no birds, no cars, no wind, no tree branches rubbing against other branches.

"Up one step," said my politely treacherous escort.

I stepped up.

"One more," he said.

My right foot jutted out awkwardly looking for the shape of the stair. I tentatively took another step, waited for a third, but found a cold, smooth, flat surface instead, slightly slippery, probably marble. With my escort guiding me, I kept walking and relaxed my gait a little.

"How much farther?"

"Ten steps forward then a staircase down," the man said.

Okay, good to know. I proceeded to a basement, probably in a sound-proofed room, which of course was a bad sign but not necessarily a death sentence. Basements were private and provided a level of spatial separation from different types of operations that might be going on in other wings of the estate.

At the staircase, I slowly took the first step holding tighter to my escort, then felt the height of the steps and descended more naturally. It cascaded to the right in what might look like a large letter "J" from above.

"Wait here," he said at the bottom.

I gripped the thick, ornately carved handrail, keenly aware right now that Derek and Ivan weren't here.

And that I was being watched.

Scuffing of a chair against a tile floor, the thud of a closing door, mumbled voices, and I realized the voices were above me in the foyer, not in the soundproofed room. Were more people coming? I wanted to check my surroundings but knew my action would be observed. I touched the bottom of the hood and lifted it up to my forehead and glanced left and right. I was in the lower foyer, which appeared large enough to host the Super Bowl, mostly dark with light coming from something to my left.

"Oh!" I gasped, startled by a face staring at me thirty feet ahead, a short, dark-skinned, thin man in a suit. He put a finger over his lips, and I nodded. Now he pointed a finger to the right, indicating a door behind him. "Staircase…goes up," he whispered, enunciating each syllable clearly.

I nodded and followed along with the charade that he was my secret ally helping me plan my escape. I was sure the opposite was closer to the truth, but I made a mental note that someone may want to help me, someone might not agree with Operation Kidnap Mari, and that there was undoubtedly a trap waiting for me behind that door. I glanced left again toward the light source and, when I looked back, the man was gone. I slid my hood back down and another door closed somewhere in the labyrinthine cavern of the estate.

Footsteps.

Slower this time, so not the same man. Woman? No. I know the sound of heels when I hear them.

"Come with me," the voice said, a different voice now. *I knew that voice,* different energy, different smell, something in between soap and maple syrup. I couldn't put my finger on it, but it was vaguely familiar.

The man led me around the staircase, through a doorway, and deposited me in a chair next to a heavy table. "Go ahead, Ms. Ellwyn, take it off."

I took off the hood, and the man turned to close the door. There was no observation window so the rest of his team could watch our conversation but of course there'd be an A/V system that would record everything, including my interaction with the man in the foyer. The man returned and sat in the chair opposite me.

I knew that face, or I knew it when it was smoother with no gristly beard, less wrinkled, and when the blue eyes sparkled a bit more. The hair that once framed his eyes was now only slightly longer than a crew cut.

"Hello, Roger," I said to Roger McGuin, who had been my Special Operations Group Task Force Team Lead within CIA's Special Activities Division. "I knew that smelled like you."

"Oh?" he said without even a hint of amusement. "Do you know...why you're here?"

And that's what I remembered most about Roger McGuin. His power, which didn't stem from ammunition or being a good shot, but from the timbre of his voice and the way he used it to persuade, command, and communicate. Roger McGuin's power came from a secret language of pauses, used alone, in combination with other pauses, and in combination with eye movements or blinking, or a ten-degree tilt to his head, and when he spoke, the rest of his body was otherwise completely still. He never scared me before, because we were always sitting on the same side of the table.

CHAPTER TWENTY-NINE

"I'm mostly thinking about how I got here. I mean, was that seriously your plan?"

The eyes narrowed; the head didn't move.

"I can think of ten easier ways to abduct someone than to try and fail to run them off the road, stop in front of them and get out with guns flashing in daylight. Seems a bit desperate and amateurish, don't you think?" I was taking a risk even talking to him right now, but I had to know what he knew and had to move this situation forward somehow.

"Your driver, or should I say drivers, eluded our operatives and wasted a lot of…your and my valuable time." He looked at the ceiling, sighed, shrugged his rugged shoulders in a suit I could tell felt confining. "Plans are only that, right? Plans. Execution, well," a pause, and that signature right-tilt to his head, "you certainly know the hazards of setting unrealistic expectations, don't you?"

He didn't expect an answer to that because he knew that part of my past as much as I did. We were there, together, on his team tracking down Jacques Martel and his team of operatives who'd been running three layers of smuggling operations off the California coast and eluding every known law enforcement agency for over five years. Interpol had tracked him successfully up until 2010 when he went off-grid. My team's investigation and research found him, monitored his movements, tracked him, and closed in. He was just one step ahead of me.

"You were there, too. What about your expectations? Or did I fail you when I had the audacity to get shot?"

"I am sorry about that," he said effortlessly, and my shoulders recoiled from the shock of hearing those words come out of his Roger McGuin's mouth.

"Really?"

"Well, if you'd followed orders and stayed long enough to properly debrief the incident, you would have heard it sooner. You recovered quickly, were unresponsive to calls, emails, texts, and you damn well should have been fired. I recommended it."

"Who dissuaded you?"

"Your father's voice is not without influence. Even now."

I looked down at the wood on the varnished table. It was dark, like ebony-dark rather than the more customary dark brown shade of *cappuccino* that had taken over modern décor, probably to offset the white porcelain tiles. Roger McGuin was a seasoned professional who carried an invisible box of assorted tools and tricks. He'd just flaunted one.

My father. My weak spot.

I knew my face had changed at the mention of him—a downturn of my eyes, a contracting of my mouth, probably a minute slumping of my shoulders. Roger McGuin had been trained, so had I, to make careful note of the ticks, twitches, fidgeting, squirming, or shifting that occurred in response to verbal stimuli and emotional manipulation. There were many types of both conscious and unconscious responses to stimuli, and I was a textbook case right now. But I had my own bag of tricks. I refused to hide my vulnerability from a man who would undoubtedly detect it anyway. I played into it. I leaned forward and put my elbows on the table, placed my two index fingers on both sides of the bridge of my nose, making it seem like I was holding back tears. Roger McGuin cared about me once, and I think in a way that wasn't purely professional. He hated his job right now, and that was the card I was holding.

He and his team had to know I had a cell phone in my pocket. I was sure this building, or at least this floor or maybe only this room had been fortified with data and IT infrastructure that could detect RF signals, alerting them to radio frequency detection on premises, and those sensors would be able to detect those signals even in standby mode. Best-case scenario was if Derek and Ivan were hearing our conversation and had a make on my location. Worst-case was that the call had disconnected. That would mean I was here alone unprotected.

"You haven't answered my question," my former boss and captor said in the true style of psychological interrogation, bringing it back to an original question over and over and over hoping to elicit different answers each time while mentally exhausting the subject and, thus, peeling down their layers of defense.

"I give up. Why am I here? You want me to stop investigating whoever's blackmailing a federal judge? I don't know the blackmailer yet. Look at my face, Roger. Am I hiding the name from you?"

His teeth were clenched, eyes unmoving. "No."

"Is that why I'm here? You obviously know about my partner and the part of the investigation he's working on, right?"

A slight smile crept into Roger McGuin's face. I wouldn't have thought he knew how. "Yes actually, your knights in shining armor are very close to here. We've been tracking them for the past hour. Not too bad actually, those two. Not the typical bunglers."

"I'll tell them you said so, if I ever see them again."

"Don't be so melodramatic. If we wanted you dead, that could be arranged with a phone call. You know that. You've, unwittingly perhaps, stumbled onto something larger than the blackmailing of a federal judge, or the strangling of a college student." He moved his chair back a few inches, unbuttoned his suit jacket and crossed his legs, returning his manicured hands to his lap.

"What do you know about her, so far?"

"Sophie Michaud? I know her brother Jonathan works for you and has been driving a big, gray van all around town tracking me. Is he a new recruit or something? Maybe you guys had layoffs and the customary training program wasn't available?"

"Don't...under...estimate...him," he said, pause-strategy intact. My stomach tensed at the words. Mental note made.

I let a full minute pass before I spoke again, using his tactic of pauses to acknowledge the leverage he'd just revealed. Was it intentional? I suspected very little accidental behavior got through for someone who'd expended such time and energy building control. It was a fortress visible in the taut skin on his face, knobby hands, rigidity of his jaw. Even a fortress, though, requires the advantage of windows for spotting incoming threats, and windows were vulnerable. But the fact remained he had just given me something for free. You want to know what I know about Sophie. Why? Either because you don't know as much as you need to, or because my knowing something is a threat to your operation. I suspected the latter. So I went through it in my head, still looking forward, and acting as I had been.

Sophie Michaud, bored, rich teenager, begs her parents to let her go to school in America, citing her dual citizenship as an obvious logistical advantage. Let's say she already had a school in mind and had started filling out the application. Why UCSD and not Stanford, or Tufts, or University of Chicago? Her brother may or may not actually reside in San Diego but he does own property there, which could mean extra support for her, a/k/a a human ATM. San Diego is also a port city on the water, and a major enough hub to catch international flights overseas without having to deal with LAX.

Sophie was a straight-A student, demonstrated a passion for visual art, worked in a studio, studied in the library on campus, had close friends, and didn't care about sexual hookups. She also had two connections to San Francisco: Hannah, who previously studied at UCSF, and her father, Nicholas Michaud, who supposedly knew Judge McClaren when the judge lived in Paris years ago. Sophie and Hannah's friendship was obviously strong enough that she'd taken Hannah to live with her at the brother's house, and then lived with her in her dorm room when they moved out after an argument.

There were a lot of ways I could answer McGuin's question, and I remember how he'd articulated it. Not just what did I know about her but 'so far'. To me, that meant he thinks I haven't had sufficient time to research her and also process what I'd learned to form any salient conclusions about the factors that might have led to her death. Not just death, but violent death. Somehow, Sophie had gotten involved in something, or with someone, that made her a liability that was too strong to leave exposed. Maybe she sought it out by soliciting danger, risky situations, and edgy people, which would have been other students, right? Who else would she meet? Other artists from San Diego? Perhaps. She also could have met associates of her brother while she lived there. I'm assuming she didn't know what he did for a living. Or did she?

I watched Roger cross his legs the other way, pretending to get more comfortable with my long silence.

Strangulation posed another wrinkle in the fabric of this convoluted case. Why that and not something easier? Not just easier but less intimate, less personal, less chance of leaving DNA and other forensic evidence on the body. And of the two types of strangulation, why manual and not ligature with some kind of tie or belt to do the work for you? This, to me, said something compelling about Sophie's killer. They'd wrapped their bare hands around her neck and pressed until she stopped breathing, causing, according to the autopsy report in Ivan's file, asphyxia leading to anoxic encephalopathy. Brain death. That almost certainly meant that her assailant had been looking in her eyes while they were choking the life out of her; the autopsy report had made note of finger marks on her neck. To me, that indicated a level of personalization, intimacy almost, that could cause that level of hatred or possibly revenge. Revenge for what? What had Sophie done, or not done? My mind returned again and again to Reggie, our law clerk/bartender who so desperately needed me to contact his former boss that he'd summoned security to my art gallery on a Sunday. Ivan was right about this case, but I needed to craft a suitable answer to Roger McGuin to get myself home tonight in one piece.

With so many choices, I decided the most prudent approach was to play into his charade, feigning ignorance and lack of sufficient time to pull together a theory.

"Not much, other than that she was an art student over here from France studying visual art and living with her brother." I still wore the same wounded expression from the comment about my father, used specifically to elicit guilt and play the victim. That was another thing I wouldn't give him the satisfaction of bringing up today. Of course, he knew of my father's whereabouts, probably Martel's as well. It's okay, Dad, I'll find you on my own.

"She lived on campus, actually."

"I hadn't gotten to that yet," I lied, and I was certain McGuin knew I was lying, and therefore he would draw certain conclusions about that lie, and build an elaborate case based on assumptions that may or may not be true.

"You might know more than you think you do," he said in a practiced, friendlier tone.

"About Sophie?"

He stared me down, unmoving, unblinking.

"How's our friend Martel these days?" I asked, changing the subject.

At that, Roger McGuin rose, slid his chair under the table, and gripped the back of it. "We'll…let you know if we need anything further."

"You could just call me next time. Might be cheaper." And quicker.

He smiled and exited the room.

I'm not dead. Good work.

Before I had time to get up, the door opened and McGuin poked his head back in. "By the way, your Morse code is rusty."

Shit.

"You spelled Lagos. Surprised your friends aren't on their way to Nigeria right now."

CHAPTER THIRTY

I had two choices right now: try the door in the hallway as shown by my secret ally or climb the stairs and head out the front door the same way I came. I chose option two and made it up the grand staircase, white marble, without issue. I headed for the front door half expecting McGuin or one of his goons to say something from the balcony, or a shooter to slip out from behind one of the ginormous pillars and take me out. I was walking too fast. Don't trip, keep going. One hundred and five steps later I made it. I turned the knob and stepped out.

Nigeria, right. From the front door, I saw Ivan's SUV peeking out behind a yucca on the other side of the exterior gate. Why the hell hadn't they brought the cavalry to arrest my abductors? I knew the reason. I knew it out of logic, from my own experience, and I knew it in my bones. These men didn't answer to local police, to the FBI; they didn't obey the rule of law in this or any other country. They had higher objectives and evolved influence, which padded them with Teflon and prevented recourse from their shadowy pursuits.

I approached the SUV and watched Derek's eyes widen, like they expected they'd have to break in. I got in the back door, closed it, and said, "Go, now." I pulled out my phone, disconnected the call, and powered it off.

Ivan, in the driver's seat, checked me in his rearview. "Is she hurt?

Check," he said to Derek who took off his seatbelt and climbed into the backseat, clasped my seatbelt, then wrapped his arms around me and held me there.

He backed away. "How are you doing?" Derek whispered. He looked like hell.

"Delighted to be not dead." I laughed, and my chest heaved, and instant tears spilled from my eyes.

"You're okay, we're right here."

"How'd you guys find me?"

"We traced you from your phone. Thank God you left the call connected," Ivan said. "I don't know why they didn't take it from you. They must have known it was there."

I nodded. They weren't trying to harm me. Just letting me know they were watching and scaring me off. "You told Derek who lives up there?" I asked Ivan.

"Yeah, and the rest of the story," he said, which meant he'd shared the details of my work, my team, my sting operation on Martel, and the outcome.

I cleared my throat and wiped my nose with my shirt. "How'd you like my Morse code attempt?" I asked.

"We didn't get to it in time to decipher it," Ivan said, "but I knew if you were making the effort to contact us, you were telling us you were okay. If you weren't, you would have been screaming."

"Have you ever heard me scream, Ivan?" I asked him.

He winked at me in the rearview.

"Shut up. It didn't work anyway. They knew what I was doing because my phone's been tapped."

"I'm surprised he admitted that," Ivan said and he was right. Because in doing so, Roger McGuin had probably betrayed their best method of tracking me.

"I know. So I need a new phone today, but I'm keeping the old one. Could be an advantage to provide false leads now that I know they're tracking me, and to keep using it from time to time so they don't get suspicious."

Ivan wound us out of Beverly Hills and then southwest to Santa Monica. "You can get a new phone tomorrow. Right now, I'm taking you home." Then Ivan turned to Derek. "Can you stay there tonight?"

Derek nodded.

"What they want is to know what we know about Sophie. They

don't seem to care about the judge and said this case is way bigger than any of that. Sophie was on to something, or someone. I played ignorant and he knew it. But right now, I think we know more about Sophie than they do."

"Maybe not. She could've gotten too close to something and they could've killed her," Derek posed.

I shook my head. "The autopsy report indicated that she was strangled, manually strangled with someone's bare hands. If they were gonna take her out, it would be with a semi-automatic pistol with a silencer, a neat, professional hit at a time when she was alone, to avoid immediate detection and to give themselves more time to move off to a safe distance. Strangulation, especially that kind, has almost no advantages and is a sign of uncontrolled rage. Speaking of autopsy reports, what happened with your press conference?" I said to Ivan.

"Didn't happen, but I talked separately to one reporter, explained the details of the mix-up, and reassured her that we were investigating the matter and would have another report shortly."

"You always were a good politician." Derek shook his head. "What does that mean exactly?"

"I'll tell you. I've been trying to track down the pathologist who conducted the autopsy initially and concluded that the victim was raped postmortem. A doctor named Cronin. Well, get this, Dr. Cronin has been missing for the past three weeks. The octopus just grew another arm."

CHAPTER THIRTY-ONE

While grateful for the company and reinforcement, I just wanted to be alone tonight. Derek had spent the past thirty minutes using up all the hot water in the shower. I got caught up with Duga using a special burner phone he'd given me a while back, which I hardly ever used. I'd already said three times that I wasn't hurt.

"They were instructed not to hurt me," I explained.

"Do you know where they took you?" Duga asked.

"Derek and Ivan traced it, and they were waiting when they released me. A mansion in Beverly Glen that I remembered from my old life."

"I'm just glad you're home now," Duga's voice cracked. He cleared his throat. "I've been doing my homework on your friend Thomas."

Reggie, that's right. "Oh yeah? How does he spend his time?"

"You were right about the Chess Park. He plays a rotation of three old men every afternoon at three and leaves at four to go to the Le Merigot Spa steam room at the Marriott."

"That's like a five-star resort. And who the hell goes to a spa every day?" I asked.

"Just the steam room. He must know someone there. He told a woman at the front desk that he has a bad back."

I chuckled. Reggie. "He's beyond neurotic. He has a bad back and he's on his feet for a living? I'm sure he has a bad back, bad feet, and takes fifteen different medications. And after the spa he goes to work at one of the bars?"

"Only three or four nights a week. On his off nights, or two of them anyway, he drives down to San Diego."

"Why?"

"He parks in front of Elise Turner's house for an hour and then drives home."

"Elise Turner? She's the other journalist, the one who wrote an article about Sophie's case. She's been missing for a month. What was he doing?"

"Just sitting there watching the house. He's there right now actually. I've been here watching him for an hour. No phone calls made. He's just staring out the window at her house, waiting for something. Maybe waiting for her to return."

"Thanks, Duga. That's a lot of late-night surveillance for you. This is helpful."

"Mr. Abernathy's with you right now, right?" he asked, reverting into bodyguard-mode.

"Singing in the shower as we speak."

It was the wrong thing to do and it was risky. But the world just looks different after you've been abducted at gunpoint.

There was no GrubHub delivery, no martinis, and no celebrating. After a hot bath and my favorite dinner of scrambled eggs and toast, I tucked Trevor into his gigantic doggie bed and crawled under my duvet. I had no sense of time, but it was dark out so I wasn't too far off.

I knew I wouldn't be able to sleep. The pervasive thought rolling around my head was that we'd been looking at this case the wrong way. The case, I knew now, wasn't about Sophie. It was about something Sophie discovered. She was an unintended victim, but that doesn't mean her death was accidental. She got in the way of something, of someone's agenda, and had to be eliminated for fear of exposure. Did she threaten exposure explicitly, or was she more of a loose end that had to be tied off?

What that told me was that whatever she'd stumbled onto was bigger than her drawings, bigger than her paintings, bigger than UCSD, and more than she could handle. So not only was it likely that she had help, but whatever she was doing was probably done on a different computer.

I grabbed my phone off the bedside table. Shit. Okay, I thought, plan B. I slid my robe over my shoulders and listened at my bedroom door for the sound of the shower from the guest bathroom. Seriously, he's still in there? How long does it take for a man to shower? I approached the door.

"Everything okay in there?" I shouted.

"Sorry, be right out."

"No rush, I'm turning in." I tiptoed into the living room, picked his phone off the coffee table, and brought it back to my room. I still hadn't bought a new one and could no longer use mine. My guest room still might have broken glass on the floor from the most recent break-in, so I convinced Derek my sofa was super comfortable. We'll see.

Sure enough, he'd saved Hannah Moraga's phone number. I took it down and entered it into Duga's burner phone, quietly returned the phone to the coffee table, and crept back to my room and typed out a text.

Hey Hannah, it's Mari, we met the other day with my partner Derek. Are you busy right now?

Hi, no, what's up

Can we talk?

Sure

I dialed the number and tiptoed from my bed to the door and closed it. I knew Derek would be getting out of the shower soon. Hannah picked up on the first ring.

"Hey," I said. "How are you doing today?"

"Why are you whispering?" she asked, amused.

"I have a friend over and they're sleeping. Listen, I was thinking about something and had a question I wanted to ask you. Did Sophie keep a diary? I know I did when I was in college."

"Mmm, sort of."

"More like a journal maybe?"

"She called it a register of everyone she'd met that had power."

I made mental note of this. "That's pretty enterprising."

"Yeah," she snickered.

"Like what kinds of people?"

"CEOs, heads of state, the staff and spouses of heads of state. I think she learned from her father about leverage."

It was an interesting comment for several reasons. The word leverage didn't seem like it would have been in her vocabulary. Leverage was a grownup's word, a political word, a word for people who didn't trust each other. Not a first-year college student.

"Did Sophie's father know about the book, or the register?" I asked.

"I don't think so," she blurted.

"So then…I have to ask this, why'd you tell me her parents were dead?"

Pause. "Sophie told me. She'd trained me to always tell people that so no one would know she'd grown up wealthy and privileged. Her father's a French government official. She was embarrassed, mortified really, by opulence and disgusted by people who abused wealth and power. She said sometimes she ran away from home and slept in a park near their house with homeless people because she felt like she had more in common with them."

"Hannah, where's the register now?" I asked, wishing now that this had been a text conversation so I'd have a permanent record of it.

Five seconds. Six. "She was always writing in it under the covers."

She'd answered a different question, but I took it in stride and kept going. "When was the last time you saw it?"

"The week she died."

"Had she met someone new that week? Someone of influence?"

"Maybe. Through her brother she met a lot of people of influence."

"What kinds of information went in the register? Do you know?"

"She recorded tips about them. Their favorite color, favorite artist, the names of their children, people they hated. Things like that."

People they hated. I was getting a picture of something. "How did she learn these things?"

"By just meeting them. You know, or maybe you don't because you never met her, but when you look like Sophie, and when you're as charming as she was, or pretended to be, people tell you anything. She knew how to talk to people and ask them things. She said more than anything else people just want to stand around and talk about themselves and impress other people. And she had a good memory. So she used those things to her advantage."

"Did her brother know about the register?" I asked.

Pause. "I don't think so. Only I knew about it."

"Do you know who she met most recently?" I asked, making sure not to linger too long on her last answer, which could be the key to everything we'd learned so far.

"Not met. She didn't meet anyone. She learned something about someone by eavesdropping on her brother."

"You're saying she was essentially keeping a database of contacts of people of interest."

"Right," Hannah replied.

"She must have had a master database she kept online somewhere, though, yeah?"

"No. The notebook was the master," Hannah replied. "The one on her laptop was the backup in case anyone found the master."

"Okay, I get it. The police must have taken her laptop a long time ago, right? After they found her?"

Pause. Here was the standoff. Hannah knew what I was really asking. I just hoped I'd been innocent enough in my delivery that she wouldn't just hang up. "The other one," she whispered.

"Other what? Were there two laptops?" I asked, pretending to be astonished.

"Yes."

"You never turned it into the police?"

"They never asked me for it." Her tone was defensive. "I would have, if they asked."

"Would you give it to me?"

Long pause. A sigh. "Okay."

"Is it password protected?"

"Yeah. The password's her favorite painting. Go to her studio, you'll see."

"So this database is something she started in Paris related to her father's government role as Minister of Culture, and later to her brother's business?"

"I think so."

"What does her brother do?"

"Some kind of art dealer. International art dealer. He travels for work a lot."

My stomach clenched. Jacques Martel was also 'some kind of art dealer'. I couldn't tell if the smoke was thicker or if it was beginning to clear.

"I need to go to sleep now." She yawned. "I have an early class."

"Hannah, do you have the diary with you now?"

"No, not here. She kept it safe, buried somewhere on campus."

"Okay, I'll come by tomorrow afternoon to pick up her other laptop. Sound okay?"

"Yeah. Text me when you get here. You can meet me in my room. Just say you're my mom if anyone asks. You're picking up my dirty laundry."

"Your mom?"

She laughed slightly.

"No problem. I'll be there around three. Does that work?"

"That's fine."

"Thank you, Hannah, sleep well."

CHAPTER THIRTY-TWO

I slipped out before six, while Derek snored on the living room couch and Trevor eyeballed me tiptoeing across the floor. Something eerie about the Santa Monica Pier, first thing in the morning, always made me believe whatever I decided there had to be true, no matter what. The hushed gray sky at dawn transformed the iconic Ferris wheel into a grotesque monolith towering over receding surf and squawking seagulls. I found myself there, sometimes with Trevor, sometimes alone but for a cup of coffee, and not thinking but deciding things, inevitably searching for signs. Did I really need something or was it a fleeting impulse I could live without? Could I trust someone, or should I listen to the warning in my heart? Trust, a tricky one. Derek, yes. Duga, certainly. Ivan, no, and Hannah…where do I start?

I walked the full 2745 feet of the Santa Monica Pier and back, over a mile, before the hordes of kids arrived and before all the rides opened at Pacific Park. The methodical rhythm of my steps geared up my brain for what would be a day of observation and analysis. I had time to think about the gallery, the artists whose work I represent, paying the rent on my dingy trailer in Fashion District, all the things I'd neglected for the past month.

Then after an hour at Verizon to get a new phone, Derek and I drove together down to Venice Beach to the Sidewalk Café, my favorite breakfast spot for huevos rancheros.

"Miss E! Howzit?" yelled one of the surfer-servers as he backed into the kitchen with a tray full of dirty dishes.

"You have interesting friends," Derek commented.

"Compared to Duga, who's like a Buddhist monk you mean?"

"Two please," Derek said to a young woman at the front, who led us inside and then out again to sit under the huge red and white awning. I loved the perfect view of sand, palm trees, and the Santa Monica mountains before all the riffraff arrived.

"Awfully loud here though."

"I know, but where else can you get first class huevos and see topless roller-skaters at the same time?"

He looked left and right. "You don't need a menu?"

"Huevos rancheros is the only thing I ever order for breakfast here," I said.

"But it varies widely from place to place, I notice. Sometimes it's just a pile of salsa on top of eggs and flour tortillas, and other places have a special ranchero sauce, others include green chili."

I studied Derek's face thinking that this man spent the night at my house last night, which seemed kind of a milestone in any relationship. "So how'd you sleep?" I asked.

"Pretty well, your sofa's indeed very comfy."

"As much as I like my independence, I appreciated having someone else in the house last night. Thank you for staying."

He studied my face, knowing that was a lie. "How about telling me where we're going today."

I'd brought him up to speed on Reggie and the updates we got from Duga on the drive here. But I hadn't yet told him what I'd learned from Hannah.

"To breakfast, and we're here," I said, innocently.

He shook his head. "Try again."

"All right. Last night when you were in the shower, I used a burner phone I got from Duga and I texted Hannah asking if we could talk."

His eyes widened. "I thought we were under some moratorium about that. Does Ivan know?"

"I told him we were going down there again to follow up on something and he said fine."

"Okay. Proceed."

The server set down two mugs, silverware, and napkins, poured coffee into the mugs and asked if we wanted menus. I looked at Derek. "Two huevos rancheros?"

"Sure," he said, nodding to the server.

"Well, I was thinking about whether Sophie kept a diary. Turns out, she kept more than a diary. It's a comprehensive register of people of influence, and she kept adding details to it to—"

His eyes widened. "She kept a database of contacts? For what purpose?"

"People of influence," I explained, because it seemed totally obvious to me. "People she'd met through her father and her brother."

"I thought her parents were dead."

I nodded, sipping the strong, black coffee. Ooh, that's good. "Hannah admitted Sophie trained her to perpetuate the lie to conceal that she'd grown up privileged and wealthy."

"Wow. Okay. But wouldn't such a myth be easy enough to debunk by one Google search?"

"I don't know, I guess. Anyway, she kept a diary hidden somewhere on campus, and only Hannah knows where it is."

"Did you ask her where?"

"No."

"Nice play." He nodded. "What else?"

"There's an online version of her logbook on a second laptop, which we're going to pick up today, and stopping at her art studio to get the password."

Derek shook his head. "So..."

"It's her favorite painting, which will apparently be obvious when we go there."

"You're a gallery owner, so it's your job to identify the painting."

"I like a challenge. So anyway, we also talked about her brother Jonathan." From there, I stopped talking knowing that this was the connection between this case and my unfinished business with Jacques Martel and, possibly, the whereabouts of my father. The server set our plates of food on the table. I stared into the eggs, trying to remember our last conversation.

"Jonathan? What about him?"

We spent the rest of breakfast and the drive to San Diego chomping on the details I got from Hannah last night. The drive south to San Clemente always seemed underwhelming to me compared with the open ocean vistas of I-5 the rest of the way. Derek offered to drive so I could admire the view, which I found so thoughtful given the position of my steering wheel. I'll never tire of the endless horizon and the beautiful monotony of blue-on-blue. It's my respite, my comfort, and my salvation from the uncertainties of life. Whatever the curve ball, I always had that vista to return to.

"So Sophie," he said, "probably when she was still pretty young, started keeping a log of who she met, their role and title, their sphere of influence, and collected data points about them."

"Not exactly a typical teenager."

"And these data points were being used, no, collected as a sort of currency that she maybe intended to use sometime in the future?"

"Currency. Good word for it," I said.

"And her brother, you said he was some kind of art dealer?"

"That's what pinged something in the center of my chest, reminding me of Martel. Well," I reconsidered, "Martel's an art dealer, yeah, covering up his career as an art smuggler, which covers up his reputation as an embezzler, an assassin, and his life as a spy. So he's smuggling secrets for different countries but disguised as a reputable art broker."

"Very sixties," he said. "And you think Jonathan Michaud's got the same kinda scam going?"

"Maybe, but to me it's all about Sophie. I think her brother may have been connecting billionaire art investors with stolen art, skimming off the top to make it economical for him, and I think Sophie was on to him."

"Sort of brings a whole new wrinkle into this case, doesn't it?"

"That's right. Suddenly Sophie's no longer a naïve art student and, instead, a very enterprising young businesswoman—"

"…who's holding a full deck, you know, with her people-of-power logbook. Is it possible that's what she was selling to Judge McClaren, and it wasn't a piece of art?"

"I really need to talk to the judge. That would clear up a lot of these questions. But if you're right about her trying to sell that register to him, maybe that's what my burglars were looking for in my house," I realized. "Does Roger McGuin think I have Sophie's register?"

"Seems like you played it pretty well with him, so maybe not. Anyway, Hannah didn't tell you where it was, right?"

I let an eerie smile creep across my mouth.
"You know where it is," Derek surmised. "Where?"

CHAPTER THIRTY-THREE

There were some places where the quality of the light is always good, and others where it's never quite right. Too bright to see an incoming text, too dark to find your keys in the bottom of your bag. Besides California, I'd lived in three other states, and somehow the light in LA had a quality that didn't exist anywhere else. Sometimes the sun was so high and bright, it bled out all detail leaving a luminous silvery cloak over the sand and surf. Then at dusk, that same beachfront hides in climbing shadows, with only small details visible beneath the streetlamps. It was this unsinkable promise of light and dark that anchored me to this place, this stretch of rugged coastline with its seagulls and secrets.

I hadn't yet told Derek about my theory: that Sophie Michaud was no gardener. I stalled the answer to his question while we wound our way across campus to North Torrey Pines Road, then to Scholars Lane, and parked in an open lot. The only empty space was next to a gray van. Very funny, I thought, realizing it was a different shade.

We started down a narrow walkway between two buildings and followed a sign that read Visual Arts.

"Another thing that's been bothering me." Derek stopped to face me. "Reggie's connection to Elise Turner."

"Which means Reggie's also connected to Sophie," I continued his thought. "What did they have in common?"

"The judge," we said in unison and nodded.

"Reggie worked for him," I said, "and Sophie knew him through her father. We still don't know how Elise Turner knew about Sophie's connection to the judge."

"Did Hannah know the judge?" he mumbled. It was an insightful question considering Hannah transferred here from UC San Francisco. Possible.

I started to answer but felt my phone buzz with a text. I stopped.

"Give me a second, it's from Carrie. Oh, cool, we sold a painting. Omg, she's too funny. Carrie took a selfie with the buyer," I explained, "some guy named Abe who came in drooling over the piece a few weeks ago." I showed him the picture of Carrie standing with a dapper man in a purple tie with dark hair and stylish glasses.

"The painting I liked and fully intended to buy? Great."

"Nope, not that one," I smiled and winked.

We continued walking and entered a large, open lobby and followed signs to the gallery.

"So you don't know what we're looking for, right?"

"Right."

"But you'll know it when you see it?" Derek asked.

My eyes scanned the large interior. "Hannah said the password to Sophie's other laptop will be obv—" I stopped. A tall blue and pink light caught my eye.

"Wow, um, wow," Derek said, and we followed the light into the main room of the gallery where a colossal image of a painting was digitally superimposed and replicated. "Do you think—"

"Yeah," I confirmed, without even thinking.

A digital lighting display extended the dimensions of the painting, so the blue of her dress spilled onto the floor and above our heads on the tall ceiling. The figure, or I should say figures, were of a Parisian woman from the late 1800s adorned in a striking cobalt, multi-layered dress, matching blue gloves, and a hat, with a tiny hint of a black slipper extending beneath the border of her voluminous skirts. The vibrant shades of color spilling down the wall from the ceiling drew me in. I'd spent ten years of my life as a gallery owner and felt reassured that I was still capable of this awe.

"Beautiful," I mumbled. "The Blue Lady."

Derek found the artist attribution on the wall, citing 'Sasha

Michaud' as the digital artist, with lighting assistance from the Visual Arts department, and with proper homage to Auguste Renoir for his painting "La Parisienne". Though translated to "The Parisian Girl," the painting became colloquially known as The Blue Lady by the early 1900s.

"Sasha?" he asked.

"I think Sasha's her real name and Sophie must be a nickname," I said, remembering seeing references to Sasha Michaud in her police file.

I never tired of watching others view art, seeing their reaction, the impact of a color field or figure take hold on the viewer's face in the widening of their eyes, the way their arms wrapped around the body as a way of studying it, moving closer and closer, to enter the canvas and become a part of it. Derek touched the wall and ran his open palm over the areas of The Blue Lady's arm as if to confirm that she wasn't actually standing there before us.

"So, she reproduced," he stopped to count the Blue Ladies, "eight versions of this painting in all different colors and sequenced them to blink on and off as if the woman is climbing down to you from the ceiling. That's stunning."

"Guess we know what her password is," I whispered, hoping it would be that easy.

We walked politely through the rest of the gallery, giving about five seconds to each painting, knowing they all paled in comparison to Sophie's work. She of course hadn't painted The Blue Lady herself, but she'd found a way to bring her back to life. If only we could do that to Sophie…

"I'd like to walk to their dorm from here. I want to see the path and gauge the distance," Derek said.

I texted Hannah that I was on campus.

Fifteen minutes, she texted back, which would give us time to walk over and make some observations.

"I see you've met her," someone called out to us from the other end of the gallery space.

We turned but no one was visible. Then footsteps echoed off the walls and a man in square-toed boots stepped around the corner into view. He stopped, looked, crossed his arms, and added a smug grin to his face. Five foot nine, reddish wavy hair, and large dark eyes framed by cartoon-like eyebrows. I wondered if he'd used makeup on them.

"You guys lost or something?" he asked.

Derek didn't move, so I took that to be my cue. "No, not lost. Just wondering, is the gallery closed?

"Oh no, come on in. We're open, we're always open."

"We were just leaving, but then you saw that, didn't you?" My eyes narrowed and I saw the man swallow a gulp of air.

"The Blue Lady, yeah, wow," Derek jumped in, thank goodness. "Impressive, especially the lighting."

"Thank you," the man said and nodded. "I did that."

"So you work here?" Derek turned toward the exhibit. "How long did this take to design?"

The man took a few steps toward Derek, maintaining a cautious distance from me for some reason. He moistened his lips, uncrossed and recrossed his arms, then stared at both of us as he backed away a few paces. If we'd been born wolves, we'd all be dead right now.

"A few weeks, and the installation took months," he said, elongating *months* and rolling his eyes.

Something pinged in the center of my chest, the part of me that only wakes up in times of danger or to alert me to something.

"Are you guys parents of a student here?" He'd executed the question perfectly, yet the undertones of who-the-fuck-are-you were clear.

Derek gave me a quick glance. "We're investigators working with the LAPD on the Sophie Michaud case. And your name is…?"

The man's mouth hung open slightly, but he quickly recovered, wiped his right hand on his pants, stepped forward and offered it to Derek. "Troy, I'm on the staff here." His eyes went from Derek to me and back and forth for a good thirty seconds. "I have a class I need to get—"

"Oh no problem, we're good here. Can you just tell me when you and Sophie worked on this piece together?"

"Ah…" The man's face turned three shades lighter at the question.

"The time period," Derek explained. "You said the installation took several months. Was just wondering which months."

We moved toward the entrance.

"Oh okay," the man said, shifting his weight from one foot to the other. I thought he might fall over and faint. "Um, last fall I think," he managed. "Terrible thing," he muttered under his breath.

"Sorry?" Derek turned back toward the man now, The Blue Lady watching us from her lofty view.

"You said terrible thing. What do you mean?"

The man released an exasperated sigh. "What happened to Sophie."

Derek nodded. "Which part?"

Again, the man named Troy stepped back three paces and put his palms up in a surrender pose.

"No worries, buddy, I'm sure it's hard to talk about. Hasn't been that long," Derek said. A master.

"Yeah no kidding. Hard enough when you hear it about someone on campus, let alone someone you know."

Derek looked at the floor, then at Troy. "I'm sorry for your loss," he said, and we walked out together, leaving Troy to the mercy of The Blue Lady and her plans.

I loved how Derek hadn't asked for the guy's card or mobile number. I said this to him on the walkway out. "I'll call Duga on our way back north later, see what he can find out about our new friend."

"I've got a better idea," he replied.

CHAPTER THIRTY-FOUR

I'd made sure I brought a brown leather messenger bag large enough to fit a laptop. I assumed Sophie's laptop would be something like my larger MacBook Pro because she was a digital artist and needed a large screen. When we approached, Hannah was standing awkwardly at the bottom of the staircase holding a white laundry basket.

"It's in there?" Derek asked. "Nice."

"You're the dad," I said.

He shot me a look. "You're the mom, and we're married now and have a teenaged daughter? I know I slept on your couch last night but, to be honest, you're moving kinda fast. Besides, you're not really my type."

"Ha!" I cracked up, a full smile like I didn't care who was watching. I suspected he was right too, about my not being his type. I wondered sometimes. Was there some part of him that looked at Hannah like she, or someone like her, could have been his daughter, and the dangers she might face navigating the world such as it is now?

"I like that pink," I said to Hannah, pointing to the fuchsia streak in the bottom half of the right side of her dark brown hair.

"Thanks." She handed me the laundry basket and winked. "Are you sure you have time to do this with your busy schedule?"

"Your laundry? Of course, gives me another excuse to see you." I handed the basket to Derek. "Could you bring this to the car, honey?" I asked Derek and tried not to laugh.

"Sure…honey."

I leaned in close to Hannah. "How's it going today?"

"I don't know. Okay, I guess. Did you go to the gallery?"

"Yep. I think I'm good."

She knew what I meant.

"We met Troy," I said, with amusement.

"Kind of a piece of work, huh?"

"He was a little, what's the word…territorial. Is he always that way?"

"He's obsessive," Hannah said.

"About his work? Or about The Blue Lady?"

"Yeah that, because he was getting his name on the wall plaque."

"I take it he's not your favorite person."

Hannah shook her head slowly and scanned the parking lot. "He's an asshole, but he was always a puppy around her."

"Sophie? In what way?"

She looked at the ground and shifted her feet. "He was obsessed with her. She spent the night at his apartment once," she said, quietly, "like after a party she crashed on the couch is all, and she forgot her jacket when she left the next morning. He refused to give it back to her, and now he wears it like every day. Kinda gross, and a little disturbing. He won't wash it either, says it still smells like her perfume."

"What kind of perfume?"

"Chloe. She wore that scent because it's her sister's name."

I'd texted Duga information about our new friend Troy before we left, asking him to do his magic and find out what he could about him before I returned Sophie's laptop.

Derek drove and I fished through the piles of what smelled like clean sheets to something cold and smooth at the bottom.

"What are you gonna do with that, exactly?" he asked.

"Do you disapprove of my methods, Detective?"

"We both have to answer to Ivan on this case. I'm just being pragmatic. What's your story?"

I opened the lid to make sure it turned on. "My story," I sighed, "is to, of course, hand this over to Ivan." It turned on, battery 2%.

"Tomorrow. I'll have to charge this first. I have a power cord at home."

•———•••———•

In light of my run-in with Roger McGuin, we decided to forego the trip to Jonathan Michaud's house and instead went to Mission Beach to see the exact location where Sophie, and also Nina Richmond, had been discovered.

"I went to Surf Camp here," I said.

"At Mission Beach? How did that go for you?"

"I got up on my board. That was miraculous. And I experienced the tug and push of the current."

"I like watching other surfers. Does that count?"

I regarded my partner as he climbed out of the car. "You never surfed? You look pretty athletic. Why not?"

"I was a flooring installer for fifteen years, which is back-breaking work and great exercise. Never surfed."

"Flooring," I said, remembering being in Hannah and Sophie's dorm room.

"What about it?"

"I'm just remembering the stain on the carpet in Hannah's room near Sophie's closet. Now I understand why you noticed it."

He nodded. "I've been studying it but it's probably food or something. If it was a bloodstain, someone would have found a way to remove it. And I didn't smell anything like solvents or cleaners in their room."

"Very observant. We're going back there to return the laptop at some point so you can take another look."

With traffic surprisingly sparse, we followed Ingraham and turned into the Dana Landing Boat Ramp to get to Sunset Point Park on West Mission Bay.

"According to the initial police report, Sophie's body was discovered at seven-thirty in the morning by a fisherman under the West Mission Bay Drive Bridge," Derek read from his phone. "It would be pretty dark here in the morning, especially around those huge concrete pylons."

I pulled my sunglasses out of my bag, put them on, and still needed to shield my eyes from the brightness with my hands. "You're saying it's a smart place to deposit a body?" I asked, in a quieter voice as I noticed a couple lying together on the grass thirty feet ahead of where we stood. We moved to the paved walkway toward the bridge.

"Depends," he said, catching up to me. "This is a popular fishing spot so it's definitely not secluded in the mornings, when she was discovered. But in the evenings, you could hide anything here."

"Interesting," I said, thinking out loud. "So you think her killer, or whoever brought her body here postmortem, wanted her to be found? That's notable."

"I'd say so."

I suggested we walk to the actual spot where she was discovered. With neatly manicured grass near the parking lot, the paved walkway that wound under the Glenn A. Rick Bridge was lined with sand on each side, some scant brush, a few slender palm trees, and large rocks leading down to the water. In all my trips to San Diego, I'd never been to either Mariners Cove or Sunset Point, yet I knew every square inch of the Santa Monica beachfront.

"Okay," my partner announced with outstretched arms, "according to the report, it's pretty much here."

The spot didn't quite constitute being *under* the bridge but was close enough to have been easily hidden from view, especially at night. It had been six months since Sophie's death. I'm sure, for weeks following her discovery, this area had been protected, cordoned off with crime scene tape, coroner tents set up to view the body and gather evidence, huddles of onlookers pushing in from the other parts of the beach, the press interviewing, photographing, researching, clinging to any detail that could begin to explain how a teenaged girl could get the life choked out of her.

Six months later, there was no taped-off area, no collection bags, tents, signs, or other boundaries the police use to cordon off an area to onlookers and foot traffic, which would otherwise disturb the fragile and very temporary evidence that lingered in the early hours after death was discovered.

The late afternoon sun spilled alternating layers of sunlight and shadows on the huge bases of the pylons, which stood like soldiers, unmoved by the roving current, unswayed by the movements of nature, and without judgment for the evils we inflict upon each other. Sophie's remains, her eighteen-year-old body, had lain here on this patch of dirt and grass, unable to tell that hapless fisherman the next morning the story of her brutality, of her assailant, and the intricate pattern of steps that inevitably led her there. She had been silenced, literally with a set of bare human hands around her throat. And someone else had gotten the last word.

Derek held his phone up with a picture of Sophie's body from Section 17 of Sophie's murder book, which contained the crime scene photographs. "Do you want to see this just to make where we're standing a bit more real?"

"It's real enough already, but sure." I grabbed the phone from his hand and studied it, reluctantly at first, but then more closely, zooming in and out. The vantage point was from about five feet away, about where we were standing now, showing most of her body from that distance, oriented with her feet positioned up the slight incline of the berm and her head toward the water. Her clothing was mostly intact: jeans that I could see were unzipped, a shirt that was mis-buttoned at the bottom, and a light jacket unzipped and with one sleeve stuck up around her elbow.

The clamor coming from the beachfront stores, restaurants, bicyclists, joggers, and foot traffic folded into a sort of white noise. The gravity of this spot and the crime scene photograph muffled out external noises, so all I heard was my own breathing. I'd been a private investigator long enough to know that the spectrum of potential investigation cases could span from cheating spouses to something significantly grittier. Someone died here, like right here beneath my feet on this very patch of earth. But then I corrected myself. Sophie was killed somewhere else and was picked up, transported, and deliberately set here. Why?

Derek took back his phone and put it in his jacket pocket. I knew we were thinking the same thing. "Pretty obvious that her clothes were removed and hastily put back on after she was dead."

"Yep," I agreed based on the mis-buttoned shirt. "Which leads me to believe in the veracity of the initial autopsy results of port-mortem sexual assault."

"That could certainly be true, judging by the haphazard condition of her clothing. But we don't know for sure which happened first: strangling or sexual assault, or if they happened at the same time." Derek shook his head.

"What?"

His eyes followed the shape of the slight hill leading from the paved walkway up toward the street. He pointed at a long, wooden staircase about ten feet away. "How did she get here?"

I looked back to the parking lot. "Would be about a two-minute walk from there to where we're standing now. Carrying a body—"

"Exactly," he interrupted. "Carrying a body, it could take five minutes, and that's a lot of potential exposure. If Sophie weighed, say, a hundred and ten pounds, that's a lot of weight and, logistically, a very tricky package to transport." He studied the wooden staircase. "What about if they carried her down that staircase? Very long and curved staircase, so probably not."

"It's possible," I said, "but there's no place to park up there."

"So the only possibility is putting her body in his car, driving her here, and carrying her out to that specific spot under the bridge?"

I thought of the autopsy report again. "What if she wasn't moved and she was killed right here?"

"The report indicated that livor mortis showed the way the blood was pooled in the body at the estimated time of death, she had not died in the location where she was found."

"I'm not a pathologist, but I think I'd like to see that report again," Derek said.

"We should go, I want to try to catch Reggie at the Chess Park if we can."

CHAPTER THIRTY-FIVE

Duga texted that he'd meet us at the Santa Monica Pier.

"Where's the best place to park this time of day?" Derek asked as we got off the exit from Highway 10.

"Just go to the Santa Monica Pier parking lot, it's like three dollars an hour and is right near the Chess Park. There's Duga's car," I commented, pointing.

"Where?"

"He has a Nissan Leaf, a pretty metallic blue, but around town like this he always drives an old, black, nondescript Nissan from like the nineties, the kind no one would ever notice."

"Except for the fact that it's twenty-five years old?"

"Hello." Duga did his signature magical appearance-out-of-thin-air act. He'd done it to me so many times I was barely even startled anymore.

Derek turned quickly at the sound of his voice and looked behind Duga. "Where did you come from?"

Duga winked at me.

"He does that," I explained. "Duga, you remember Derek Abernathy, my new partner in crime, ha ha."

Duga, dressed in a black t-shirt, black jeans, black tennis shoes, and a black baseball cap, extended his hand. "Don't turn around but

Reggie's playing chess at a table right behind you guys."

"Does he see us?" Derek asked, without turning his head.

"I don't think so. Why don't you park and meet me right here. Let's walk away from the Chess Park," he motioned, "and we can come back up the other side and observe the game undetected."

Derek parked, and we walked across the sunny concrete. Then we followed Duga, who immediately started talking about our new friend Troy from the UCSD gallery. "Troy Garrity, thirty-two, has worked for UCSD for ten years in the Visual Arts department, teaching classes, assisting with installations at the gallery, and does setup and takedown of other events on campus."

"Criminal record?" Derek asked, of course, pragmatic as always.

"Nothing recent, but he was arrested twice when he was seventeen, and the records were sealed by court order because he was a minor."

Derek and I stopped walking at the same moment.

"Keep going," Duga said, pointing to the south end of the boardwalk and a staircase leading down to the beach and the chess park: a seated area where all the tables were chessboards. "The staircase will be a good vantage point."

I could see Reggie Barnes' back, his dark orange, short-sleeved shirt, forearms on the chessboard table and his head angled down toward the board. His opponent looked to be forty years his senior and was sitting back observing the surf. Three elderly men sat beside him on the same side of the table. Four on one side, Reggie on the other. Odd arrangement.

"You're sure that's him, right?" I asked Duga, who nodded soberly. "How long has he been there?"

"Thirty minutes maybe," Duga said. "Usually his games are shorter. He's playing a different opponent today."

Duga was facing Reggie, and Derek and I were facing Duga to keep out of Reggie's view. Duga laughed and shook his head.

"What?" I asked.

"Hilarious."

"What is?"

"Those old Chinese men sitting around the chess board, including his opponent, are talking about game tactics in Mandarin. They don't realize Reggie speaks Mandarin, and now Reggie's about to win."

"Reggie speaks Chinese? Where would he have learned that?" Derek asked.

"How do you know this?" I asked Duga.

"His LinkedIn profile. Certainly could be considered a professional advantage."

"And I'd like to know why he speaks Chinese."

"Game's over," Duga said, angling his head down. "He's walking this way. How do you want to play it?" Ahead of us was the Ocean Front Lodge on Arcadia Terrace, a parking garage. Spilling onto the sidewalk right now was a school bus filled with elementary school students. Perfect.

"Derek and I will say hello to him when he walks by. He'll run, and you cut him off on the other side of the hotel."

"Okay." Duga nodded.

"I'll stay here and Derek can go get the car. We'll bring him to Fashion District."

"How do you know he'll run?" Derek asked me as Duga walked away.

"Because he's slippery and has something to hide. Watch."

Reggie Barnes stepped quickly through the crowd along the boardwalk, pushing past a woman with a stroller, angling awkwardly into an old woman with a scarf on her head, now stuffing his hands in his pockets. Derek and I were huddled near some tables, appearing deep in conversation as he approached.

"Now," Derek whispered.

I turned slightly toward the water as Reggie passed. "Oh, hey Reggie, how's it going?" I said in my flirty voice.

He slowed but didn't stop, paying more attention to Derek, and looking around to see if we had reinforcements with us. "Oh hey, Ms. um, Ellwyn, I'm sort of in a hur—"

"I was hoping I could talk to you for a minute. Can you—" I followed. He sped up, glancing around. I jogged to keep on his heels. I knew he was looking for Derek, who had gone for the car. "Or would you prefer to chat somewhere else?" I shouted. He turned back, stopped, and stared me square in the face.

"I'm good, actually. I gave you my message from the judge the other day at the gallery," he explained, with a shoulder shrug and a hapless smirk on his tense face. He was trying to look targeted and confused, but his wild eyes gave away his intentions. "Why are you harassing me down here?" he said now in a louder voice with outstretched arms, planning to make a scene and have witnesses.

"I live here," I explained and pointed. "Like five minutes from here. It will be much easier for both of us if you give me five minutes."

"Okay sure, just give me a—"

He turned, mid-sentence, and ran up the slight incline toward Oceanview Lodge, to the walkway on the right side of the lobby. I ran up the left side, scanning the street for Derek's car and wondering if Duga was in position.

Reggie. What was he running from this time?

I caught sight of Derek's Land Rover live-parked next to an old red convertible about ten steps from where the hotel walkway ended. My handbag thudded into my side as I ran, and now I wish I'd worn running shoes instead of flats. My poor high arches were forever in the wrong shoes. I headed toward Derek and waited for Duga, who was nowhere in sight. WTF?

Derek rolled down the passenger window. "Where are they?"

I still couldn't see either Duga or Reggie. "Reggie may have continued past the hotel and kept going. There are two more parking lots back there." I pointed.

"Or he could be hiding out in the hotel somewhere."

"No, I don't think so. The sight of me sent him in a panic. Let's just wait." I leaned against Derek's car. The warmth felt good on my lower back. I reminded myself to keep my eyes peeled in all directions, not just where I expected them to be coming from. My phone buzzed. Duga.

"I got him. We're in my car," he said. "Trailer?"

"We'll be there in a few."

CHAPTER THIRTY-SIX

Every time I turned left onto the forgotten dirt path leading to the rented trailer of "Mari E", I remembered the tangled threads of my family dynamics. It would never be okay to the Ellwyn family to be a private investigator, and only occupations with the requisite cocktail party cache would suffice. Gallery owner, as it turned out, made the short list. Today, I wasn't wearing a gray hoodie, or driving my PI car and, worse, Reggie had been to my gallery, so now he'll add his name to the list of those who've seen both sides of my career. Both sides of my double life.

Derek and I got there first. I texted my friend Bobby Bishop on the way for additional reinforcement. Not that I expected it would be needed, but the idea was to sufficiently intimidate Reggie Barnes such that he might crack open and tell us all his secrets before we hauled him into the Crenshaw precinct. On what grounds? It seemed every day more reasons arose for why we might suspect Reggie of involvement in any of the related circle of crimes that had taken over my life over the past two months:

1. The murder of Sophie Michaud
2. The murder of journalist Nina Richmond
3. The disappearance of journalist Elise Turner
4. The blackmailing of Judge Conrad McClaren

5. The break-in at Judge McClaren's office
6. The two break-ins at my house

Octopus, as Ivan had said. I was afraid to ask how many more crimes might occur before one of us finally solved one of them.

The door to my trailer opened as I stuck my key in the lock.

"Oh, hey Bobby, you scared me!" My hand landed on his chest, and he took the opportunity to wrap his arms around me in a hug that lasted two seconds too long. Derek looked quickly down to the floor. Great.

"This is my partner, Derek Abernathy." I went inside to consider the seating arrangement in the main room, leaving the two men to do their posturing. "It's not gonna work." I dropped my handbag on the floor and crossed my arms over my chest.

"What's not gonna work?" Derek moved inside.

"This arrangement." I circled my finger around the room. "Duga's gonna be here in a minute. Bobby, quick, what do you have in your office?"

"Is this some kind of interrogation or something?"

"Pretty much," Derek answered. "We need a small room with three folding metal chairs and nothing else in it."

"No desk or table?" Bobby asked.

"Right."

"I've got a small room, not sure about the chairs. Lemme go check." Bobby disappeared through the back door of the trailer that led to his adjacent unit.

"Butterworth's?" I asked Derek, referring to Butterworth's *Library of Investigations.*

"Sort of a combination of that and a few other books I've read about the psychology of interrogations. Sit the detainee in a hard straight chair with nothing in front of them, so the entire body can be seen, and proper attention can be given to small changes in body language," he said. "What they do with their hands is always very telling, but also their feet, arms, head movements, facial expressions. Reggie's nervous and fidgety anyway, so this should be interesting."

"I just can't picture you as a flooring contractor," I admitted.

"Why, you don't think contractors are introspective?"

I shook my head. "Because I imagine it's very solitary work, and I can tell you need to be around people."

"Some people maybe."

Bobby opened the back door the same time as a car pulled up out front. It had to be Duga and Reggie. Bobby nodded toward the front door. "We're ready," he said.

"What do you think, Detective?" I said to Derek.

"Leave him in there alone for five, ten minutes, then you and I go in and see what he knows." Derek looked at Bobby. "No table?"

"No table," Bobby nodded.

"Right on. Thanks."

"Do you want me to stick around?" Bobby asked.

Derek nodded soberly. "This guy's pretty slippery. Can we wait in there?" he said to me, pointing to a storage room. "Duga needs to just walk him through here and then into the interrogation room."

"Sure." I opened the storage room door and Derek and Bobby walked inside. "These walls are paper thin, so we'll hear everything."

I closed the door and the three of us stood about a foot apart, heads angled down, arms crossed. I heard one car door outside, and a second only after about twenty seconds, which meant Duga had likely handcuffed Reggie and put him in the backseat. Duga gave his signature knock of one-twothree-four and the door opened.

"Go," I heard him say.

One of them tripped on the way in, probably Reggie. I'd already texted Duga about my very specific handling instructions: place Reggie in an empty room with no table and three chairs. Position two chairs on one side of the room, and seat Reggie in the lone, single chair. Leave him alone in there handcuffed, then stand outside the door and wait, and don't respond to anything Reggie says. Duga followed my instructions and stepped out of the room.

"You can't keep me here, you know." Reggie bellowed to the closed door in front of him, five seconds and already unglued. Derek, Bobby and I exited the storage room, and the two men sat in the leather chairs in the main room. I walked through to Bobby's trailer to see Duga.

"Hey," I whispered.

Duga leaned in close. "He's unraveling."

Perfect.

CHAPTER THIRTY-SEVEN

"Can you grab a water out of the fridge?" I said to Duga, referring to the thirty-inch mini fridge that sat on top of a foldaway table next to some piles of file boxes and a stack of real estate books left over from the previous tenant. I wondered how many shady deals had transpired in this room, within these sad vinyl wall panels. Duga handed me the chilled plastic bottle. Derek was poised for battle just inside the door.

"Has he asked for his lawyer yet?" I asked.

Derek nodded, amused.

Duga opened the door and walked into the holding room. "Can you shut up?" he asked Reggie in his hood voice. I knew he had one, I'd just never heard it before.

"Listen to me, you can't just—"

"Are you capable of shutting the fuck up? Because the longer you whine in here, the longer you'll be in here. Got me?"

"Yeah yeah, okay. But—"

"Dude?"

Reggie went silent.

When Duga exited, I gave Derek the nod that it was our turn. I looked at Duga and pressed my thumb and index finger together and rotated my wrist left and right, lip-synching "key".

"Handcuffs?" he asked.

"Yeah."

Now armed with comfort and compassion, Derek and I entered the room. OMG. I tried not to laugh. The only light in the room was flickering like something out of a Quentin Tarantino movie.

I went in first. "Hey, Reggie," I said in an apologetic tone.

"Hello again." Derek nodded.

Reggie watched us carefully, waiting, his eyes shifting from one to the other making quick, calculated assumptions, silent decisions, because maybe for him everything was a chess game. Which piece did he see himself as right now?

"I probably shouldn't have run, I guess," Reggie admitted. A drop of sweat beaded and dripped off his forehead onto his pant leg. He closed his eyes and sighed.

Derek sat in one of the empty chairs and I walked slowly behind Reggie.

"Why'd Duga handcuff him?" I asked Derek and winked. "Let me get these off you. Duga can be kind of a pit bull sometimes. I brought you some water." I removed the cuffs then handed him the cold bottle.

I took the seat directly across from Reggie now, all three of us seated, no table. So awkward. Derek's a genius for suggesting this. Reggie downed half the bottle, then probably guessed a bathroom might not be an option in this place. He capped it and set it between his knees.

I rose and opened the door a crack. "How about turning on the air in here," I shouted into the hallway, hoping Bobby was still here. A moment later, I heard the same thunk of the chiller that I heard in my trailer and the cold air streamed in before I'd even sat down. At least something worked well in this place.

Reggie sighed. "Thank you," he said with his eyes directly on me.

"You were asking for your lawyer a minute ago. Why?" Derek asked.

"Because you can't keep me here, that's why."

"We're not detaining you, Reggie," I said. "We're not the police. You can go whenever you want. We just wanted to ask you a few questions, and you ran off. So I asked Duga to try to find you and we came here because it's a little more private than out in the open on the beach. We're talking about very confidential matters."

"I—" Reggie laughed, shaking his head—"I can just get up and go?"

"Sure," I said.

"And your friend, out there. What about him?"

"Hmm, there's that," Derek said.

I leaned forward. "I just wanna know what you're doing here, Reggie."

He shook his head with a bewildered expression.

"Not here in this room, I mean here in LA. I met you with the rest of Judge McClaren's law clerks a few months ago. You, all of you, had what seemed like super successful careers in enviable spots within the justice system. From that post, you could go anywhere."

Reggie listened while I talked. I could tell Derek was three steps ahead of him.

"Something must have happened to make you completely change course, leave your promising career, move down here to live with your mother, play chess, and tend bar."

Just silence. He didn't move his hands, didn't twitch, or fidget, drink more water, or fumble with the plastic cap on the bottle. He breathed in and out, staring straight ahead, blinking occasionally, and purposefully not answering my question. This guy was more controlled than I originally thought, which meant he was capable of feigned composure. What else was he capable of?

"How about *my* questions? I have two." Derek crossed his legs.

"Sure," Reggie replied.

"Where were you on August 28th last year, and why do you speak Mandarin?"

Slight laugh, and a glance at me as if to say, 'where'd this guy come from'. "That's random, but, okay sure. Um…how do you even know that?"

"It's on your social media profiles, and obviously it's something you've used to your advantage, meaning language proficiency is a huge career differentiator."

Reggie tilted his head to the right as if considering this theory.

"I also don't think your chess opponents know they were giving away their strategy for free back there."

The man shrugged. "Chess is about using every possible advantage without losing anything, or without losing too much. There's no false advertising here. They made an assumption that I can't understand what they're saying, giving them the mistaken impression of advantage. I'm just using what was handed to me for free. Opportunistic? Sure. Unethical, no."

"Okay." Derek nodded. "But why? Mandarin is not a language you learn over summer vacation. It's complex."

"I started out with Go, and all my Go trainers were Chinese. If I wanted to learn from the best, I had to be prepared to speak their language." It sounded pragmatic the way he described it. I just wasn't buying it.

And right now, Reggie was giving us a lot of intel for free. Derek circled back to the question of August 28th, after which Reggie crossed and uncrossed his legs.

"It was kind of a long time ago, so you might not remember," Derek added. "But it would really help us out in another investigation we're working on."

"I don't think I remember offhand, no. What day of the week was it?"

"A Saturday," Derek answered quickly, which may have been the truth.

"Yeah, I'm not sure. Depending on our docket at work, I could have been in the library that time of night."

"Sorry, what time of night?" Derek stared unblinking now. Everything stopped. Bingo. "I just said August 28th."

Reggie cleared his throat. Another shoulder shrug. "I thought you said nighttime. What I'm saying is that I sometimes spend Saturday evenings, even Sundays, researching case law in the library."

"Which library?"

"The Ninth Circuit Library. There's one in our building and other branches throughout the rest of the nine western states that make up the circuit."

"I see. So there were probably other people there that same night?"

Reggie nodded. "Probably, yeah."

"That's great. It would help, you I mean, if you can give us the names of anyone who might have been there on that particular night, like any coworkers, or employees that might have seen you."

At that last point, the interview irrevocably changed. Thomas Barnes' eyes widened. He started looking around the room again, then back to alternating his gaze from Derek to me and back again. You're a suspect, you know something, and now you know that we know.

"Is this conversation official or unofficial?"

"Unofficial, of course. Why do you ask, Reggie?" I asked.

"Well I was just wondering what the other case is that you're working on. Because I thought I was here today about the judge's blackmailing case, since of course that's the reason I came to your gallery."

It was a risky opening on his part, because now when we mentioned Sophie, his reaction would be under even greater scrutiny. But what I couldn't figure out was how he was missed the first time around. Section 12 of the Murder Book on Sophie Michaud included the list of suspects, and Section 14 the list of witnesses. There was no record of Thomas "Reggie" Barnes in any part of Sophie's casefile. I was dying to know how Derek would play his next move.

In the room were three people sitting in chairs, with no table to hide behind, no paper cups full of bad coffee and powdered creamer, no lukewarm water, pens, legal pads. Amazing what you take for granted when suddenly your whole case reduces to the head of a pin.

"A missing journalist," Derek answered.

"Oh really?"

"Yeah. She's been missing for—" Derek looked to me for corroboration— "this is four weeks now, right?"

"About that, yes," I said.

"And we're now going back a ways," Derek continued, "and looking into a related crime that occurred last August, which is why I was asking you about August 28th, which I know you've said you don't remember."

"I said I was researching." Reggie's voice was sharp, probably sharper than he intended.

"Oh, okay, because I thought you said you didn't specifically remember but that you sometimes did research on Saturday evenings in the Ninth Circuit Library."

Blinking, nodding, shaking his head. "Uh, okay, yeah that's right. I did say that and that's what I meant. Right."

"Is there a Ninth Circuit Law Library in San Diego?" Derek pressed.

"I—no, I don't think…I don't think there is."

Derek looked at me. That was my cue. For what, I wasn't sure.

"Well, we were just looking into this today and—" I started, winging it.

"And turns out there is one at the Thomas Jefferson School of Law in San Diego," Derek said. "So, in theory, you could have been there researching on the night of August 28th. I'm just saying it's possible, right?"

Laughing now and rubbing his palms on his pants. "I've never even been there," he said to the floor.

"To San Diego?"

"No, to whatever fucking law school you mentioned!" He'd raised his voice now, and that escalation couldn't be undone.

"Okay, calm down Reggie. We're just talking, right? Just talking." I watched him watching me watch him. What a game. "When was the last time you were in San Diego?" The way I was sitting, I could see Derek if I shifted my eyes left even without moving my head. He literally hadn't moved an inch in the past ten minutes. A master.

"I-I-I don't know what you think you're—"

"Answer the question." Derek's voice was firm but calm.

Reggie sighed. "Look, I think I'd better call off this line of questioning because it's getting a little—"

"Reggie, are you uncomfortable?" I asked in my most annoyingly gratuitous voice, with a tactic that had worked once before on another potential witness. "You look a little bit uncomfortable. Can I bring you some more water, or any—"

"No!" His temper erupted in a different tone of voice now; his face flushed and his hands wiped down on his pant legs. Derek's face was the same: firm and calm.

"Answer the question, Reggie. Unless you didn't understand it. I'll ask it again. When was the last time you were in San Diego?"

Reggie closed his eyes.

"Was it August 28th of last year?"

"No," he said through gritted teeth.

"Could it have been three nights ago?"

Reggie's eyes snapped up to meet Derek's, momentarily, and without moving his head.

"Is that more likely?"

He shook his head back and forth, quickly, then slowly.

"Do you know someone named Elise Turner, Reggie?"

Another snide chuckle, showing his teeth, then he rubbed his lips together as if to gather his thoughts. The room was completely devoid of sound; for some reason the air conditioner had gone off.

"The reason I ask that is because we know you were staked out across the street from Elise Turner's house three nights ago. Mind telling us why you were watching the house of a journalist who's been missing for four weeks? How do you know her?" Still, Derek's voice was like cold water, calm, even toned, without emotion.

"I don't—" Reggie started, then sighed.

"Okay, Reggie," Derek continued. "You can play it that way, and we can continue this conversation down at the LAPD Crenshaw precinct, because we now have probable cause that you could be a witness in a case involving a missing person, and under these circumstances we are allowed to detain you, handcuff you, and bring you in. Would you prefer that, Reggie—to talk to a detective and have them fingerprint you and—"

"I know how it works, for God's sake."

"Well, for some reason it's getting warm in here again and I think we'd probably all like to call it a day. Tell me here and now how you know Elise Turner and why you were watching her house three nights ago or we c—"

Reggie's palms went up, and when he shook his head sweat dripped off his forehead.

"She's my wife."

CHAPTER THIRTY-EIGHT

Sweat rolled down the back of my neck as I processed this new piece of information. I couldn't believe, in this moment, that at one point I liked the décor of this place, even the ugly paneled walls. These trailers had to be at least fifty years old.

"Reggie, we need you to repeat what you just told us to someone else we're bringing in. Are you okay with that?"

A single nod. He looked wiped out. No defenses left.

A car approached; that had to be Ivan. I'd texted him before Derek and I went in for two reasons: one, to cover our asses and, two, in case Reggie confessed to something significant, which he had just done. We left him alone in the room for a moment while Derek and I talked briefly outside the door.

Ivan and Derek shook hands, which somehow made me a little uncomfortable. "Thomas Barnes goes by Reggie. He was a law clerk for Judge McClaren, in—"

"Your blackmail case." Ivan pointed to me.

"Right."

"He was seen staking out Elise Turner's house in San Diego three nights ago. We asked him why and he said she's his wife."

"Ah, a new wrinkle, which also means he's now a suspect. He needs to say it to me and at the station so we can get an official statement in order to use this information in our investigation."

"I know," I said, "but he'll say it to you here right now so you know that this conversation was a legitimate lead."

Ivan raised his eyebrows and tipped his head, always to the left side. His signature move. "I didn't doubt you, or you either," he added, looking at Derek. "You two make a good team, you know that?"

I ignored the comment and knocked on the door before opening it. Reggie had been sitting with his hands covering his face.

"Reggie, this is LAPD Chief of Detectives Ivan Dent."

Reggie rose and shook Ivan's hand. Ivan's old-world sensibility would appreciate the formality.

"So, I hear you know our missing journalist," Ivan said in a way that somehow made it all seem a little less grave. "You wanna tell me about that?" Both men were still standing.

"Elise Turner's my wife."

"Your current wife, or ex-wife?"

"Current."

Ivan nodded. "Okay, thank you, that's an important detail and I'll tell you why. In a missing person's case, the missing person's spouse is always the first potential suspect. So what I suggest is to bring you down to the station and have you give a statement about where you were the night she disappeared and everything you've learned about what might have happened to her so we can clear your name quickly and get on with trying to find her. Okay?"

Reggie nodded.

"Now, I'm not gonna cuff you, and you're gonna sit in the front seat with me. This is gonna be a respectful, easy process for both of us. Sound good?"

"Yes, thank you."

"Say what you want about Ivan, but that was slick." Derek grabbed two waters out of the fridge and passed one to me.

"You were pretty slick in there yourself, I have to admit."

"I liked your doting mother routine with the water and the AC. That sorta snapped him. Did you know that was gonna happen?"

I smiled. "It worked once on someone else."

Bobby and Duga took off while Ivan brought Reggie to his car. I seriously wanted to pour the entire bottle of water over my head.

"Let's get in my car and put the air conditioning on," Derek said. "Your car's still at the beach."

"That's right." I grabbed my purse and locked the door to both my trailer and Bobby's, and happily got into Derek's car, running my hot face over the cold air blowing out of the vents. "Why's it so hot today? My God, it's only March."

"You know what this means, right?"

"Sure. If Reggie's married to Elise Turner, it might mean he knows everything she knew about Sophie."

"That's right," Derek agreed. "It could also mean that if Reggie killed Sophie, he might have also killed Elise Turner for fear of being exposed by her research."

"Killing his own wife?" I asked.

"Do you know how many husbands kill their wives every year?"

"No. Do you?" I joked, grabbing a scrunchie from my bag. I did a quick ponytail/bun to get my hair off my neck.

Derek's theory didn't feel right. "I don't think so," I said.

"Why not?" he pushed. "He was pretty controlled in there, you said so."

"I know but he was also very unstable." I shook my head. "He's just too nervous and neurotic. I think he could plan something like this but executing it? No way. And if he killed his wife, why would he be staking out her house? Duga said he was there for at least three hours, and he was literally staring at the house the whole time."

"You think he expected her to come home?"

"I'm not sure, but why isn't he living there? Why is he living in LA with his mother?"

"Do we know if he was living with Turner before she disappeared?"

"My District Court security guard contact, DeRon Richards, said Reggie hadn't worked there in three or four months."

"So, it's possible he could have been living with Turner and, when she disappeared, went to live with his mother. But then why was he working in San Francisco? Were they separated?"

"I can ask Duga to go down and talk to some of Turner's neighbors tomorrow, check her mail, see if it's in both their names. I already asked him to run surveillance on our new friend Troy Garrity at the university."

"You're giving Duga a pretty heavy workload. You must pay him pretty well," Derek said with a sly grin.

"He has many special talents, and yes, I do pay him for surveillance. He also has underlings, people he subs out odd jobs like this to. I'll talk to him and see if they're available tomorrow."

CHAPTER THIRTY-NINE

Before I ever had a dog, an old woman told me once that I had the soul of a Great Dane. I didn't know what to make of this until the first time I looked in Trevor's big, soulful eyes and pretty much fell in love at first sight. He's a canine and I'm a human, but after spending three years with him I can see that we're very similar in how we look at the world and how we relate to others. Both tall, too trusting, and don't eat much.

We finally got back to my house, so Derek and I could dig into Sophie's other laptop. I felt Trevor's powerful paws on the kitchen floor before I even touched my key to the lock.

"I'm coming, I'm coming," I said and opened the door wide enough for Trevor to see Derek. "Look who's here!"

Derek held his fist out as he walked into the house. "Hey, buddy, remember me?"

Trevor sniffed, licked his hand, and sniffed it again.

"That means yes." I set my handbag and Hannah's laundry basket on my kitchen table so I could indulge in our nightly ritual. I stood in front of Trevor and kissed him on the top of his head ten times, because that was how we said hello to each other. I pulled back, still holding his face, and looked in his eyes.

"I know. I love you, too. How are you today?"

Trevor licked my cheek on cue.

"Make yourself comfortable," I said to Derek. "I just want to feed Trevor and change clothes."

Derek took Sophie's laptop from the bottom of the laundry basket. One of Hannah's t-shirts fell onto the floor. Trevor sniffed the shirt, looked up at me, then grabbed it in his jowls and ran out of the room.

"Trevor, get back here!"

"So, is everything on here password protected?" Derek asked, connecting her computer to the MacBook charger already plugged into the outlet by the sofa.

"Macs let you password-protect a folder but I don't think individual files."

After our experience with Reggie and being in that hot room, I craved a cool shower. I kept the water lukewarm so it didn't shock my hot skin, soaped up from the neck down, and rinsed off in a matter of two minutes. Clean clothes. Relief.

When I came back in the living room, all the food in Trevor's dish was gone and Hannah's t-shirt lay in a soggy wet pile on the floor under the table. Great. I brought in two cold beers from the fridge.

"Thirsty?" I handed one to him and took a long gulp of mine.

"Look at this," he said hunched over Sophie's MacBook. "It's weird because there are all these random files scattered on the desktop, and then this one folder called Renoir."

"Is it encrypted?" I asked, remembering what Hannah had said about her password.

"That folder isn't, no."

"What's in it?"

"All the files on her artwork. They're all INDD files, which I think are Adobe InDesign."

"We're supposed to be finding her log, or her ledger, as Hannah put it, of all the intel she'd gathered on people of influence. I assumed it would be an Excel file or something and that it might be pretty long considering she probably poached a lot of intel from her brother and his contacts. Or, if she had a really extensive list, she could have used something more sophisticated like a database program, MySQL maybe. Are there any other folders?"

"Not that she created; only system folders," he said.

"So, whatever we're looking for must be in the Renoir folder. Something in that folder must be password protected. Keep looking," I said, took another sip, and went to check on Trevor. I called to him, and he returned with his leash in his mouth.

"Sorry sweetie, not time for a walk yet. We'll go soon. Go lay down now. You just ate."

"That's odd," I heard Derek say.

"What?"

"I found another folder but it's not visible on the desktop."

I considered this. "How'd you find it?"

"In a backup folder."

"Show me," I said, standing behind him. He clicked Finder, and then MacKeeper Backups, which had another folder in it called *La Parisienne.* He double clicked to open that folder and a window popped up asking for a password. "Okay, here we go. Do we know what the password rules are?"

"No. But presumably Sophie set this password herself, so it might be something easy." He typed 'The Blue Lady'. Incorrect password.

"Try an 'at' symbol for the a."

He typed in The Blue L@dy. Incorrect password.

I moved to the sofa and sat, thinking. "How about The Blue Ladies plural? Her gallery piece is of several blue ladies."

"Good idea." He typed it. "Incorrect password."

"We might be here a while then. Keep checking, I just got a text," I said, hearing my phone buzz in my purse, which reminded me that I hadn't charged it in the car on my way back. I pulled it out, plugged it into the charger on the kitchen counter, and saw the sender's name. "Hannah."

"Is she okay?" Derek said, looking up.

My hand involuntarily covered my mouth as I viewed an eerie image she'd sent of a glow-in-the-dark, spray-painted message on the wall of her bedroom. It read, "I know what she buried and I know where she buried it." Jesus.

Derek put his hand on my shoulder and took the phone from my hands. We spent the next fifteen minutes arguing about the potential hazards of my driving down to UCSD this time of night. It wasn't late; it was barely even dark out. But my traveling alone, in light of the gray van abduction last week, just wasn't a good idea. I knew it; he knew it. Derek wanted to stay here and work on Sophie's laptop.

I'd already asked Duga earlier today if he would take me back down to San Diego to do surveillance on Troy Garrity from the Visual Arts gallery, and a newer assignment to see what he could find out about Elise Turner and Reggie Barnes from Turner's house in Del Mar. Duga showed up fifteen minutes later. He beeped once and parked on the street.

I grabbed my purse.

"Call me if you find anything." I opened the side door.

"I'll be calling you anyway. I still don't like it."

I cracked up when I saw Duga in a green jumpsuit, green baseball cap, tall boots, and driving a "Roy's Gardens" branded truck. "Lookin' good," I chided.

"I'll be mowing Elise Turner's lawn," Duga explained, "pruning her rose bushes, and installing an irrigation system in her front yard. She's got a retired neighbor on the left, a single older woman who sits outside reading all day. On the right is a family with twin infant boys and a mother still on maternity leave."

"That's perfect. How long will it take us to get to UCSD this time of night?"

"About ninety minutes. What's going on down there?"

I held up my phone so he could see the image of Hannah's wall.

"That's disturbing. She's being targeted. Why?"

"I'm calling her right now."

"Kinda loud in here. Sorry," he said, and it was.

"No problem, I have earbuds somewhere." I dialed Hannah.

"Hey," she answered in a whisper on the first ring.

"Hey, I'm on my way down there right now. Are you okay?"

"Thank God." I heard her sigh.

"Are you in your room right now?"

Pause. "They spray painted it over Sophie's bed, not mine."

"Okay." I wasn't sure what that meant.

"Someone, who got into my room, knows which bed I sleep on so I'd be sure to see it when I turned the light off. Scared the fuck out of me."

"I can imagine. Keep the light on and stay where you are. Don't open the door for anyone."

"Okay."

"Have you had any visitors tonight?"

"No."

"Anything going on in your quad or in the residence halls tonight?"

"Just the usual noise, inconsiderate people screaming and running up and down the halls, smoking weed, slamming doors. No events or anything though."

"Okay." I thought as I talked. "Who had or has a key to your room?" I put Hannah on speaker phone and held it between us.

"Um, I have my set of keys. Sophie's might still be in her purse, wherever that ended up."

"I can check with the PD on that. Anyone else?"

"She told me she gave her key to Troy one time to pick up a painting from our room. But she told me he gave it back."

"Troy Garrity, from Visual Arts?"

"Yeah," she confirmed. Interesting.

"When was this? Do you remember?"

"I—not too long ago. A few months before she…you know."

"Okay, so that would have been last summer, around June? Did you guys stay on campus for the summer?"

"Sophie did because her parents live abroad and she wasn't getting along with her brother at that point. I went home for a couple of weeks and then came back here."

"Okay. So as far as access goes, there was you, Sophie's set of keys which I'll try to track down tomorrow, and Troy. Anyone else? Like anyone else on your floor in case you got locked out?"

"No. Well, Adam has a key, but he doesn't live on our floor of course."

Duga and I looked at each other. "Who's Adam?"

"Adam Bouvet. Sophie's therapist."

CHAPTER FORTY

I told Hannah to sit tight and I'd be there in forty-five minutes, then called Derek to fill him in.

"Adam? I don't recall that name from any of the suspect or witness reports in the case file," he said. "Do you?"

I sighed, exhausted by the number of details surrounding this case and more than a bit appalled at the original investigation. The lost autopsy report was bad enough. Now Sophie's bike, and now Adam. "No."

"Had Hannah ever mentioned him to you before?"

"No. As far as a therapist goes, I have no idea what he was treating her for, and I didn't ask Hannah about that over the phone."

"She's probably too upset tonight for any more questioning anyway," he said, right of course.

"I might ask her about it when I see her. We'll see. I'll try to get her to go to the PD tomorrow and file a report. In the meantime, can you call Ivan and give him the name of Adam Bouvet and have him check him out? Normally my driver would be doing that but he's busy right now." I looked at Duga's serene face smiling back and felt a moment of calm in the chaos.

"You got it. I'll bring Sophie's laptop to my place. Will Trevor be okay?"

"He might not want you to leave without taking him for a walk. I didn't get a chance."

"Oh, I'll take him. Trevor, go for a walk?" I heard him call out.

"Watch out, he'll be jumping all over you. Walk and cookie are his triggers. So you're taking Sophie's laptop straight home right now, right? No stops anywhere?"

"Straight home," he reassured me. "How about you—are you guys coming back tonight?"

I turned to Duga.

"I was gonna sleep in the truck and start on the lawn early in the morning. You don't mind sleeping in here, do you?"

"Yes, Duga, I mind." I knew he was kidding. "Yeah, we're driving back tonight," I confirmed to my partner. "I'll call you in the morning, or if you find anything in the meantime let me know."

"You bet."

I texted Hannah from the lot outside her building. Duga waited for me in the parking lot. On my way up the stairs, I reminded myself that this new puzzle piece by the name of Adam Bouvet had a key to Hannah and Sophie's dorm room, and Troy Garrity had a key once and very well could have made a copy before returning it.

"Hey," Hannah said, standing over me on the top of the outdoor staircase.

"Hey," I said, gently. "How are you doing?"

"I can't be in that room anymore." Her customary soft voice was barely a whisper today.

I caught up to her and gave her a quick hug, trying not to be too maternal. I wasn't her mother, after all, nor was I responsible for her. She felt thin and frail in my arms.

"You really need to give a statement to the police about this. Would you consider letting them come here to talk to you, or we could take you there tonight if you're up to it."

"I can't sleep anyway, so, sure. Who's we?" she asked, looking down at Duga and his ridiculous gardening truck.

"A friend of mine gave me a ride south from LA. Do you mind if I take a few pictures upstairs first?" I watched her face carefully, observing the change in her expression from amusement back to cold fear. "You can stay out here. I'll just be a minute."

"Okay."

I remembered how to get to her room. The door was already wide open with no lights on. I could see the glowing words from down the hallway, obviously sprayed or written with luminescent paint, and it reminded me of crime scenes I'd seen in the movies, not something you expect to see in a freshman year college student's room. I used my iPhone to photograph the phrase, both vertically and horizontally, then one shot of it close up to see the script:

I know what she buried and
I know where she buried it

Buried what? Her log? Obviously "she" referred to Sophie, and the phrase was positioned on the wall opposite Hannah's bed on purpose. But why? Someone knew something and threatened to go public with it. Why would Hannah care, though? I stepped around the room carefully, studying the photos I'd taken. On the closeup photo…OMG. Was I seeing this clearly? I swear the "a" in the word "what" looked like it was originally an "o". Did the perpetrator intend to write 'I know WHO she buried'?

I needed to get out of there. I took a quick picture of some paperwork on what had been Sophie's desk and another picture of the carpet stain for Derek. Some unspeakable cue drew me to Sophie's closet. I took two pictures of the top and two of the bottom, not really sure what I was seeing but determined to exit the room leaving as little forensic evidence as possible. Of course, I'd let the PD know that I was in there, but my forensic evidence could get in the way of other forensic evidence that might have been left by our spray paint artist.

Someone had entered this room in daylight using an illicit key, spray painted the walls, then left and re-locked the door. A planned, brazen, calculated act of someone with an organized, analytical mind.

Hannah was still perched in the same place at the top of the stairs. I told her I would have Duga drop me off at the Visual Arts building.

"You're looking for Troy?"

"Yeah," I said, knowing that earning her trust could be advantageous in several respects. "I wanted to follow up with him on a couple of things." Hannah's face made a very slight twitch when she said his name. "Do you want to walk over with me?"

"Sure," she said, and I knew she wanted to be anywhere but in her room. I told Duga where we were walking, and like the dutiful bodyguard that he was, he got out and shadowed us, staying about fifty feet behind. He had his phone in his hand as he walked, presumably to have a flashlight to illuminate the dark walkway, but I knew it was to be able to either call for backup or take a picture if needed.

"What do you think of him?" I asked Hannah, seeming casual but actually choosing the question with great care and precision.

"Who, Troy?"

I couldn't see her face as we were walking now, but there was a lilt to her voice when she said his name.

"Weak, insecure on the inside, full of himself on the outside."

"Do you guys ever hang out?" I asked.

She laughed, slightly. "Troy doesn't really…hang out with anyone. He's always working on secret art projects and he'll never show them to anyone until he's ready to unveil them at an official opening."

"Does he have studio space over here?" I pointed to the building as we approached a nicely lit walkway.

"No one really has studio space here, or not individual rooms. But Troy made himself a sort of studio on the lower level in the back, in a part of the building nobody uses."

"What's he doing in there?"

"I don't know, honestly."

"Have you seen this secret studio?"

Hannah shrugged. "Nope. Only one person did."

"Sophie?"

Hannah widened her eyes to affirm. I desperately wanted to ask her about Adam Bouvet, Sophie's therapist, but the moment had to be perfectly timed. Right now, my presence was a comfort to her. Don't blow it.

"Down here," Hannah said.

I followed her through the length of the Visual Arts gallery. The back wound around to the left where long tables and professional lighting were set up.

"Did Sophie work here in this room on her Blue Lady?"

"She mostly worked in the digital lab. She ordered large scale prints from an art supply store downtown, and she and Troy did the mounting here on these long tables."

I tried not to laugh, but that got me thinking about Troy and Sophie, remembering how he acted when Derek and I questioned him. I felt like my intuition combined with my observation of human behavior would let me know right away if Hannah and Troy had been lovers.

Hannah disappeared behind a door and returned a moment later. "He's not here," she said.

"No problem. I can come back another time. Is this his?" I gestured to a pile of charcoal drawings stacked on a metal cabinet.

Hannah came over to look. "Um..." She picked them up. "That's weird."

"What is?"

"Sophie drew these," she said in a dreamy voice. "I don't...know why they're here. They were in our room."

"When was that?"

"This is me," she said, looking straight at me. "I posed for her. Not nude or anything, she was practicing figure drawing. She told me I was beautiful."

"You are," someone said, a man walking toward us: Troy Garrity, wearing running attire and sweating. He wiped his forehead with his forearm.

"What are you doing with these?" Hannah grabbed the drawing and held them up, obviously annoyed.

Troy took three steps toward us and shrugged. "You brought them here. How else would they get here?"

"I haven't been back here in months."

"You think I took them?"

Now I felt in the way of this rather personal dispute and wondered, suddenly, about Duga. Did he see Troy approach? Would he do one of his magical acts of appearing out of thin air? Troy Garrity might have broken into their room to spray paint his message and took the drawings on this way out. Or someone else did it and planted the drawings in Troy's studio. But why? Troy shook his head and bent his left leg back to stretch his quad, then did the other side. I loved that stretch.

"You were obsessed with her," Hannah said, her voice cracking. "She's dead and you're still obsessed."

"Can I help you?" Troy said to me, ignoring Hannah's comment. The bastard. She's obviously in love with him. "Oh sorry. You were here yesterday. What can I do for you?" he asked me.

"I wanted to ask you..."

Hannah ran out of the room wiping her eyes.

I grabbed my phone and texted Duga to keep an eye on her. "Um, sorry—"

"No, I'm the one who's sorry about that unfortunate display."

"I'd like to understand what work you were involved with in the development and installation of Sophie's project."

"Sasha?"

"Sophie Michaud. You know, The Blue Lady."

He nodded. "Her name's Sasha." He said it in a way that more than just corrected a mistake. I couldn't put my finger on the nuance, but there was something.

"But Sophie's her nickname. You didn't call her that?"

"No."

"Okay, sorry about that," I said, revising what was obviously a grave error. I was more interested in Hannah's safety than Troy's ego. "So, Sasha's Blue Lady. You were listed as Lighting Support."

His hands plunged deep into the pockets of his track pants and he studied my face. "Do you always interrogate people this time of night, detective?"

"I'm not a detective, and I'm not the police," I answered, calmly. "I thought this was a conversation."

"Is that what you think it is?" A smug look took form on his hardened face, which made me wonder if Derek had been right about him.

"You seem kinda nervous, Troy. Do I make you uncomfortable?"

Slight laugh. "I *seem* nervous? That's interesting. Do I look nervous to you, Ms. Ellwyn?"

"Nervous people are defensive, and you've behaved that way during both of our meetings. Nervous people also do things like put their hands in their pockets as a way of concealing their feelings."

"What a crock." He took them out and crossed his arms. "What does this mean? That I was in love with my mother? Hated my father? Any other observations you'd like to share?"

Where was Duga?

"Just one." I took four steps toward the main gallery corridor. "When I was here before, I never told you my name." I smiled and did the eyebrow raise my maternal grandfather had taught me, as a way of saying "Gotcha" with just your eyes. Yeah, Troy, gotcha.

CHAPTER FORTY-ONE

I'd texted the pictures of the dorm wall to Derek before Hannah and I walked to the gallery. Derek wrote back telling me to call him. I started with Duga because I wanted to know about Hannah's location and her state of mind. He met me outside the Visual Arts building.

"She's gone back to her room."

"She told me she didn't want to be there anymore. Did you speak with her?"

"I asked her to let me walk with her for her own safety. She said yes but only if we didn't talk. I gave her a brass elephant."

"Awww. I love the little trinkets you leave in the pockets of my jacket, in the console of my car. They're like little good luck charms."

He smiled. "Exactly. I think she's okay. I saw her in and she locked the door."

"She's in love with that guy," I said.

"And jealousy makes people do crazy things."

I narrowed my eyes, because it was an interesting comment. "Jealousy?"

Duga shrugged.

"There's something I need you to check on tomorrow during your landscaping job," I said.

"You mean besides the nature of Elise Turner's relationship with

Reggie, and where she is now?" he joked.

"I want to know where Elise Turner's from. She's not on any social media, which in this day and age is unusual, unless she's elderly, and in which case she wouldn't likely be married to Reggie."

"You're wondering if she's not from California or not from this country?"

The evening breeze blew a waft of cool air over my face and hair. I smelled a faint whiff of low tide. I wrinkled my nose. "I want to know how Elise Turner knew about Sophie in the first place. She's probably in her thirties, and Sophie was an eighteen-year-old college student from France. Not exactly in the same circles."

Duga blinked, listening. "She's a journalist. What makes you think it's more sinister than her getting assigned to investigate a local murder? I checked and she covers these types of high-profile stories."

"Come on, Duga," I sighed. "Yeah, I checked too and, sure, she typically covers features related to socially and politically motivated scandals. So a teenager found strangled on a beach would be within her wheelhouse. I know. I just know there's more to it than that."

"Why?" He wasn't asking to disagree, and there was absolutely no emotion in that one word. Duga had been my friend for ten years and, like a good kindred spirit, he sometimes challenged me to ask myself hard questions. Why was there more to it than this? What assumptions had I made about Elise Turner?

"She seems to care more about this case than a journalist normally would in the course of their job."

"What about Woodward and Bernstein? Their investigation of Watergate started out as an assignment and turned into their life's work. You're not thinking right now, you're feeling something. What?"

I shook my head as an admission that I lacked the answer to another straightforward question.

"I'll see what I can find out tomorrow."

"Hey," I said, answering Derek's call.

"On your way back?" he asked.

"Yeah, I'm in an Uber."

"Uber? That's expensive."

"Not too bad. Duga's sleeping in his truck so he can get started with Elise Turner's yard first thing in the morning. I didn't want to stay in a hotel because, well, I like my own bed."

"How's Hannah doing?" he asked.

"I've just had a very interesting hour, to say the least. Hannah's afraid to be in her room but she's apparently in there safe now. She's in love with Troy; she accused him of being obsessed with Sophie. Even now, Troy only knew Sophie as Sasha. One last thing, Troy checked us out."

"Meaning what?"

"He called me Ms. Ellwyn. I didn't tell him my name the other day. And you only told him your first name."

"Sasha, huh?"

"Yep."

"You think he called the police to inquire about us?" he asked.

"I don't think so. I think Hannah told him, and I think they're sleeping together, or they have."

Derek sighed, and I heard typing in the background. "That sort of complicates things, doesn't it?"

"What are you doing?"

"I've been looking at the photos you sent me of Sophie's desk and closet on a bigger screen, and I see something here that sort of reminds me of what I'm seeing on Sophie's laptop, and of something you just told me."

"What?"

He didn't answer right away. "Sort of hard to say. I'll have to show you in person."

"Let's meet at my favorite coffeehouse tomorrow morning. Around nine?"

"Where are you right now?"

"I'll be home in thirty minutes."

"Text me when you're in."

"Oh, come on, don't be so paranoid," I said, and instinctively glanced at my driver. He hadn't uttered a word since I got in and that was fine with me.

"Seriously? Maybe you forgot that you were kidnapped last week."

"Okay, okay, I will definitely text you when I'm locked safely inside my house."

Okay, I'd been home for fifteen minutes and still hadn't texted

Derek. I liked him looking out for me, but it threatened my need to feel unleashed. I fed Trevor, opened all the windows to let the cool night air inside, changed clothes, and shuffled out to my mailbox in my cozy slippers, remembering when I'd been getting threatening notes every week. Three bills, a political leaflet that hadn't been mailed but had been stuffed inside, and…what the hell?

No index card this time but instead a package in a white envelope. It felt like a book, with no labeling at all. I glanced behind me and all around me observing the dark, tree-lined street of my little microcosm. I loved this street. I walked back inside, closed and locked the windows and closed and re-locked all the doors. Then I called Derek.

"Hey. Um…"

"Did something happen?" he asked.

"Nothing. Or nothing much. I got something in my mailbox that hadn't been mailed."

"Another note?"

"No. It feels like a book. Have you ever heard of a bullet journal?"

"No."

"It's a sort of book of lists used as a planner, organized into bullet points or boxes that you check off. Looks like someone was using this as a bullet list and also a diary." I flipped through the smooth, white, high-quality paper in the front. "Wait," I said, finding something different when I flipped from back to front. "This looks like…hold on…" I knew I was mumbling. "It's two journals."

"Okay…" Derek said, trying to keep up.

"Sorry, it's nothing dangerous, no threatening notes, and it's not about me."

"Whose journal is it and who sent it to you?" Derek asked.

"Not sent. Don't forget, someone hand-delivered this. I think it was Sophie's. I see references to TBL, which I think might be The Blue Lady, which is her art project and her favorite painting."

Derek sighed, typed more, then cleared his throat. "Are the references to The Blue Lady in the front or the back of the book?"

I checked. "Front. Why?"

"What's in the back?" he asked.

The first page from the back of the bullet journal was blank, I told him, then the next page had a bullet list of people's initials. Half of them were checked off, and the next page had some general journaling.

"About what?" he asked.

"The number of steps between the different buildings on campus."

"Odd," he commented, "keep going."

"The next page has a hand-drawn map of something called Roger's Community Garden with the number of steps between different areas, or plots maybe, and the next page has another bullet list of initials."

"Wait a minute," Derek said. "Go back. I mean go back to the front of the book. Can you read something from a diary page in that part?"

I flipped to the front of the book. "Here she's gushing about The Blue Lady's dress, wondering about the pigments Renoir used to come up with the different shades. She also mentioned Henriette Henriot, the model who posed for that and several other Renoir paintings. It's written in a sort of stream of conscious admiration. She obviously loved this painting."

"Interesting."

"Why?" I asked.

Another long sigh. "I've been examining the pictures you sent me of Sophie's desk and the inside of her closet."

"It was dark in there and I don't think my auto-flash was working. Sorry," I said. "I was trying to get out of there quickly and not leave too much of my own evidence, knowing the police would be going up there probably the next morning to take photographs."

"Okay, I'm emailing you four pictures right now. Can you get online for a minute?"

I'd charged my laptop last night. I retrieved it from the cedar chest at the foot of my bed, where I often closed and left it if I was working before turning out the light. I opened the lid, connected to my home Wi-Fi network, and opened Gmail. "I got 'em."

"Look at picture 1," he directed, and then look at 2. What do you see?"

Picture 1 was the top of Sophie's closet on the left side. It contained a messy pile of hoodies, sweaters, and t-shirts sort of all mixed in, unclear which were clean and which were dirty. Probably clean, I surmised, because I remembered it smelled fresh in there. I relayed this to Derek.

"Picture 2…" I leaned in close get a clearer image. "Wow."

"Yeah," he confirmed.

"I see that…um…Marie Kondo is a student at UCSD."

He laughed. "Exactly."

"Counting here...sixteen folded t-shirts, arranged by color, and below it a makeshift shelf containing what looks like folded sweaters positioned in the same color blocks as the t-shirts. All folded exactly the same way using the KonMari method, which requires time, patience, and care. That's suggestive."

"Of?" he asked.

"Well, she's uber organized, but," I looked again, "kind of a duality, making me wonder if it's the same person's closet. I wish I'd photographed Hannah's closet now, for comparison."

"Now look at pictures 3 and 4," he said.

Picture 3 had a messy pile of what looked like ten or twelve pairs of shoes, and picture 4 had four pairs of nearly identical women's Chuck Taylor sneakers in navy, light blue, dark gray, and white, positioned next to each other in a long, perfectly neat row. "Okay, I see it."

"What's interesting about Sophie's other laptop, which I've been reviewing for the past few hours, are more examples of that same duality. For instance, on her computer desktop is a huge array of disorganized files, with the icons overlapping in a complete mishmash of file types, like she'd never organized them before and just haphazardly stored stuff on there. I imagine it would take at least an hour to find any one thing here."

"I'm sensing a however coming," I said.

"Yeah. Well, there's only one actual folder on the desktop, and inside it is two folders, both encrypted: one called Hot and one called House."

What sounded like a tractor trailer rumbled down Highland Street, and I heard Trevor's paws scratching the hard wood floors as he scrambled to get up. "Just a truck, buddy. Go back to sleep." Returning my attention to Sophie's computer, another thought came to mind. "Did you see anything interesting in the picture of her desk?"

"Your flash didn't engage and it was too dark. Did you hear what I said ab—"

"I heard you, I'm just processing it all. Were you able to get into —"

"Just one, the Hot folder, not the other one."

"What was the password?"

He snickered. "The Blue Lady but with an *at* sign for the 'a' and lady was spelled with an 'ie' on the end. That took like 50 tries."

"Nice job. What's in it?"

"Another folder called Stuff, also encrypted, no luck yet. And no-go on the House folder so far. I'll keep trying."

CHAPTER FORTY-TWO

I suggested calling Hannah to ask about the other encrypted drives, because I also wanted to find out whom she'd gotten to deliver Sophie's bullet journal to me. I was a business owner and used social media, so that meant much of my otherwise personal information was publicly available, and I was sure the property tax records on my home made my address Google searchable. Had she come up here herself to deliver it earlier today before I saw her on campus tonight, or did she know people in LA who would do it for her? So many unknowns.

First I emailed Carrie about our recent gallery sale, making sure that she'd taken the deposit to the bank, logged it in our accounting system, removed it from our inventory, and marked it as "Sold" on the website. I'd be lucky if she'd completed one of those tasks so far.

How are you doing? I texted Hannah.

Okay, in bed now, I tacked two sheets up on the wall to cover the message.

You're gonna go to Campus Police tomorrow morning like we agreed, right?

I will, she typed back and I believed her.

I want to talk to you later about Troy. You were pretty upset back there. But for now, can you help me with something on Sophie's laptop?

I don't know, I never touched it and she didn't tell me much about it.

Somehow I didn't believe that last statement, but I kept going. *She has more than one encrypted directory and we're having trouble with two of them. Can you think of what other passwords she might have used?*

What's the folder called? she typed.

Something called House.

I waited and had a feeling I might wait a while for this one. I texted Derek to let him know that Hannah and I were in a text conversation.

My phone buzzed at the same time my eyes landed on a phrase in Sophie's bullet journal, in the front part. It was on one of the diary-written prose pages and the phrase read, "I'm sorry. I'm so sorry for the things she does." I typed this out to Derek, then picked up my phone again. It kept showing Hannah typing, then stopping. More typing, then stopping. Was she editing and uncertain what to write, or typing a long text, or was she falling asleep?

House is where the host and alter live, Hannah finally wrote back. I typed that in a message to Derek.

WTF does that mean? Derek typed back.

OMG. I knew, only in this lightning moment of clarity, what this meant. *Text me your address, I'm coming over. I'm leaving now.*

My epiphany about Sophie completely overtook what would normally have been a voyeuristic impulse to finally see how and where my partner lived. I felt puzzle pieces snapping into place. I rolled down all the windows to feel the night air on my bare shoulders.

"Street parking?" I called to him from the street outside his house.

"Did you teleport or something? How are you here already?"

"It's midnight, there's no traffic."

"Just park behind my car in the driveway."

"Tudor," I said when he opened the front door, then stepped back to gaze up at the embellished stone doorway, steeply pitched roof, and signature half-timbering, which I adored. "I love this house."

"Let's see what you think about the inside," he said and opened the heavy door wider so I could enter the foyer, which led to a cozy, wood-floored den. He stood opposite me and stared. "You have fire in your eyes. What is it?" He motioned me to a white, leather club chair; there were two of them, with a matching loveseat, which probably reclined on both sides, and a long sofa.

"Do you need a drink?"

"Actually yes," I said and rubbed my temples, then steadied my breath, to quiet the frenzied pace of my brain. My kind partner handed me a glass of white wine and I held it close to my chest. "House," I said and sighed, "is where they live."

"Who?" he asked. "Sophie?"

"Yes."

"And…who? Hannah?"

I shook my head and stared. "House is a sort of colloquial name for the intellectual container in which people live." I paused and let the words sink in.

"People," Derek repeated after a moment, nodding slowly. "Duality?"

"Right."

"So you mean…wait, Sophie and Sasha are the same people, or person?

"No," I shook my head slowly. "Sophie and Sasha are not the same person. They're two different people."

Derek's living room turned into a vacuum, devoid of all sound or movement. No cars, planes, or street noise.

"Living in the same…body?"

"Yup. Hannah said, in her words exactly, 'house is where the host and alter live.'"

"Alter? Which is which?"

"I think Sasha's the host and Sophie's the alter," I said and shrugged. "Just a theory."

Derek leaned on the side of the chair and crossed his arms. "How do you know about this?"

"I watched something on it a number of years ago. The effect is called DID or dissociative identity disorder. It's replaced what used to be called multiple personality disorder. I should also add that after doing more research tonight, most psychologists no longer believe this disorder is real anymore and it's no longer listed in the DSM, which is the official catalog of psychological disorders. But in the absence of any more recent ways of characterizing it, I'll just share what I learned."

"Okay, noted. Keep going."

"The host is the biological individual, and the 'alters', as they're called, are the other personalities that live inside that person and emerge to protect them from trauma or of the symptoms of the PTSD effects from that trauma."

"Excuse me for one moment." Derek disappeared. I was dying for a tour of his house, but that could wait. This couldn't. He returned a minute later with what looked like scotch and water.

"So Hannah knows about this?" he asked.

"She must. She's the one who told me about the terms house and alter. House describes the relationship or container, I think, for the different alters, like housemates all living in the same house, or brain, and all the alters are there to protect the host."

"Do they know about each other? Do they remember what one does from alter to alter?"

"From what I've read, basically yes, but I think it depends. In the stories I saw on this case study documentary, the three examples did know what the other alters were doing, and they sort of lived peacefully together, but they were completely distinctive people with different ages, sometimes genders, accents, identities, personal style, and had very different memories. It was amazing to see this intricate labyrinth the mind could create on its own as a means of protecting the host from the emotional pain of a trauma." I realized suddenly I'd placed my hand on my heart. "Again, current sentiment among the psychology and psychiatry communities doesn't really support this thinking anymore."

"What was the trauma?" Derek asked, of course zeroing in on the most important question.

"I don't know but whatever it is, I'm sure that's what her therapist was working on with her. We need to go see Adam Bouvet. Tomorrow."

"Another question that comes to mind is whether Sophie's killer intended to kill Sophie or Sasha."

"More likely Sophie."

"Why do you say that?" he asked.

I got up to walk around the room. I needed to move right now to help me puzzle this out. I had my glass in one hand, swishing the wine around in little circles. "Sasha was the artist, she was romantic, she loved color, clothes, landscapes. Her diary was sort of as dreamy as you'd expect a young girl in her first year of college would be. Innocent, sort of sheltered. Sophie, on the other hand…sorry, do you remember the witness statements we read in Ivan's file?"

"Yeah. Which do you mean?"

"The ones from her housemates in her dorm building."

"Yes," Derek said, "they were all over the map. I remember words like sweet and thoughtful and also bitchy and manipulative, depending on whom you asked. They were all investigated and cleared. Wow. They may have been talking about two different people. Amazing."

"Sophie has shown us that she had a lot of secrets and had a lot to hide." I pointed to her laptop. Derek nodded. "Sophie was, thinking about her closet now, no-nonsense, hyper organized, patient, controlled, manipulative. Here's another thing, and I have no conclusive evidence yet, but I think Sophie was highly sexualized."

"Really. Why?"

"Her part of the bullet journal in the back had lists I was telling you about, right? I think they were names, as in conquests. And another thing—"

Derek pointed to the wine. "Why don't you take another sip. You're talking nonstop."

"Something stronger please, actually."

"Coming right up. Would you like a martini, even though you think you can make a better one than me?"

"Yeah, that'd be good," I said, feeling sufficiently creeped-out at the moment and wondering how inappropriate it might be to ask to sleep on his couch. Of course I didn't want to leave Trevor alone all night, and of course I was perfectly safe. But now, this entire case had tipped sideways and my head felt the same way.

"Try this, it's proven to be good medicine in the past."

I sipped once, nodded, and sipped again. "Very good, Detective."

"Are you okay?" he asked, knowing I was anything but.

"The handwriting's different in both halves of the bullet journal. What the hell have we gotten ourselves into here?"

"Thinking about Sophie's log, where she kept secrets she learned about people of influence, do you think she used sex to buy this information?"

I thought about this, and felt the alcohol relax my chest and stomach. "No," I said. "I think she was using sex to get people to let down their guard and tell her secrets, and then sold that information to the highest bidder."

"Whoa. Now what would make you think that?"

"I found out earlier today that Sophie had $40,000 in a savings account in her name at a Chase Bank near campus."

"What the hell?" Derek sat on the sofa opposite me, legs crossed, arms crossed over his chest, eyes deciding something.

"I know. Another thing Ivan didn't know about."

"Kind of a lot of money for a college student, even one who came from wealthy parents." I knew what he was thinking. Follow the money.

CHAPTER FORTY-THREE

"Good morning, sunshine," Ivan Dent said, with a grin too big and white for this early.

I'd had a fitful night sleep with dreams of being chased and locked out of buildings, and I kept waking up sweating.

Ivan held the door open and we followed him into the main lobby. There were no empty chairs, so we stood in a semi-circle for a quick huddle before we headed back south to campus. Derek brought him up to speed on our discovery and recent events. He blinked and listened carefully, taking in every word. Listening was one of his best and most surprising qualities, I had to admit.

"Mari has on her 'I need a favor' face. What is it today?" Ivan asked.

"There's no such face and I don't need a favor," I replied.

"Yeah, she does," Derek said. "We need your permission to interview a new witness in the Sophie case."

Ivan's brow wrinkled. "Who?"

"Her therapist," I answered. "We're following the money, trying to find out what specifically Sophie sold and to whom, if our theory is correct," I said.

"It's in her logbook. We just haven't found it yet," Derek added.

"Before you go." Ivan reached over the front counter to grab a file folder, "I have an update of my own. He pulled out two stapled sheets of paper. "This is the graphology report on Thomas Barnes from our handwriting specialist, Louise Chen. I haven't read it." He slid the sheets back into the folder and held it behind his back, standing in one of his signature stances.

"What?" I eyerolled and tipped my head to the side.

"I want to know about the role Judge McClaren has played in this drama. Was Sophie selling something to him, or was he selling something to her?"

"We're not there yet, but we concluded earlier on that Sophie sold him some piece of art," I said.

"And you thought that was why your house was broken into, that someone was looking for that artwork?" Ivan recalled.

"We now think they were looking for Sophie's log. In fact," I said to Derek, "that's most likely what the message on Hannah's wall referred to."

We barely talked leaving LA. I think of Carlsbad as the halfway point between LA and San Diego. Just passing Encinitas, I started reviewing the list of questions I had for Psychotherapist Adam Bouvet. I'd made an appointment by calling at exactly 9:01 this morning, explaining that I was a prospective patient and I'd brought my husband with me to make sure he too was comfortable with my choice of a therapist. There was no charge for the initial consult, a woman explained.

I introduced myself as Marie Chambers here with my husband. The receptionist asked us to have a seat and Dr. Bouvet would be with us shortly. I picked up a Parenting magazine and looked at the pictures, then tossed it back down on the side table. The door opened and a dapper man with stylish glasses and a bright blue tie entered the lobby. Derek and I exchanged glances.

"Abe?" I said, rising from my chair. I pulled out my phone and found the photo Carrie had sent of our recent customer who bought the David Korty piece. I showed it to Derek.

"I'm Dr. Adam Bouvet. Please come in," the man said.

"So, are you an art collector, Doctor, or are you keeping tabs on me for some reason?"

"I do collect art. Why do you ask?"

I held up the photograph.

"Oh, okay, yes that's the woman from the gallery. Is that your daughter?"

Derek laughed and I elbowed him. "My daughter? Very funny. I'm the gallery owner."

"Nice gallery. Think I got a good deal on that piece?"

"Dr. Bouvet," Derek interrupted, "we have some questions about a former patient of yours. Sophie Michaud."

"Sasha Michaud, you mean," he immediately corrected.

"Well, both," I added, watching his face closely.

A little smirk appeared on his lips. "Who are you?"

"We're investigators working with the LAPD on Sophie's case," I said.

We were all still standing awkwardly in the doorway of his office. Bouvet closed the door gently.

"First of all, you can start by telling us where you were on the night of August 28th of last year."

"How do I know? What day of the week was it?" Dr. Bouvet asked.

"Saturday."

"Probably in session. I keep late hours on Friday and Saturday nights. My admin can go back to that date and give you the names of the patients I was seeing."

"Great," Derek said. "How long were you seeing Sophie Michaud?"

Bouvet motioned for us to sit, and he moved behind his large, protective desk. He sat and tried to cross his legs under it but was unable to fit them in the opening. Love it. He scooted back in his chair a few inches and readjusted his glasses, trying to recover. That was three nervous movements. I made note.

"Sasha, not Sophie, as I've pointed out, was a foreign exchange student doing a year abroad from her home in Paris. As a favor to her parents, I came with her to San Diego as additional support for her in this new environment. I'd been Sasha's therapist since she was eight years old."

"What were you treating her for?" I asked, this time, curious how and whether Bouvet would answer.

"Sasha suffered, since adolescence, from something called DID or dissociative identity disorder." I nodded. "You know of it?" he asked.

"I've read about it, yes. Was she on medication?" I asked. Why was he answering our questions so openly rather than citing doctor-patient privilege and the legal protection of confidentiality?

"We'd tried a number of them and most recently I had her taking Venlafaxine, which is a serotonin and norepinephrine rebuke inhibitor for depression, anxiety, and panic disorders. That worked the best for Sasha with minimal side effects." The man sighed and looked down at his desk. "With DID, the host endures some kind of physical or emotional trauma that it's not mature enough to process, so the personality splinters, in effect, causing the emergence of another personality to take over and deal with the situation. These other personalities are referred to as 'alters'.

"I've been reading about the controversy surrounding dissociative disorders and how there's heated debate among the psychology and psychiatry communities. Just wondering what your thoughts are."

"There are believers and non-believers, about any number of things. While I respect the more modern evidence-based approaches to diagnoses, I'm a believer because I've been treating Sasha for most of her life."

"Sasha was the host and Sophie was the alter?"

The man stared unblinking and without speaking. "Using terminology relative to DID, yes." His shoulders dropped and he seemed to resign himself to something. He looked, wide-eyed, at Derek and then me.

"Why did you have a key to Sophie's, sorry, Sasha's and Hannah's dorm room?"

"In case of emergencies, of course. Sasha had a potentially life-threatening mental illness that frequently results in suicide or a complete mental breakdown and inability to function. I think she functioned extraordinarily well, all things considered."

"How did she do that?" I asked.

"Well, as I said, through precise dosages of medication to help minimize the adverse symptoms of her illness and with the perfect release outlet, which was her art. Are you familiar with—"

"The Blue Lady?" I interrupted. "Yes, we've seen it. It's… extraordinary."

"I believe Renoir's Blue Lady, or La Parisienne, as she was officially called, gave Sasha something to focus on, something visually beautiful and something technical, in the digital scale and formation of the gallery installation. I used to think," he paused, then continued, "The Blue Lady saved her life."

"What's your theory about how Sophie died?" Derek asked, and I knew he said Sophie on purpose, hoping to provoke the doctor.

The doctor again admired the surface of his wooden desk and evaded the question.

"What was your relationship with Sasha?" I asked.

"She was my patient since she was a child. She was like family to me," Bouvet answered, with a look of anguish on his face.

"What's your relationship with Hannah, her roommate?"

"Sasha was very close to Hannah, sometimes too close. Hannah knew everything about her and was a wonderful support during troubling times."

"And your relationship with Hannah?" I pressed.

The man looked confused. "I know Hannah. I'd talked with her at length about Sasha's condition, I counseled her about how she could help her. That's it."

"Do you know of anyone who would have benefitted from Sophie's death?" Derek asked.

"No. If there's anything else, I need to see another patient shortly and I'd like a few minutes to focus. This subject is, as you can guess, very upsetting."

"What was the trauma, Doctor?" I grabbed my handbag from the floor and perched on the edge of my chair. "The trauma that caused Sasha's mind to create an alter identity. Something related to her brother?"

The doctor rose, hands in his pockets in front of his desk. I could see the full spectrum of his outfit now, appreciating the color coordination of his blue tie and glasses. Someone who expended energy shopping for very specific, expensive clothing, someone who cared about engineering someone's first impression of him, making a statement, and being visible. "Indirectly, yes," he replied, finally.

"Meaning what?" Derek probed.

"Sasha's parents live in Paris. Her stepmother is her father's second wife. Her birth mother killed herself and Sasha discovered the body. She was seven. Her mother had a history of mental illness, and it's not unusual for it to run in families like this. Sasha's brother Jonathan is actually a half-brother who came from a previous relationship of her father's, which is why he's so much older than Sasha." The doctor took a breath and a sip of water from a glass on his desk.

"How was the brother involved?" Derek moved a step closer to the doctor.

"According to family folklore, Sasha's biological mother was a nurse and gave a patient an incorrect dosage of a heart medication, which resulted in the patient's death."

"Was she prosecuted?" I asked.

"It was determined to be accidental because it wasn't otherwise a lethal dosage. It was to the patient because the patient had already overdosed on several other medications before arriving at the hospital. They only found out later. So Sasha's mother was cleared of all blame, but she never forgave herself and fell into a deep depression. Jonathan, identifying the deceased patient as a close friend of his, blamed the mother and accused her of both murder and negligence, and threatened to re-open the investigation to prove it and send her to jail. This conversation happened the day before the mother's suicide. Little Sasha found her mother the next morning in the bathtub, and her fragile young psyche just cracked."

"So tragic," Derek commented. "When did you come into the picture?"

"I'd just gotten my doctorate and set up practice in Paris, and Sasha's father, Nicholas, found me and told me about his daughter. He asked me to treat her for grief and trauma, to help her get over the painful memories and move forward."

"Who have you had more success with, Sasha or Sophie?" I asked.

"Success?" He laughed. "I've never thought of treatment that way. I've certainly known Sasha much longer than Sophie. Sophie didn't emerge until Sasha was around thirteen. Sometimes, in our sessions, it would be Sasha; other times Sophie. I worked on creating a calm, safe environment for her to talk about whatever feelings were coming up for her, whoever it was."

"Did Sasha have any serious boyfriends?" I asked.

Half-second pause and a shift to his eyes. "She was interested in guys but thought they might interfere with her artistic pursuits."

"What about Sophie?" Derek interjected in a courser tone of voice, and the doctor at hearing the question immediately looked at the floor as if we'd caught him in a lie he hadn't yet told.

"What about her?" The doctor replied, raising his chin.

"Did she ever talk to you about guys she was interested in, or sleeping with?"

The palms went up and I knew the conversation was over. "I really, really need to keep my schedule with my next client. We'll have to pick this up another time. Ms. Ellwyn," he said grabbing my hand, "and Detective, you won't mind if I don't see you out."

"No problem, thank you for your time." Derek followed me out.

"That was interesting," I said in the car. "I mean, an interesting way you articulated that sentence. Was that deliberate?"

"Yes."

"Why?"

"Ever watch that old retro TV show, Columbo?"

"That was your Columbo impression?"

"Sort of. I always loved the way he had just 'one more thing' to ask at the end of an interview, and it was always the juiciest, most controversial detail. Doc's face turned white when I mentioned Sophie sleeping around."

I'd noticed it too. "Why, though? I would think he'd view Sasha as his daughter since he'd been treating her since she was eight."

Derek shook his head as he drove out of the medical building parking lot. "I don't think he thought of either Sasha or Sophie as his daughter. Definitely not."

"It's common for patients to fall in love with their therapists. Are you thinking Sasha or Sophie was in love with Bouvét? Or vice versa?"

CHAPTER FORTY-FOUR

After Derek dropped me off in Santa Monica, I picked up an oat milk latte and croissant at Cognoscenti's and drove to the lot diagonally across the street from Reggie's mother's house.

Reggie saw me almost immediately after he crossed the street. We locked eyes.

I leaned my elbow out the window and made my most glamorous smile. "How's it going? I'm alone today."

"I can see that. Your pit bull was busy?"

"I'm sorry about that."

"I doubt it. Look, what are you people doing about what should be a routine missing person's case?"

"You people? Come on, Reggie, you know we're not cops. We're private investigators assisting the LAPD with Sophie's case, which you also know is tangentially related to the case of your wife's disappearance."

Reggie turned his back to me and ran his hands through his hair. "Who the fuck is working on that case, and what leads have they come up with? No one's fucking returning my calls, which I've made every morning for the past month."

"I'm sorry. Missing persons cases often go slowly, and there might not be anything to report yet. But given your connection to her, they should be contacting you weekly with progress. I'll check on it."

He bit his lip and regarded me carefully. "Thank you. So what can I do for you today?"

I set my coffee back in the cup holder and wiped my mouth with a napkin. He took two steps closer to my car. "You said Elise Turner was your wife. She's your ex-wife," I said, having gotten that tidbit from Duga after he spent an afternoon trimming Turner's shrubs and pruning her rose bushes.

"Wasn't my idea," he said.

"When were you divorced?"

"Last year."

"Okay. What I really need to know about is Sophie and Judge McClaren."

Reggie gave me a blank stare that seemed genuine. "What do you mean?"

"Can you tell me what happened when she came to see the judge?"

"Like which time?"

"It was more than once?" I asked.

"She came to see him all the time," he said, like he thought I should have known that. "He invited her into his private chambers, when almost nobody else was allowed in there. She never stayed long. She used to bring him her artwork, like drawings and stuff, for him to critique. He was a collector."

"Did he ever buy any of her art?"

"I think he was planning to buy one piece, but I never saw it and I don't know if he ever did."

"What did you think of her?"

Reggie's face tightened. "I thought she was fine, but some of the other clerks I worked with thought she was risky, like she had the judge wrapped around her little finger."

"Did she?"

He shrugged. "I didn't pay that much attention, to be honest. Sophie was very attractive, and I've never felt comfortable around obviously attractive women, especially women who try to be attractive."

"And you think Sophie was in that category?"

He laughed and nodded. "Um, yeah," he said, like it was obvious.

"She was workin' it, huh?"

"Well, she worked hard to conceal it but I saw through her."

"What do you think she really wanted from the judge?"

Reggie looked up and down the street and moved closer to my car when a motorcycle drove past us. "Access."

I sat back, thinking. "What did you think when you learned about the article Elise was writing with Nina Richmond about the judge?"

"Are you fucking kidding?" he blurted. "I was mortified. What do you think? McClaren's one of the most respected of all the district court judges. His reputation's…untouchable."

"But your wife didn't allege anything specific in her article, just—"

"No, but, you know, the innuendo was pretty obvious that she was calling his character into question and alleging a kind of sordid entanglement between the judge and this young, beautiful, college student."

"Whom he'd known since she was a child, though."

"Even so. It was potentially so damaging to the judge, the credibility of the institution of the district court, not to mention my job. Nothing came of it, or not so far, but to be honest, that's why I left. The judge was horrified by the implications the article left. He blamed me for it, and he said it would look bad if he fired me so he suggested I quit. I did."

After Reggie took off, I left Derek a voicemail containing these new details, and followed up with Ivan to coordinate two San Diego PD detectives to officially interview Adam Bouvet. Unofficially, Duga already had him on his personal watch list.

I left my car in its spot near Reggie's mother's house and walked with my croissant and large latte four or five blocks to the entrance of the Santa Monica Pier, my favorite morning ritual, my reassurance that despite how it seemed, the world was okay and we were all okay in it. I took off my shoes and sat on the edge of the pier watching the rippled current flecked with late morning light, sea lions, and a few anglers fishing for mackerel, perch, sea bass. I loved the ocean's promise of renewal, that no matter what you'd been all your life, or what you were today, when the tide went out and came back in, it was always a fresh start.

I liked the ease with which my conversation with Reggie had unfolded, him standing casually by my car, me asking non-threatening questions. I suspected the good cop/bad cop routine with Derek, even though we weren't actually cops, worked into his psyche that I wanted to help him. And I guess I truly did, in a way. I didn't trust him, but nothing in Louise Chen's report raised a red flag that Thomas "Reggie" Barnes could be capable of murder, which disappointed me. He'd been my wild card all this time. Not that it wasn't possible, but the graphology report indicated more uncertainty and insecurity than overt aggression and hostility.

CHAPTER FORTY-FIVE

"This seat taken?" Duga sat beside me on the edge of the pier. Without even looking at him, I grabbed his hand, which I recognized by the unique, jagged scar between his thumb and index finger.

"Tashi delek," I said and half-bowed, using the traditional Tibetan greeting. *I honor the greatness in you.* Nothing could be truer in this case. Duga bowed back, today adorned in gold aviator glasses and dressed all in white. That meant he was going up to the Tibetan Buddhist meditation center.

"Where's Derek today?"

"I wish I knew," I said. "Haven't been able to reach him. How about you? Anything to report on my two suspects?"

"Is that what they are now?" he asked, being coy.

"You tell me."

He turned to face me. "Troy Garrity's gone."

"What? Like…skipped town?"

Duga nodded.

"You mean like moved out of his apartment?"

"No, but he took a sudden leave from work and said he'd be gone at least two weeks."

"Do you know where?"

"I'm working on that."

"Sorta makes one look guilty, doesn't it?"

"Depends," Duga said in a dreamy voice, returning his gaze to the water and the fisherman on shore. "There's a new art installation coming up next week and he'll miss that. So he's either chasing something, or he's being chased."

"Don't look at me," I said, "we've only casually questioned him a couple of times. No police involved, and I already checked and he wasn't interviewed the first time around, meaning right after Sophie's body was found. Can you have someone try to track him down?"

"Already working on it. In the meantime…" Duga stood up and pulled something out of his pocket and handed it to me. It looked like a purple rubber glove stuffed in a zip lock bag.

"Not exactly a tiny, brass elephant. A rubber glove with…dirt on it." I looked up. "Whose?"

"Two rubber gloves previously worn by Adam Bouvet."

"Oh my God." I rose and took off my glasses. "You didn't break into his house, did you?"

"Of course not, I know the rules of evidence collection. Your suspect is a compulsive neat freak. I had someone watching him for the past twelve hours. He's an obsessive hand-washer, for one thing, and he wears rubber gloves for everything, carries a box of them in the front seat of his car. He was walking on Mission Beach this morning, which is suggestive in itself. He stopped to sit on the grass and realized there was a dog turd a little too close to his towel. He pulled a pair of gloves from his pocket, put them on, picked up the offending material, moved it a foot to the right, rose, and peeled the gloves off, and put them in an open trash can on the beach before he left. Posed as a vagrant, my contact fished them out for you knowing how they undoubtedly contain trace amounts of Adam Bouvet's skin and could be used for DNA testing. Merry Christmas."

"And since he deposited them in a public trashcan and you witnessed this, that would most likely be admissible as evidence. I'll get this to Ivan right away."

"Another interesting detail about him." Duga cocked his head sideways, to indicate a loose thread.

"What's that?"

"Some kind of injury to his back or shoulder or something. My contact reported that a kid threw a ball as your suspect was leaving the beach, and he ducked out of the way, winced, and held his stomach.

I'm looking into it. Let you know if something turns up."

"Thank you for that, and this." I held up the zip lock bag.

"Be careful today," he said and half-hugged me, leaving me standing on the pier with what could be the most important key to this case so far.

Ivan called me as I was driving to see him at the precinct.

"Are you a mind reader or something?" I asked.

"Why, were you thinking about me?"

"I'm on my way. Are you at the precinct?"

"Yeah, and my crew just got back from picking up Mr. Bouvet from his office."

"I can imagine how that went."

"Badly," he sighed. "He was verbally abusive to my two officers the minute they set foot in his office, he refused to let his Admin confirm his alibi for August 28th, and he assaulted one of the officers outside while resisting arrest."

"Lord. Did they get anything out of him other than requests to speak to his lawyer?"

"He said he did have an appointment the night Sophie died, and that appointment ended at seven p.m. Sophie's time of death was determined to be, what, three a.m. or something? Would have given him plenty of time."

I pulled into the Crenshaw station parking lot, reminded of the tacos that I still hadn't tried. I'd asked Ivan to meet me in the lot. He was walking out as I pulled into his designated space.

"Aren't you funny now," he said seeing this. "Where's your partner today?"

"I don't know but finish your story. What'd you pick him up on?" I had my window rolled down and he leaned against the next car, facing me, shaking his head.

"I had one of the officers ask him where he was the night Sophie was killed, and then what his relationship was with her, the latter of which unglued him to the extent he had to be restrained and physically carried out to the squad car."

"What part specifically unglued him?" I asked.

"He kept correcting us that her name was Sasha, not Sophie."

My stomach caved in hearing this.

"And after that he apparently screamed that her name was Sasha not Sophie and that he loved her like the rest of his patients. We've got him locked up and he's gonna stay that way for the moment."

"Did he give an official statement?"

"No, he hasn't even processed in yet."

"So if he finished with a patient at seven the night Sophie was killed, that means he had opportunity to get to her, and he most certainly had access, maybe more than anyone else, given how well they knew each other."

"That's right, and we're still only halfway there. We don't have motive or evidence to link him to the crime scene."

I held up the zip lock bag containing the rubber gloves. "Now you have evidence," I said and explained what was in it and where it came from. "Run this through your crime lab and compare it with the forensic evidence reported on the coroner's report."

Ivan nodded. "This has Duga written all over it. Was this an illegal search and seizure? You know it won't—"

"Yes, it will, the suspect dropped it in a public trashcan, and my guy witnessed the drop," I said. "This is solid. Run with it."

"Good work," Ivan said, turning his back on me and heading toward the building. "Call you later."

I texted Derek again before driving out, quieting the paranoid voice in my head. *Where are you??*

He wrote back immediately. *Meet me at the trailer.*

CHAPTER FORTY-SIX

Derek opened the Voice Memos app on his iPhone and pressed the red button. "State your name please."

"Marilu." The woman cleared her throat. "Marilu Duff."

"Do we have your permission to be recording you right now?" Derek asked.

"I'd rather that than have to go down to the police station."

"You may need to do that anyway depending on what you share with us tonight," Derek said and eyed me. He'd called when I was en route explaining that he had his newspaper contact person with him and this was the only way she'd talk to us.

Marilu Duff, the old woman sitting in front of me, face wrinkled from decades of cigarette smoking, had to be Derek's former client.

"No one else is in here except you and her?" the woman asked, looking right through me.

"No one, and no one's coming in," Derek said. I nodded and had already sent Bobby Bishop a text to leave us alone here for an hour or so. "Why all the secrecy, Marilu? You and I have known each other a while now."

"Nothing against you," she explained in a hushed tone, "just that I think someone's been watching me lately…when I'm at work."

"Someone who works at the newspaper?" Derek asked.

I sat back and listened, assuming he would be asking all the questions. My feet ached, and accumulated fatigue from five poor night's sleep weighed down my eyelids.

"Nobody I recognize," the woman said.

"Okay." Derek rose and walked around the room. He seemed to do his best thinking when he was either walking or pacing. "Explain to my partner here what your role is at the paper."

The woman cleared her throat. "I'm the staff dinosaur," she snickered. "I've been replaced by apps like the one you're using on your phone right now to record me. Years ago, to record someone you had to use big, heavy, expensive equipment. Now you push a button on something the size of a cracker. I've been employed for thirty years as a Video Editor. I don't record the videos, and nowadays I don't even edit them, as there's software that does that, too. I view the final mockups to make sure the content isn't violating any of the newspaper's publishing policies, FCC regulations, privacy laws, and so on. So there's nothing artistic about what I do. I'm more of a video content overseer to maintain policy compliance."

I nodded. Marilu blinked back, appraising my clothing, sizing me up. It's okay, I was doing the same thing, and dying to know what case Derek had worked on for her.

"Do you know Elise Turner, and did you know Nina Richmond?" Derek asked, now leaning against the wood-paneled wall in the trailer.

"Yes and yes, I knew them both. My office is upstairs, and their desks are directly below me. Through the heat vent I could hear everything they were saying, even the annoying clicking of their fingers on their keyboards. Elise Turner is about the fastest typist I've ever seen, or heard, and Nina's just, well, was just out of college." The woman lowered her eyes.

"I'm gonna interject something here," Derek said, eyes on me. "I called Marilu last week to ask about any other articles the two journalists published about Sophie's case." He looked at Marilu now. "And what did you tell me?"

"Written? Yes. Published? No. There were three articles written by both writers. Only the first one was published," she explained.

"Why?" I asked.

"Our managing editor wouldn't publish them because especially the second article made a startling allegation about who likely killed that poor young girl but without any conclusive evidence. He basically said to go and find evidence and then he'd consider publishing it and, until then, it was grounded."

I opened my mouth to speak. Derek held up his hand. "Marilu, are you aware that Elise Turner's been missing for the past four weeks?"

The woman shook her head. "She's not missing."

"What do you mean? Do you know where she is?" Derek asked.

"No, but I know she's not missing. She's in hiding."

"Why?"

"After Sophie was killed last summer, and then Nina was killed two months later, very likely because of the article she and Elise were working on, Elise started getting threatening notes in her mailbox."

"What kind of notes?" I asked.

"Written on index cards with a marker. Messages like 'stop'."

I listened but my eyes were widening. Those were the same type of notes I was getting in my box up until two weeks ago.

"She continued her research?" Derek asked. "How do you know she's okay and still working? Have you heard from her?"

The woman hung her head, breathed, then sat up. "I'm in email contact with her. I'm the only one she'll talk to now."

"Okay," Derek said, pacing again. "Tell us about the second article. You don't happen to have a copy of it, do you?"

"I wouldn't give it to you if I did. Our managing editor trusts me." Her eyes were ice. "Trust is hard to come by and it only lives once."

"Understood. Can you tell us anything about it?"

I put up my index finger. "I'd like a minute to turn up the air conditioner and get us some water if that's okay."

Derek nodded. I exited and was back the conference room in thirty seconds.

"The first article, as you probably know," the woman said, "was mainly about Sophie and her life here in San Diego, her school relationships, her artistic talent, and how random and senseless her murder seemed, like out of nowhere. Another unsolvable crime. It talked about her connections, like to a federal judge she'd known since childhood, and a piece of art she apparently sold him. I think Elise thought of him as the killer at first." Marilu opened one of the chilled bottles of water, took three long sips, and cleared her throat.

"Thank you," she said directly to me and continued. "The second article, though, was all about Sophie's mental illness."

"Can you explain what you mean by that?" Derek asked.

"In one part of the article, it referenced a controversial video that Sophie, or I should say Sasha, posted on YouTube called 'MultiMe' where she came forward and openly shared her story of anxiety and depression, and eventually her somewhat debilitating mental illness. In this video—it was a series of them actually—she introduced what she called her alter-personality, that was Sophie, and she showed live on the video feed where she turns from sweet Sasha-the-artist to Sophie, who talks different, walks different, dresses very different, even the way she plays with her hair is like a completely different person. And she was."

"That sounds like a brave thing to do. What was controversial about it?" Derek asked, sitting now in the chair beside Marilu.

"Sophie talked a lot about sex, and that part got pretty graphic, speaking openly about what she liked in bed, what she liked to do to her partners, have done to her. Then she sort of giggled talking about her current partner without naming him. The person shooting the video was a man's voice, told Sophie to shut up, just repeating it over and over, interrupting her, and his voice was getting louder. Sophie laughed seeing that she was upsetting the guy. She kept pushing it and I could tell in the video that she thrived on that kind of risk, liked the edge. Her words got more and more graphic, taunting almost, and in an instant the tone of the video changed, Sophie's eyes got really wide and followed someone from the other side of the room like they were coming at her. The last thing she screamed before the video cut out were the words 'Adam no'."

I'd involuntarily put my hand over my mouth while Marilu recited this. "And the video was pulled down from YouTube?"

"The next day, yes," Marilu replied. "I think someone at the paper leaked a part of the article and, within a day, the video was deleted from YouTube. Elise, from researching Sophie's mental illness, already knew about her therapist, Adam Bouvet, and she naturally concluded that Adam had a motive to kill her."

"How did Elise find the video in the first place?" Derek asked.

"She was obsessed with Sophie's story. So was Nina. Nina was about Sophie's age, too. Elise used the types of media that eighteen-year-olds use: Instagram, YouTube. After Nina saw the video and they'd sent a draft of their second article upstairs for review, it was squashed pretty quick because of a lack of evidence. And Nina was more than just a little upset. She said Bouvet was a predator and she wasn't going to stand for him getting exonerated on a technicality. I stayed quiet upstairs so they wouldn't hear me shuffling around in the office, and I heard Nina say she was going to catch him outside his office to interrogate him about it."

"Help me with the timeline here, Marilu. What month was this?" Derek asked.

"October I think. The night the two of them had their blowout about Adam Bouvet was late October. Elise didn't want her to go because it would be too dangerous and because it would endanger the credibility of the work they'd put in on Sophie's story." Marilu took another sip of water and looked at her watch.

"Do you think Elise Turner blames herself for Nina's death?" Derek asked.

Marilu nodded. "I think that's the real reason she's in hiding. I blame myself, too."

CHAPTER FORTY-SEVEN

Derek and Marilu Duff left the trailer first. I followed a few minutes later heading back to Ocean Park. My head swirled with too many new details and not enough time to process them all, though the details of our investigation seemed to be heading in the same direction as my gut. For once.

An hour later, I answered my doorbell in my robe and slippers, drink in-hand.

"Could I have that special martini now?" My partner looked wrung out, face glossy from the heat, wrinkled shirt, eyes barely open.

"Take a load off, Detective. Adult beverage coming right up."

I'd just made myself one, so the gin, vermouth, lemon, and peeler were already out on the counter. Trevor was so good at sensing someone's mood, mine in particular, but he quietly sniffed around Derek's legs and feet and then rested his face on his lap as if to say, "I'm here for you." If that dog had been born human, we'd be married by now.

"We need something to connect Sophie's and Nina's murders. Forensic evidence."

Derek closed his eyes and sipped the drink I'd just handed him. "Oh my God, that's good."

"Instant revival?"

"Literally." His eyes were wide open and he sipped again, slower this time to savor the flavors. "Interesting."

"I ran out of my favorite citrusy vermouth, so I used extra lemon rind and broke it in a few places to release the flavor."

Derek's glass was completely empty.

"Dude, you chugged it like a frat boy. This is a very special beverage—"

"Could I have another?" he blurted.

"You're funny. Sure. But what we need is that video," I said, in the kitchen again making myself another as well, and realizing that I'd hardly eaten all day.

Derek took the glass and looked up from the sofa. "I have it."

"Have what?"

"The video. It's on Sophie's laptop."

"Oh my God, you opened the locked directory?"

"There's only one file in it, an MP4 video file called MultiMe." He set the drink on my coffee table, and I sat on the edge of the sofa.

"Did you watch it?"

"Yeah. And it's just as Marilu said. It's incriminating to Adam Bouvet, but more than that, I found it very disturbing. The video shows someone filming Sasha Michaud talking about her…well, I'll show it you so you can see for yourself."

"My God, tell me."

"Sasha was like this sweet, sugar and spice college girl, bright-eyed and full of promise talking about her passion for making art, her inspiration to teach art to low-income students, socially conscious, facing the camera and talking earnestly about her mental health history, and how she's lived with two distinct personalities, the other is called her Alter, as she describes, and that person is Sophie. They know each other, they co-exist, though not always peacefully, meaning that sometimes they disagree, but she knows Sophie exists to protect Sasha."

"From what, or whom?" I asked.

"The video didn't go into that, just that they work together and, with medication, Sasha is able to be a college student and live a somewhat challenged version of a normal life. And that all sounded very rational and very evolved, to be honest, for someone so young. Then she said she was feeling 'twitchy'—that's what she called it, saying that her throat always hurt when Sophie was about to come out. She held onto her throat, swallowed a few times, and moved away from the camera, stopped smiling and, geez, the body language totally changed from that sweet, innocent girl to this sort of vampy, edgy manipulator."

"Why manipulator?"

"The speech she used was different, I mean, a different style of talking but a different vocabulary, too. Sasha spoke like an educated girl and Sophie was guttural, less eloquent, frequent cuss words, rough around the edges. Sophie unbuttoned two of the buttons on her blouse and tucked it into her jeans, rolled up the cuffs of her jeans, took her shoes off and sat with her knees up to her chest. Trying to be provocative while trying to be coy and offensive almost."

I asked him about the ending when she was taunting her videographer.

"I agreed with Marilu's assessment there, too. She was taunting him, talking about his method of thrusting into her, saying he seemed sexually inexperienced, and how she didn't like that, and looking at him and laughing at him the whole time."

"So it was obvious that Adam Bouvet had been sleeping with his patient, Sasha Michaud?"

Derek raised a brow. "Um…yeah. Very. Now we just need—"

"Wait," I interrupted. "The very end though, did he attack Sophie?"

"The video didn't show her being attacked specifically, just that the camera came closer to her, she looked up into it and screamed, 'Adam no!' just like Marilu described. It would be chilling to watch if I knew nothing about her." He took another sip.

"Well, if it's any consolation, we might be a step closer to finding what we need. Duga brought me a pair of rubber gloves that Bouvet wore at the beach this morning to remove dog poop from his beach towel. He tossed them in an open trashcan at Mission Beach and Duga picked them up. Ivan's got his team working on it now to get a DNA sample and compare it to the forensic evidence the team gathered from the crime scene."

Derek shook his head. "What was he doing there? Sophie was killed at Mission Beach; so was Nina Richmond."

"You think he's scoping out a site because he's planning another murder?" I asked.

"Maybe."

"If Bouvet killed Sophie, and we still don't have a motive other than the video, he eliminated one obstacle, Nina Richmond. Elise Turner could definitely be seen as a loose end. What if she's next?"

"Call Reggie," Derek said.

I dialed his number.

•———•••———•

Reggie's voicemail picked up. "Reggie, it's Mari Ellwyn. Please call me immediately, it's urgent." I hung up and waited. My phone rang a moment later. "Hey," I said, "I'm putting you on speaker, I'm here with Derek."

"Hey guys, what's up?" Reggie Barnes asked.

"We just talked to someone from the newspaper where Elise has been working."

"Marilu?" he asked.

"Yeah. She said Elise is in hiding, not missing."

Short pause. "I know," he replied.

"Listen to me, Reggie," I said, "we need to know where she is so we can protect her. And it might already be too late."

CHAPTER FORTY-EIGHT

The fitness requirements of Great Danes included walking an hour a day, not only for health and wellness but to keep them used to the normal socialization of being around other dogs and humans. Besides, I needed to clear my head.

So, I left Derek at my house to see what he could get out of Reggie man to man, and Trevor and I walked around the neighborhood. Today, Mrs. Whittimore was digging up plants in her own yard and appeared to be changing their locations, moving a rose bush to the shady side. I waved to her with my free hand. She waved back with dirt dripping from her fingers, frowning at the size of Trevor.

Dirt.

I hadn't forgotten about Roger's Community Garden, and how Sophie, or more likely Sasha, had a plot there and had been gardening. There hadn't been time to track down that lead yet. It couldn't be Duga. This detail needed to be me. I also hadn't checked on Hannah in a few days. Never enough time.

This case right now felt like a package getting wrapped up with string coiled around the length and girth, but the string kept coming up short to make a bow at the top. I could shift things around so both ends of the string would meet up, but the bow would inevitably be too short and come untied. As an investigator, the string was constructed of details of the crime: access, motive, and evidence. I had everything but motive at this point.

Sure, Sophie had been taunting Bouvet in her MultiMe video, which could be considered motive, but sufficient motive to kill? It seemed too flimsy to convince Ivan to make an arrest, and to hold up in court. Bouvet was calculated, not impulsive. The impulsive side of him might have taken over and attacked Sophie to turn off the video camera and silence her, but not silence her for good. Motive had to be something else. I could pull and pull on the string, but the limitation of its length was unrelenting. We had more work to do.

I'd put my headphones on before Trevor and I left, and I had my phone tucked into the back pocket of my jeans. It vibrated with an incoming call.

"Wait, Trevor, wait," I said.

As a puppy, he'd been expertly trained by Pet Whisperers in San Diego. He stopped long enough for me to put the leash in another hand and pull out the phone. Duga.

"Hey there, what's up?" I asked.

"Hey. When we were observing your suspect, I mentioned he favored one side, right? He looked like he had some kind of injury. Well I looked into it and found out he had an ER visit last year."

Duga paused, which I knew meant he was waiting for me to draw a conclusion. "Last year, like when last year? You're saying…summer?"

"I'm saying August 27th."

"Holy shit. Okay, for what?"

"A stab wound to his right side."

"Stab wound? Stab wound," I repeated, working through it mentally. "How long was he in there?"

"He wasn't admitted so probably left that same day or night."

"What time of day, Duga? This detail's critical."

I heard the flipping of notebook pages. "Looks like he drove himself to the ER, Sharps Memorial, at 9:05 p.m., and said he'd been stabbed by a stranger outside his home."

"Did he file a police report?" I asked.

"Nope."

Interesting. So he wanted medical help with his injury but didn't want any other permanent record of the incident and didn't want legal retribution. Another cover-up for Adam Bouvet.

"But why would he still be favoring that side if the injury was last year?"

"If it cut deep enough, especially into the muscle, it could still be sore now."

I thanked Duga, thought about turning around to go home, but Trevor whined and tugged on his leash. I called Derek and brought him up to speed. The wind howled, suddenly, making it hard to talk outside. "Can you hear me?"

"I can hear you fine," Derek said. "That's good intel. We still have a missing piece though."

I sighed as Trevor and I took Highland to Raymond and then continued back on Highland towards Beverly and Joslyn Park, one of three parks in the neighborhood and Trevor's favorite because of the soft sand and even ground.

"Well, unless his Admin is covering for him, we confirmed that he saw patients up until seven p.m. the night before the morning Sophie died, which was August 27th." I paused to let a gust of wind blow past us. "So let's say he was stabbed at 8:30, he got something to stop the bleeding and drove himself to the ER and got checked in by nine, that seems at least possible unless it was a large stab wound, in which case driving himself to the ER might not be plausible. And as you said, that's assuming he did actually see that patient at seven. If he didn't, why did he lie about it and, more importantly, why would his Admin be willing to cover for him?"

"Sorry, but how did Duga get the ER report?" Derek asked, which meant he didn't yet understand Duga and his methods. I wasn't certain he hadn't broken the law to get it, but it was easy enough to confirm via a call to the PD officially requesting the records, and a court order would be easy enough to get at this stage of the case.

"I didn't have time to ask," I replied, which was true. "But the missing piece is that we don't know who stabbed him or why. What's the date or time stamp on the MultiMe video?"

"Looking," Derek said, as Trevor and I got to Joslyn Park.

"Might get loud over here," I said. "Is that Bruno?" I said to Trevor about his friend, a gorgeous, mature Husky we knew from the neighborhood. The two majestic animals barked briefly at each other, then sniffed each other, tails wagging. Trevor tugged on the leash. "No running today, sorry sweetie."

"Bingo," Derek interjected. "August 27th, which was the night she died."

"What time?"

"7:05 p.m."

"It's pretty clear that Adam was the one who recorded the video for MultiMe. So he and his Admin are lying and there was no seven o'clock session."

"Looks like it, yeah, unless that was the session. What else has he lied about?" Derek asked with the question of the day.

Derek took off and, right now, loathe to admit it, I needed Ivan. But first I texted Reggie with a command and a promise. I wrote, *Have Elise call me. It's my mission to protect her.* I wasn't specifically promising I would or even could protect her, but Bouvet had taken two victims so far. And I knew he hadn't gone to Mission Beach yesterday to sunbathe.

Ivan's text reply said he was in a meeting and could meet me in an hour. Finally I had time to try Worldwide Tacos and, naturally, after I'd parked in the PD visitor lot, the taco line was around the block. I walked up and read the menu of literally 84 types of tacos and burritos.

"What do you want? I'm buying." I recognized Ivan's voice behind me.

"Just lemonade, I'm not hungry," I answered, secretly glad to see him.

"Why—are you sick? What's the matter?"

I looked up and gave my ex-lover, Detective Ivan Dent my longest, deepest sigh, comforted somehow that he knew me, knew what exasperated me, knew when I felt defeated.

"Where's your partner?"

"You had to say 'partner' that way, didn't you? He's only my working partner, Ivan, nothing to get upset about."

Normally, Ivan would have run through his "Upset? Who's upset?" routine. Today, he hooked his arm in mine and said, "Let's take a walk."

When we got inside the station, I sat on the other side of the wide desk in his office.

"I sense a question hanging in the air," he said. "Just say it."

"You know what I'm gonna ask," I said, and I was sure he did.

"Look, I don't know how or why we missed Adam Bouvet the first time around."

I leaned back in the hard, black chair. "You talked to her roommate," I argued.

He spread his palms in the air. "She didn't mention a therapist, not to my team anyway. You have a special way with people; we know this. She trusts you."

"What about Elise Turner, Ivan? We've established that she could be Bouvet's next victim. I thought you picked him up for questioning. Is he still in custody?"

"Do I have probable cause that he could be a suspect? There are still some holes that need to be filled in."

"He lied to Derek and me about having a client the night Sophie died."

Ivan leaned toward me. "It's not against the law to lie to a private investigator, and how do you know this, anyway?"

"I received a report that he was stabbed the night of her murder and he had an ER visit around the time of what he said was his last patient of the day."

"Where's your evidence?"

"I gave you the evidence yesterday, the rubber gloves," I whined, in a tone I had better control. "How long will the analysis take?"

"Three days. Actually one to three but they're backed up right now. Maybe tomorrow but probably Friday. What are you specifically looking for?"

"A DNA analysis of Bouvet's genetic material on the rubber gloves, which can cross-reference with Sophie's and Nina Richmond's case. Can I see the DNA Analysis Report on Sophie?"

"I have it here, I was just looking at it again." He picked up his computer mouse and started typing. "Here we go. Cause of death was cerebral hypoxia from manual strangulation, manner of death was homicide," he paused to scan the document, "evidence of subcutaneous scratching, compression, and bruising, with ruptured neck muscles and tissue engorgement above the impact zone, fracture of the thyroid cartilage and larynx, which is common even in non-fatal strangulation," he added.

"Lab report?" I asked.

"Swabs with red-brown stains from the victim's nose, nail

scrapings, and clippings of the victim's left-hand fingernail with blood and tissue sample detected that is consistent with the profile of the victim, Sasha Michaud. And DNA typing results obtained from Sample B-04." He looked up. "I'd have to check to see what B-04 is, a mixture of two distinct blood types—one identifiable as belonging to the victim, and the other from a second individual."

"Yeah, her killer."

"Maybe," Ivan countered, still reading. "You think that second blood type belongs to Bouvet. Okay, let's see what the lab brings up. The minute I know something, I'll call you. In the meantime, why don't you have Duga keep an eye on his movements."

"I already did," I said.

Ivan rose and looked down, towering over me. "You know, I think you're blaming yourself for this girl's death. Why is that?" he asked.

"I'm not. What are you talking about?"

"Or are you blaming me?"

Lord. I didn't want this conversation now. But I sought him out today. "I think you may have missed some things the first time around. No, I don't blame you."

"Go eat some tacos, they'll make you feel better."

I sauntered slowly out to my car thinking about Duga's magic evidence bag, knowing how much power it would likely have over the final disposition of this convoluted case. I still wasn't hungry, but the line was down to just a handful of people and, after all, I had time to kill now waiting for the crime lab.

"Marissa," Ivan called to me from the door.

I turned and liked hearing that name, at least in this moment. He was holding something out for me.

I jogged back to him. "You're gonna ruin it for me, you know, the line's gone down and I was about to try it."

"Get the Garlic Chicken Taco. Here…" He placed a key in my hand.

"Where'd you get this?"

"You had me send a team down to Jonathan Michaud's condo. We found Sophie's Vespa. Following your instructions, we found this key in a little leather coin purse in the seat compartment. Do you know what it's for?" he asked.

I knew. In my bones, I knew what this key would open. Pandora's Box.

CHAPTER FORTY-NINE

I spent an unscheduled hour at the gallery to escape the sordid details of strangulation into the more alluring, maybe even comforting, world of color, texture, and inspiration. Carrie reported the sale of five of our sculpture miniatures, all from the same buyer, an old woman, which meant a nice 15% commission for Carrie. I'd always been too generous with commissions because I knew about the laws of reciprocity when it came to sole proprietorship. Accordingly, Carrie had brought me three coffees already and offered to order me lunch. Almost relieved when a call came into the gallery's landline, I closed my office door and picked up.

"Emmy Fine Art," I said.

"Marissa Ellwyn please." A hushed, cautious female voice.

"This is she. Can I help you?"

"I rather think we can help each other."

I didn't recognize the voice. "Who is this?"

"My name is Elise Turner."

Unsure whether I should laugh or cry at this point, I scanned both sides of the street for gray vans, cars with tinted windows. "You're English." What a stupid thing to say, I scolded myself.

"So it seems."

"What can I do for you?" I asked, erring on the side of formality.

"Thomas, you know, my ex-husband, has informed me of your investigation and I know who you're hunting."

Jesus, I thought. This woman's crazy. "Do you also know that you may be next on his list?"

"Yeah, I do. But it might not be for the reason you think."

•———•••———•

Okay, I might be veering towards paranoia. But it seemed at least possible that all my phones had been bugged, and I'd do anything right now to prevent another Mission Beach victim to add to the list. So I used one of the burner phones and asked Ms. Turner via text to meet me at an ice cream shop called CoolHaus on Washington Street in Culver City. It had indoor seating and, frankly, it was the last place anyone would probably look for either one of us.

I arrived first and got two scoops of Bananas Foster. I took a black stool against the wall and settled in with a hardcover book I'd brought with me. A group of five boys around ten years old, huddled around the ice cream display case suffering from the excruciating tension that comes with deciding on just one flavor. With my eyes aimed down toward the book, I heard the ring of the door open and light steps on the floor. I kept my eyes on my book.

"Mind if I sit here?" said the same British accent I'd heard on the phone, and I had to try not to laugh. Elise Turner looked like a runway model badly disguised as a teenager to avoid the press. Baseball cap worn backwards, boyfriend jeans rolled up over high-top sneakers, and a boxy, oversized t-shirt.

"Please, go ahead." I slid my book a few inches closer to my ice cream. When our eyes met, I used my spoon to tap my ice cream cup, hoping she'd comply so we both looked like we belonged here. She moved to stand in line behind the giggling boys.

"Uh…I'll have a scoop of Black Sesame please."

There were exactly five black stools, I was seated in one, and the five boys obviously wanted me to move so they could sit together. No way, I thought, smiling back at them. And like a sudden gift, the cashier turned on the stereo system, which played hip-hop. Perfect. Ms. Turner joined me and dove right in where we'd left off.

"I was part of the American package," she began.

I had no idea what she was talking about. "What does that mean?"

"I lived in the same area as Sasha's family," she said in a normal speaking volume, which was always the best cover, so we'd add to the general white noise of the atmosphere. "I was a student, you see, studying literature in Paris. I'm a runner, and I met Conrad on the running trail one day and, later, through him I met Nick, Sasha's father," she added, gauging whether I was keeping up. I continued eating my little cup of heaven and listened, riveted.

"Conrad, as in Judge McClaren?"

She nodded. "He and his wife took me to the Michaud's for dinner one night and I eventually became this sort of mentor, you could say, to Sasha starting when she was fifteen."

"So you were studying abroad like Sophie did later."

Elise Turner shook her head. "I'm French, actually. My parents are British citizens but have lived in Paris for twenty years. I'm over here on an H1B work visa sponsored by the newspaper. Anyway," she finally took the first bite of black sesame, which was one of my favorite flavors, and closed her eyes. "Omigod, that's amazing."

"I know, mine is too.

"Anyway, Sasha talked about going to art school here in the US even when I met her, but her mother, well, stepmother actually, wouldn't hear of it. Sasha was troubled, you see, but you know all about that I suspect."

"Only recently, but yes," I admitted.

"The only way she'd support it was if Adam, her psychotherapist since childhood, accompanied her, as well as me. That way, she'd have him to monitor her illness and me to sort of help keep her on the right track."

I couldn't even imagine the cost and logistics of transferring a doctor and his practice to another country. I was facing the front door and carefully monitoring everyone who came in and out but with my sunglasses on. "Had the Sophie alter already come out when you first met her?"

"Oh yes, she'd been with Sasha for several years, but Sophie didn't often reveal herself to me. I mainly helped guide Sasha's decision-making, what to wear to go out to dinner, what electives to take, and then life-skills issues like how to ask for help, how to set up a bank account, how to talk to boys, that sort of thing."

"Do you realize that you've been registered as a missing person for nearly a month?"

"Can't be helped. Thomas asked me, begged me actually, to stay with him in his mother's house. I couldn't even stand going there for dinner once a month, let alone living with them. Too much dysfunction. I'm holed up in a different hotel every few days, paying cash, of course."

I pointed to her clothing. "Nice tradecraft."

She laughed. "Not exactly my normal attire. So you know about Adam, and now you know about my connection. Do you know about the mother?"

"About…" I tried to find the right phase, "Sophie, I mean Sasha, found her, right?"

She nodded. "Which is said to have directly caused the psychological break that caused the formation of Sophie as a coping mechanism, or so Adam believes anyway. In a way, as Adam described it to me, Sasha's very sheltered by Sophie, and Sophie's a lot grittier than her because she's seen so much more than someone should have at her age."

"Makes sense. And Jonathan's an interesting part of the story—"

"Well," she interrupted while taking another bite of ice cream, "that's where I was going next. I really don't think either Sasha or Sophie knew anything about Jonathan's responsibility in the mother's suicide. So there's this duality in their relationship with him. Sasha adores her big brother, and Sophie always blamed him for the mother's death."

"How does the brother feel about Sasha's illness and Sophie?"

"He's much older than her. He left home around the time I met the family, but when he came home for visits, summertime primarily, some holidays, he would have these endless conversations with whom I thought had been Sasha in their basement. But now looking back, I think it was Sophie pumping him for information about tradecraft, to employ your word."

"Why?"

"Sophie always said she believed her brother was a spy, and she wanted to be just like him. He of course laughed it off, citing his legitimate career as a financial advisor brought in for M&A IPOs."

"I'd heard he was an art dealer," I countered, making mental note of this new data.

"Perhaps, but Sophie watched him like a hawk, memorized his movements and mannerisms, the way he talked, his rapport with the influential circle of people surrounding her father, whom of course is a

French cabinet member."

I nodded. "The log."

"Well done, Ms. Ellwyn. You've been busy. I actually hadn't had regular contact with Sophie in several months leading up to her death, which was unfortunate but couldn't be helped based on my work schedule and the research I was doing for several high-profile stories. But there were two copies of her logbook, as she called it, containing critical information about important contacts within the French, US and German governments, as Nick did a lot of traveling and took Sasha with him on many of his trips, for education purposes, you see. So, while Sasha was her Daddy's traveling companion, I suspect it was Sophie who actually had the 1:1 contact with these foreign dignitaries. So she had ample opportunities to not only meet but become friendly and favored by some of the most important political figures in Western Europe. She had a wonderful memory and memorized the birthdays of key political figures as well as the names of their children, where they were going to school, and other key details of their personal lives—"

"Which could be considered terribly valuable intel in the world of industrial espionage," I said.

"Bingo. Little innocent Sasha was the one who gathered all these disparate factoids, and enterprising Sophie commoditized them—"

"By devising a system to sell them," I interjected.

"Exactly," Elise confirmed.

"That's what she was doing in San Francisco with Conrad? She was selling him information about someone?"

Elise Turner's eyes widened but she didn't confirm either way.

The music went off in the ice cream shop and, suddenly, we were the only ones in there. "Are you guys closing?" I asked someone behind the counter.

"Not till six," someone replied.

I turned back toward Elise, who was down to the nib of her ice cream cone. "Why are you moving around so much now?" I asked.

"I was getting notes left in my mailbox, threatening me if I continue investigating Sophie's murder. Now let me ask you something. How close are you to nailing Adam Bouvet?"

I sat back, deciding whether to show all my cards. "Where are the two logbooks?" I asked, deflecting her straightforward question.

"Sophie kept one, Adam kept the other."

"Why are there two? I mean, doesn't that just create unnecessary redundancy and logistical issues with keeping them both in sync?"

"It was Adam's idea," she said, "I think in case one of them, Sasha or Sophie, felt the need to destroy it."

"Did Adam know what was in there?" I asked.

"I can't say for sure. I assume so."

"Does he still have the other copy?" I studied Elise Turner's eyes and saw something jubilant, almost triumphant there. "You stole his copy, didn't you?" I asked, astounded.

A sly grin crept across her lips.

"To do what with it? You're in a very dangerous position," I whispered now, even though the music had been turned back on.

"I need to take off now but it's been lovely meeting you." She offered her hand. "And thanks again for letting me borrow your book. I read quickly."

Without seeing her do this, Elise Turner had managed to grab my book off the counter and replace it with a book that she'd pulled out of I don't know where, because she wasn't wearing a jacket and had no visible pockets large enough to hold a book. And when I looked down at my ice cream cup, the phrase "Page 47" had been written in black pen such that it was barely visible. A pro. But what kind of pro?

CHAPTER FIFTY

I relayed almost everything to Derek as we were talking in the same room of my work trailer, just like the day we first met. Him in one of the black leather bro chairs, as I called them, and me on the mismatched brown leather sofa.

I hated the way the floors moved up and down when you walked on them, the 1970 paneled walls, the lightning-charred exterior and horrible décor. But it reminded me that I'd managed to escape my birthright life of privilege and was carving out my own path, my own albeit gritty career using skills I developed on my own without a single penny or favor from the Ellwyn dynasty or lineage. My intelligence career, even the art gallery had each been influenced by some degree of separation back to my family. And this horrendous trailer anchored me to the glimmering truth that I didn't need their vast resources.

"So where is it?" Derek asked, of course honing in on the most important detail.

"I haven't opened it yet."

"You're seriously not telling me where you've hidden it?"

"Your grammar was incorrect there."

"So was yours! You can't end a sentence with a preposition."

I loved this useless banter, and I was not about to reveal something that could put his and my life in danger.

"I give up," he joked, raising his arms. "I'm assuming that's what your home break-ins were about. Someone thought you had the logbook all along?"

"That's what I assume, but I don't know why they thought I'd have it," I replied. "I think that's the reason for Judge McClaren's break-in as well. Since Sophie had been up there a number of times, it would be a reasonable assumption that she could have left it with him, with one of his clerks, or at least shown it to him."

"So where's Elise Turner now?" Derek asked.

"Hotel-hopping and I think she intends to keep doing that, probably until we manage to bring in Bouvet. I've already told Ivan to call off his investigation in her missing person's case and that I met with her."

My phone buzzed and wriggled on the round end table. Derek grabbed it and passed it over. "Speak of the devil."

"Good morning," I said to Ivan. "You're on speaker, I'm here with Derek."

"Hey guys, I've only got a minute but wanted to give you some news on your rubber gloves."

I turned up the volume.

"I heard back from the crime lab just now that they pulled hair and skin fragments from the inside of the gloves that matches the DNA of samples taken from *both* Sophie Michaud's and Nina Richmond's case files."

Derek and I high fived each other. "Without a motive, though," I said, "I know that's not enough to prosecute him with any degree of certainty."

"That's right," Ivan said.

"You guys released him the other night after you picked him up?"

Pause. "We released him."

"But this should certainly be enough to pick him up again." My voice was hopeful.

"My team's on the way down there now. I gave them his home and office addresses. Assuming we find him, we've got enough to detain him, process him in, and question him on his relationship with Sophie and the alibi he lied about. I gotta go. Sorry. Talk to you guys later."

"Thank you," I shouted and pressed the red button to disconnect. "Feel like taking a drive south?" I asked Derek.

He looked outside. "My schedule's open today and I can never say no to that drive. But we should take I5 all the way. I heard about two accidents on 73 South."

"Don't you want to know where we're going?" I asked, gathering my phone and handbag.

"I suspect there's only one person who can fill in the motive question. Hannah. Does she know we're coming?"

"No, but she said she'd be around today. And though I don't know if she'll be able to add anything, I want this interview in person."

"Look in the eyes type of thing?" Derek asked leaning in with a jovial stare.

"Yup," I said and locked the door behind us.

I had another agenda for this time as well. I'd prepared a spiel in case one of the staff project advisors at Roger's Community Garden stopped us.

"Sophie rented a plot here?" Derek looked confused.

"Sasha," I corrected.

"Do you have a map?"

We weaved in and out of the walkways where individual rented plots of herbs and lettuces were interspersed with aquaponics and other covered structures for fragile plant species.

"I don't need one," I mumbled to Derek, and pointed to a plot ahead to our left. Like the rest of the twenty-five square foot raised planter beds, this one had what looked like dino kale on each end, followed by sunflowers closer to the center, and a single blue dahlia in the center, about fifteen inches high.

"Wow, that grew fast," a young man commented walking past us."

"The dahlia?" I asked.

"Yeah, last time I was here it was barely half that size." He walked away toward his own plot three rows over. "You should see what she's got growing inside," he said.

I looked at Derek, signaling him to take the bait. I leaned down to get a closer look at the sunflowers, one of my favorites, and could hear their conversation.

"There are a bunch of greenhouses here. Is there a map somewhere?" he asked.

"Online there is, but if you walk back that way, you'll come to a bunch of aeroponic structures. You'll see it."

"See…what exactly? Was So-Sasha growing something there?"

I turned to watch the exchange, thankful that Derek had remembered the name Sasha in time. The boy stopped moving to observe him. "If you knew her, you'll know which one is hers."

The property appeared to be one large rectangle connected to a smaller rectangular area by way of a narrow, shaded footpath. We followed the path and reached a smaller area of gray-tented structures held up by poles. I looked inside each of them as we passed, seeing nothing but tiny sprouts so far. I suggested we split up to cover more ground.

"Orchids over here," Derek said, "and more orchids." I stopped and crossed my arms to think about what we were doing. "More over here, wow these are beautiful. But I don't— Wait."

I turned. "Do you see something?"

"I didn't think blue orchids grew naturally. I thought they were injected with dye."

That's when I realized we were on the right track.

"What?" he asked when I met him in front of a white-tented dome.

"There's one," I corrected, remembering my research, "native to Australia. A natively-grown blue orchid called Blue Lady." I set my bag down on the dirt and crouched low to see inside the tent. Of course, in homage to her favorite painting, Sasha had planted a single row of twelve blue lady orchids in a bed of what looked like a lot of soil additives.

"She's got some mulch and corn husk fiber in here," Derek said, fingering a handful of the topsoil. "That's good, they need quick drainage."

"How deep is the soil bed do you think?"

"Eight inches or so, maybe ten." He fumbled with something on his belt buckle and pulled something out of his back pocket. "This," he said of a Leatherman-looking tool, "has a retractable metal tape measure, which might fold if the soil's hard but could help determine whether there's something other than soil down there."

I moved my purse out of view and rolled up my sleeves so we looked a little more like legitimate gardeners. Derek dug gently into the soil beneath the first six plants using his hands and the tape measure. Then he laid flat on the ground and shimmied under the planter to see underneath.

"Are you napping down there?" I asked him. "What are you

doing?"

"This planter is built on top of a sort of platform. It's raised up about a foot. I'm trying to see if—hold on, I got something."

I stood and brushed some loose dirt off the back of my pants and arms. "Something that doesn't belong in a bed of soil?"

Derek nodded. He had both hands in the soil on each side of the first orchid in the row. "I'm touching the left and right side of what feels like a book," he whispered. "Do you want me to pull it out?"

I shook my head. Making note of the first orchid in the row, I made sure Derek replaced the soil so it looked exactly as it had before we got there. A light-haired man approached from the other side of the property.

"Put your jacket on, quickly, button it, and cross your arms so he can't see the dirt on your hands," I said.

"Who are you talking about?" Derek blurted, but he did as I asked.

"Hey guys, can I help you? You just looking around?" the man's easy expression failed to mask his suspicion.

"That would be great," I said. "We're working in conjunction with the LAPD on the case of Sasha Michaud. Her roommate told me she maintained a garden here."

The man nodded and stepped back a few paces. "And I see you found her plot, or one of them anyway. She's got some sunflowers growing in the adjacent area, as well as tomatoes and I think mint. I'll leave you then, let me know if you need any help."

"Who's maintaining her plots now?" Derek asked. "Will someone else take them over eventually?"

"I've been looking after her orchids and one of our project leads is taking care of her other plots. We hadn't quite decided what to do with them, longer term, I mean."

We'd found what we were looking for. In theory, I didn't need the second copy of the book because they were supposed to have been duplicates. But now at least I knew where to get it if I needed it. The exact location of this second book, especially since I now had the first one, felt like a spicy little insurance policy, which I might need sometime. Who knows? I remembered the key that Ivan had given me, which would presumably unlock both of the diaries, as well as the note, 'Page 47, that Elise Turner had written on the cup of her black sesame ice cream.

CHAPTER FIFTY-ONE

I texted Hannah from the parking lot outside the gardens.

Hey Hannah, I've been thinking about you. How are you doing? Have time for a visit? I'd like to see you and make sure you're okay.

I'm good, in my room, smells like paint in here LOL.

Did you paint over the message?

Yes.

Good. I'll be there in a few.

Derek and I knocked on Hannah's already open door a few minutes later. I got a momentary sick feeling in my stomach as my eyes landed on that reddish-brown spot on the carpet.

"It's open," Hannah said in a quiet voice.

"Are you sleeping?"

"No, just lying down." Hannah Moraga sat up when she saw Derek. "Oh, sorry, I thought you were here alone," she said to me.

"Do you want me to wait outside?" Derek asked.

"No, it's fine. Watch out for the wet paint."

"What are you doing inside? It's such a beautiful day," I said.

"Is it?"

"Isn't it? I peered at her and noticing how her eyes looked red and puffy. "Did you just paint this?" I pointed to the wall.

"Yeah. Couldn't stand it anymore. What are you guys doing down here?"

"Mainly checking on you," I said.

The girl pinched the bridge of her nose, no doubt to stop herself from crying. "I'm leaving soon."

"To go out?" I asked.

She wiped her eyes and reached for a tissue from the almost empty box on the floor. "To go back to UCSF. I can't be here anymore."

"Wow, that's a big decision. I admire your courage."

"Courage," she snickered.

"We need to ask you some questions, Hannah. Do you feel up to it right now?"

"Sure, why not."

I looked at Derek and he nodded, giving me tacit support to jump in while we still had the chance. I motioned to him to sit on Sophie's bed across from Hannah, pointing to the wet wall.

"Who shot the MultiMe video?" I asked.

Hannah recoiled slightly at hearing this. "How did you find out about that?" She glanced from Derek to me and back.

"The file was on Sophie's old laptop, in the encrypted drive. Remember?"

She sat fully upright now, wriggling her legs onto the floor and maneuvering her feet into a pair of slippers, as if something in our conversation had changed. "Right," she said. "Adam recorded it."

"Whose idea was it to make that video?"

She looked at me like I had six heads. "There was a whole series of them. Only the last one was on her laptop. They made the first one to bring visibility to Sophie's illness and because Adam thought it would be good therapy for her to talk to others about it. To stop her from feeling shamed by her illness and bring support. There's a whole community of people with DID-type symptoms who share stories and ask questions and make videos to chronicle the progress of their illness and, sometimes, recovery."

"Were you aware of this illness before you came to school here and met Sophie?"

"No."

I took a minute to pause and rethink my next question. "Hannah, did you ever think that Adam had a different relationship with Sophie than he had with Sasha?"

An exaggerated, raised brow and the eyes widened. "You could say that."

"What do you mean?"

"Adam was," she sniffed and grabbed another tissue, "he was in love with Sasha."

"Not Sophie?"

She stared. "He hated Sophie."

"How could that be? He'd been treating both of them since she was a little girl."

Derek turned toward me. "Was Sasha in love with Adam?" he asked Hannah.

"I think she was a little afraid of him, or maybe overwhelmed by him. He thought she liked the attention, but she was uncomfortable with the fact that he was her therapist and that he was so much older than her."

"Were they sleeping together?" I asked the million-dollar question.

"A few times, yeah."

"And it was consensual?" Derek interjected.

Hannah nodded. "For the most part. They made a date. I helped her pick out what to wear, we picked out lingerie in case it got to that point, but I think she knew she could say no if she wanted to."

"Okay, let's go back to what you said a minute ago. You said Adam hated Sophie. How do you know this?"

"He was mean to her. He yelled at her in their sessions. She said he was disrespectful, argumentative, that he refused to treat her, only wanting to give her higher doses of medication to dope her out so Sophie was less likely to emerge." Now a flood of tears came, and she was out of tissues. I pulled my emergency stash from my purse and passed it over.

"I'm right here Hannah, no one's gonna hurt you. Now, can you tell us what happened the night Sophie died? Were you there?" I asked, carefully.

"Yes," she answered in a different voice now, a deeper, more mature voice.

"What happened?" I asked.

"They shot the last video. By this time there were a series of them, I think eight or ten, thousands of YouTube followers posting comments, questions, and words of encouragement every time they uploaded a new one. Sophie talked about sex, intending to make fun of Adam because of his infatuation with Sasha. She taunted him throughout the whole video. You guys saw it. It was bad. He attacked her, and she said his name on camera. He shot it with Sophie's phone, Sophie emailed the file to me, and I uploaded it that same night. She asked me to. Adam found out we'd posted it." Hannah shook her head. "He knew it would be incriminating to him, so he told me he'd kill me if I didn't pull the file off YouTube. He made me remove all of them that night."

"He threatened you?" I asked. "Did you tell anyone about this?"

"Only Sophie."

"How long was that last video up before you removed it?" Derek asked.

"It was filmed in the afternoon on the night she died, so, a while. Five or six hours at least," Hannah replied. "Sophie was upset when I told her Adam threatened me. She became withdrawn and took a nap, which was usually what happened when she went from one to the other. She woke up as Sasha, and had a date already scheduled with Adam for that night."

"Did she go?" I asked. "And where was it?"

The eyebrows again. "His place, if you know what I mean. He told her he was cooking dinner for her, but she knew that meant skipping dinner and having sex."

"How did she feel about seeing him after what had happened earlier in the afternoon?"

"She wanted to talk to him about me and was gonna use their date as an opportunity."

"Did she tell you what happened?" I asked.

"Some. She said they did eat dinner, but halfway through the meal he got up and started rubbing her shoulders and that led to the next phase of the date. They had sex, and then had an argument."

"Meaning Adam and Sasha had sex, right?" Derek asked.

No answer.

"Did they argue about you?" I asked.

"No. About Sophie," Hannah said, her voice now completely composed. "They had sex and when they were finished, Sasha started laughing like Sophie laughed in the video, and Adam sort of snapped. So, Adam thought he had been having sex with Sasha, who he was in love with, but he was really having sex with Sophie, who he hated. She'd tricked him to try to punish him."

"For what?"

"Sophie was jealous that Adam was in love with Sasha but not with her. He hated Sophie and tried to punish her, and she was so hurt by that. Adam broke Sophie's heart."

"What happened next?"

"Sophie confronted him about his feelings for Sasha and for her. It turned into a screaming match, and Sophie laughed at him again."

I kept my eye glued to Hannah, wondering how she could be so composed.

"He choked her to stop her from laughing. Sophie had slipped a steak knife off the dinner table, and she stabbed it in his side. His hands were still around her throat at this point, and he kept squeezing. He must have known if he took his hands away, she'd stab him again. So, he strangled her and the knife eventually fell to the floor. In his house. That's where this happened."

I grabbed Derek's forearm and dug my fingers into the sleeves of his jacket.

"How do you know all these details if you weren't in the room with them? Were you there that night, Hannah?" Derek asked.

Hannah got up, pulled another box of tissues from her closet, grabbed her phone off the desk, and started looking for something. "It starts here." She handed me the phone, to which a video was already cued up, so she must have been watching it before we got here.

"Sophie recorded the whole thing." Hannah's voice was ice.

"Did Adam know that?" I asked.

"I don't think so. You can see when you watch it that she started recording as soon as she picked up the steak knife from the dinner table, almost like she knew this might happen."

We scrunched close together to watch the video in silence. "How did you get this?" I asked her.

"I didn't hear from her when I was supposed to, so I went over there. Both of them were gone but the door was unlocked, so I went in. Sophie's phone was on the floor facedown under the table and covered by the leg of a chair that had tipped over. There was blood all over the carpet. I grabbed the phone and ran out of there and sent myself the video when I got home."

"You still have her phone?" Derek asked.

Hannah pointed to her closet and nodded. "That spot on the carpet, it's blood. I think it was on my shoe when I was walking around in his house. I tried to clean it, but it just made it worse. That's why I can't stay in this room anymore. Or this school. Or this town. I'm outta here."

CHAPTER FIFTY-TWO

Derek and I delivered Hannah to Ivan so she could provide an official statement. Considering her breadth of knowledge of Sasha, Sophie, their illness, and their relationship with Adam Bouvet, she would undoubtedly be a significant witness in the trial. We also handed in Sophie's phone as material evidence against Adam.

Even though her real name was Sasha, I still thought of her as Sophie. Out of homage to her and what she endured in her short life, I went to the Visual Arts building again to see her exhibit. Troy Garrity had returned, explaining away his sudden disappearance as a spontaneous surf trip to the north shore of Oahu in Hawaii. He walked me through all of the new exhibits in the space, ending with Sophie's *The Blue Lady*. She transfixed me the same way she had the first time I saw her. Only this time I realized all the different versions and colors cascading down from the ceiling represented the different sides to Sasha Michaud's fragmented personality. Sasha, Sophie, perhaps there were others only she knew about.

On our recommendation, Ivan picked up Reggie for the second time, holding him at the station in an interrogation room. Two officers stood outside. Ivan was in the room with Reggie, prepared to record the conversation. I entered first, giving Reggie as much of a reassuring smile as I could muster. He nodded back, then his eyes dropped when he saw Derek. We sat on each end of the table with Ivan, and Reggie sitting across from each other. Seating selection, an overlooked social dynamic. Thanks to Derek, I'd never think of it the same way again.

"Hey, Reggie," I started, nodding to Ivan to start the recording. "You know why you're here, don't you?"

"Not really, no."

"I think you need to tell us why you've been sending blackmailing texts to Judge McClaren for the past few months, why you put threatening notes in my mailbox, and in Elise Turner's, your ex-wife's, as well."

Blinking, headshaking, palms raising. "Why would—"

"Cut the crap, Reggie, we know it was you," I shouted.

"I don't think—"

"Reggie," I said in a louder voice now, Ivan staying quiet to watch the drama unfold.

"Dude, you left your fingerprints all over the place. It was very sloppy work," Derek interjected.

"I-covered-every-track," Reggie said with clenched teeth, realizing only after that he'd just admitted to a felony. He gave Derek a death stare and kept his eyes fixed on him while his hands clenched into fists. The room was a vacuum, no one breathed.

I sat back and looked at the ceiling. "Reggie, why?"

He relaxed and took a breath, looked around the room, and seemed to realize there was no way out now. "He never paid me any money."

"You mean Judge McClaren?" I asked for clarification.

Reggie nodded.

"Say it."

"Yes, Judge McClaren never paid me anything," Reggie clarified.

"So essentially your blackmail attempts failed," Derek said.

"Why?" I pressed.

Reggie hung his head. "It was Elise's idea, as a sort of sting operation." He looked up now, at each of us one by one. "Elise felt that if I could get the judge to pay me, it would be evidence on his part that he was trying to cover up the crime of murder."

"Of Sophie Michaud?" I asked, surprised.

"Right. In my text messages, I said I had evidence that he killed Sophie and unless he paid me, I would go to the police and he would lose everything."

"But you didn't have evidence, and neither did Elise." I waited for his response.

He shook his head. "No, and in fact, as Elise continued investigating, she realized the killer was more likely Adam Bouvet, but by then I'd already started down the path, so to speak."

"You put notes in my mailbox and Elise's mailbox. Why?"

"I knew Elise was in danger. I put them in her, well our, mailbox early on to try to scare her into stopping her investigation and reporting," he said.

"And mine?"

Reggie sighed. "You're smart. You were getting too close, and the closer you got to Elise, the more risk there was to her. I was afraid for her life. I still am."

"What about the break-in of the judge's chambers?" Derek asked.

Reggie kept his eyes focused on me.

"It never actually happened, did it?" I said, remembering that my security guard contact, DeRon Richards, who hadn't known about it, which would be highly unlikely. "You came to my gallery that day to see how much I knew about Elise and about Sophie's murder and used a false report of a break-in as your excuse."

"You got me all figured out, I guess."

"Well, I'm a terrible chess player, but I do all right I guess." I smiled at him. I could tell he wanted to smile back, and that he liked me, trusted me, even, though at this moment he was likely calculating his future. I turned to look at Ivan, passing the proverbial baton.

"Reggie, listen," Ivan said. "Regardless of whether the judge paid you, threatening a federal judge, you must know, is a felony and punishable by up to five years in prison."

Reggie nodded slowly. "I know. Do me a favor. Find Elise and keep her safe. That's all I care about."

CHAPTER FIFTY-THREE

When I got home, Derek's car was parked on the curb in front of my house.

"Have you always lived alone?" he asked, when we'd settled in with plates filled with pizza slices and arugula salad.

"Ivan and I never lived together, not officially, which I think is what you're really asking."

Smile. "Why not?"

"I think it's time for a martini."

"Sorry," he said, "if that's too personal…"

"No, it's fine. I just don't like feeling caged."

"Does marriage necessarily mean that?"

"When I first met Ivan, he was my flying instructor."

"I know, and it was love at first sight?"

"Ha! For him maybe," I said. "For me, our flying lessons unlocked a feeling of freedom I'd never felt before. And for a while, a long while maybe, I felt that freedom with him. So, we sort of gravitated towards each other, but for different reasons."

"What happened? You guys seem like such a natural couple whenever you're together."

Martini time. I got up from the table and hoped there was still a lemon on the fruit stand. Two left.

"Ivan's an old lady," I whined. "Dinner at five-thirty every night of his life. He has to eat meat, vegetables, and potatoes literally every night for dinner, he's super rigid in his thinking and way too set in his ways for me. People either crave or abhor structure. He's one, I'm the other." I set two of my prettiest martini glasses on the table, and I did a stellar job with curling the lemon rind.

"He took a sip. "You really missed your calling, you know that?"

"Don't get me wrong, Ivan's got a lot of wonderful qualities, but we're not a match. We were a complement. I want a match." And just as I said that I remembered that I'd gotten a delivery notification earlier today from UPS. "Oh, wait here." I walked quickly to the front door and looked out the bay window. "She's here!"

"Who?"

I opened the heavy front door and picked up a long, flat package from art.com and brought it inside, hoping my scissors were still in the pen holder on the phone table.

"What's that? It's a *she*?" Derek stood aside. "Want some help?"

"I got it. Trying to be careful here." He helped me open the exterior box.

I pulled her out of the box and removed the plastic wrapping, then turned her around to display to Derek.

"Wow. No way. You bought one."

I rotated her toward me, then spun it around to confirm that the mounting had been installed with a hanger on the back. As blue as I expected, and more beautiful in person.

"Where are you gonna put her? You don't appear to have a lot of extra wall space."

I gave Derek a *come with me* motion and we walked through the house to the half bath off of my bedroom. Outside the bathroom on the left side was a perfect fourteen-inch-wide space. The Blue Lady, mounted on Masonite, measured 12 x 20 inches.

"I see you've been waiting for her." Derek touched the nail I'd already positioned, watching my face.

I pressed the picture to the wall; the teeth on the mounting hardware dug into the nail on the first try.

"A little crooked," Derek said, moving to the other side of the bed for a better vantage point. "Move it up a little to the right. There. Perfect."

It was. I never got to meet Sasha or Sophie Michaud, but this was a little part of her that I'd keep for myself.

"I'm gonna take off, I think," he said.

I walked Derek out to the front door and downed the last sip of my martini. Some of the liquid spilled on my arm. I wiped it off, but a drop fell onto my watch. Derek's father's watch.

"Sorry." I wiped the tiny drop of alcohol from the watch face, which turned into a silent moment of vigil.

"Think you'd better keep that for a while longer," he whispered.

"I'm gonna keep it forever."

•——•••——•

After Derek left, I fed Trevor so I could retrieve something I'd hidden inside his doggie bed. I'd cut out part of the bottom fabric and sewn Sophie's logbook into the stuffing, stitching a Velcro pull-tab for quick access. I removed the bullet journal and put the bed back in its special spot on the cedar chest at the foot of my bed. And for the first time, I pulled the tiny key Ivan had given me out of my purse pocket and stuck it in the lock. It clicked. It felt sordid, almost, opening the private journal of a dead girl and reading the secrets she'd gathered about people all over the world. I wasn't sure who knew there were two of them, and when Adam Bouvet went to trial for Sophie's murder, the book would undoubtedly be used as evidence. I needed to see something before I handed it over to Ivan.

Each page was hand-numbered in blue ink in the bottom center. I flipped straight to page 47 remembering Elise Turner's cue written on my ice cream cup. The text was organized in fields, on this page and every other page, where each page was devoted to one individual, intending for there to be room to add more content later, I assumed. My heart stopped when I saw the name in the first field on the page.

> Name:
> Richard Ellwyn
>
> Year met:
> 2017
>
> Place met:
> Paris, Jardin de Plantes
>
> Description:
> Tall, neat salt and pepper hair, handsome, quiet,

dimple in left cheek, blue eyes

Traits:
Walks with a slight limp favoring his left leg, said he had an accident ten years ago that fused his left ankle

Other:
Wears Canali suits, reads nonfiction, who he loves most is his daughter Marissa

I sipped the last swallow of martini from Derek's glass and returned to the chair to read it again, though I wasn't really absorbing what had been written about him yet. What I couldn't get past was what in God's name my father was doing in Sophie Michaud's logbook.

Praise for Ninety-Five By Lisa Towles

"A delightfully peculiar, intricate, and engaging mystery." - *Kirkus Reviews*

"Punchy narration and pithy dialogue, fast-paced yet introspective fiction. Suspense and technical jargon abound in this internet-age thriller." - *US Review of Books*

"Marked by its striking execution and razor-sharp dialogue, the novel places Towles among the best of the genre. Readers will look forward to more of Towles's work." - *The Prairies Book Review*

"A riveting thriller, will keep you on your toes and eager to know what will happen next." - *San Francisco Book Review*

"A well-written romp through college and adult underworlds… a standout in the genre of new adult thriller reads." - *Midwest Book Review*

"This sprawling tale of crime and intrigue is a winner and it is hard to not get engaged with the realistic and likeable young protagonist...A compelling thriller and a propulsive read for fans of crime and YA fiction." - *The Book Commentary - 5 stars*

"Ninety-Five travels, one might say, at 95 mph, and Lisa Towles breaks up the narrative into sixty seven short chapters, so the pace is relentless. The novel is a dazzling trip into a dystopian techno-nightmare – a place where Alice Through the Looking Glass meets The Matrix, with more than a touch of Twin Peaks." - *Fully Booked*

"Towles' writing is sharp, witty, and engaging. She sets up an intriguing puzzle that gripped me from the first chapter and wouldn't let go." - *M.M. Chouinard, USA Today and Publisher's Weekly bestselling author of the*

Detective Jo Fournier series

"A wild, intelligent, and imaginative page-turner." - *Sarah Lovett, Bestselling author of Dangerous Attachments and Dante's Inferno*

"Heart-poundingly intense and palpably realistic, Lisa Towles' new thriller yanks you into a story that you cannot put down." - *Louis Kirby, MD, Bestselling author of Shadow of Eden*

"Ninety-Five is a heart-pounding, non-stop thrill ride with a devilish puzzle at the heart of it. Forget edge-of-your-seat, you'll be up and pacing around the room. Highly recommend." - *Benjamin Bradley, Author of crime thrillers such as Welcome to the Punkhorns*

About the Author

Lisa Towles is an award-winning crime novelist and a passionate speaker on the topics of fiction writing, creativity, and Strategic Self Care. Lisa has eight crime novels in print, including *Hot House*, *Ninety-Five, The Unseen, Choke,* and under the name Lisa Polisar *Escape, The Ghost of Mary Prairie, Blackwater Tango*, and *Knee Deep*. Her next title, *Salt Island*, is the second book in her E&A thriller series and will be forthcoming in late 2022. Her thriller, *Ninety-Five*, was released in November 2021 and won a Literary Titan Award for Fiction. Her 2019 thriller, *The Unseen*, was the Winner of the 2020 NYC Big Book Award in Crime Fiction, and a Finalist in the Thriller category of the Best Book Awards by American Book Fest. Her 2017 thriller, *Choke*, won a 2017 IPA Award and a 2018 NYC Big Book Award for Thriller. Lisa is an active member and frequent panelist/speaker of Mystery Writers of America, Sisters in Crime, and International Thriller Writers. She has an MBA in IT Management and works full-time in the tech industry in the San Francisco Bay Area.

Acknowledgements

Warmest thanks to the following people whose love, support, encouragement and care were of immense help to me during the writing of this book:

To my parents Connie and Dick – there are no words that can capture how grateful I am for all you have given me and continue to give. I feel your constant love and support, and with that I continue to push myself, strive to be better and continue learning. You are lifelong teachers and I've learned so much from you in the past year about authenticity, survivability, and resilience. Thank you for teaching me how to not only live but SHINE.

To my smart, wry, and wise sister Missy - thank you for reading all my work and providing feedback, and for being such an inspiration for juggling multiple priorities. I don't know how you do all that you do, but you are my barometer for success.

To Olivia and Cassidy – watching you grow into amazing young women is one of the most precious gifts of my life.

To my beta readers - Gail, Missy, Lee, and Ana - thank you for the insightful questions, comments, suggestions, encouragement, and time you contributed to help make this book publishable.

To my publisher, Lisa – thank you for your support, guidance, advice, marketing, patience, creativity, and expertise. You are amazing.

To my amazing editor, Cindy Davis – your expertise and guidance continues to help me mature as an author and a storyteller.

To my cherished MWA NorCal and SinC NorCal friends and fellow authors - thank you for your daily companionship, advice, wisdom, care, and constant inspiration. I learn so much from you and you are a treasure.

To my dear Karuna Circle – through our deep work together over the past year, I feel like everything is possible now.

To Lee, my beloved husband, whose devotion, understanding, acceptance, wisdom, and tireless humor bring me the greatest happiness of my life.

And to my readers – my most sincere gratitude for buying and reading this book. I hope you enjoy the journey, and books 2 and 3 in this series will be forthcoming soon. If you like this book, please submit a review about one thing you liked about it on Amazon and Goodreads.

To all of you, Thank You

CPSIA information can be obtained
at www.ICGtesting.com
Printed in the USA
LVHW030447060922
727616LV00003B/172